SERAPHIM ACADEMY 1: WICKED WINGS

ELIZABETH BRIGGS

Elizabeth Briggs Books

Cover Designed by Jessica Allain

ISBN (paperback) 9781677399840

ISBN (ebook) 978-1-948456-20-3

www.elizabethbriggs.net

Chapter One

OLIVIA

*S*eduction is a dangerous game, but one I have no choice but to play. And, as I've learned from my mother, seduction and deception often go hand in hand.

They do tonight, anyway.

I move through the party and try to ignore the growing hunger inside me. It's hard at times like this, when music is pulsing, drinks are flowing, and bodies are dancing a little too close. Inhibitions are down, temptation is in the air, and boy does it smell sweet. To me, at least.

I find a corner where I can survey the crowd, trying not to get too close to anyone. College kids at various levels of drunkenness dance, play beer pong, and try to talk over the loud beat of the music. A guy standing off to the side catches my eye and gives me a warm smile. He's got the face and shoulders of a small-town college football hero, and for a second I'm tempted. I picture digging my nails into those broad shoulders as I ride him hard, but I quickly glance away. He looks like a nice guy.

The kind who brings you flowers on your first date and wants to take it slow. The kind I avoid.

Trust me, I'm doing him a favor.

A guy with sleeve tats and a dark goatee walks into the room with a "don't-fuck-with-me" vibe. I bet these rich snobs invite him to parties for one reason alone: he sells drugs. He's exactly the kind of man I need tonight.

Chester's hand clasps my elbow possessively. "There you are."

"I was waiting for you." I flash him a fake smile. He's one of those kids who only got into USC because his parents bribed someone. Sandy blond hair with a perfect curl over his eye, dark green polo shirt, expensive smile—you know the type. His confidence makes him more attractive than he really is, as does his money. This is his house—bought by his parents so he wouldn't have to live in a dorm with the common folk—and his party. It's St Patrick's Day, he's wearing an "I'm Not Irish, Kiss Me Anyway" pin that lights up, and his breath smells like whiskey. It takes a good bit of acting not to cringe away from his touch, but Mother taught me well.

We met in the bar where I work, where he flirted with every girl he could before I took him home. Now he only has eyes for me. What can I say? I have that effect on people.

Chester pulls me up against him. "I missed you. Let's go back to my bedroom."

I play with the buttons on his shirt. "Only if I get a drink first. I'm dying for one of those green beers everyone's got."

He nuzzles the side of my neck like a ravenous bear. "Can't it wait? I need you now."

I might have gone a little too far with him last night. I swat his chest playfully and put on a cute pout. "Everyone's had a drink but me. Please?"

He has no idea I'm doing him a favor. If we sleep together again, he won't survive it. Humans can only handle one night with a succubus—or even a half succubus, like me.

"Fine," he says, but he tightens his fingers around my arm. "One drink and then you're mine for the rest of the night."

His mouth crushes against mine, and I can't help but take a little of what he's offering. His lust for me is delicious, but every second our lips touch puts him in more danger. The guy is a possessive, snobbish jerk, but I don't want him dead.

I push him away before I can do any real damage. "Go find me that green beer, and then we'll continue this."

His eyes are glazed and unfocused, his face a little paler than it was before, and at first I think he won't let go. Did I take too much? But after a second the daze passes, and he stumbles off to go get me a drink.

I blow out a long breath and search the room for that tattooed guy I spotted earlier. He's easy to find, with a group of entitled students passing him money in the corner in exchange for something in a little baggie. I use a tiny bit of my powers to catch his attention, and his gaze locks on me. Others in the room turn too—both men and women—and I know I can have any one of them if I want. Desire is powerful, and succubi are hard for humans to resist when we put on the charm. The only people immune are those in true love, and they're few and far between, especially in places like this.

He pushes through the crowd and makes his way over to me. "You alone, baby?"

"Not anymore." I rest my hand on his arm and tug a little with my magic, making his emotions flare.

He suddenly grabs me around the waist and plants his lips on mine, kissing me hard. Oops, I tugged a little too hard. Mother would chide me, but I'm still getting used to these powers and the thirst that comes with them. I hear it now, the little voice in my head that tells me to yank open his jeans and climb him like a tree. That voice is getting harder to ignore with every passing day.

I end the kiss slowly. "I could use some fresh air. Let's go onto the balcony so we can continue this."

He grunts and leads me outside, his hand on my ass. Subtle, he is not. I lean against the balcony and he leans against me. From below, the sound of people laughing and splashing in the pool filters up. It's a perfectly clear blue Los Angeles day and the sun hits my bare shoulders, filling me with warmth. I'm wearing a little red dress that shows off all my curves, and my new friend is definitely enjoying the view.

His hands circle my waist. "I'm Trey. What's your name?"

"Olivia." I toss my hair back. "But everyone calls me Liv."

Chester comes barreling outside at that moment and yanks the guy off me. "What the fuck, man? You think you can come into my house and touch my girl?"

"We were just talking," I say.

"Looked like a lot more than that," Chester snaps. He shoves a green beer at my chest, and a little of it foams over. "Here, take your damn drink while I kick this guy's ass."

I grab the beer from Chester. As I do, I brush against his hand and unleash a little more of my power, heightening his emotions.

"I'd like to see you try," Trey scoffs as I take a sip of the green beer. It's disgusting, but I gulp a bit down anyway.

Chester gets right up in Trey's business and he's so angry now his face is bright red. "Stay away from my girl."

Trey takes a step closer and actually lets out a growl. "What are you going to do if I don't?"

Chester throws the first punch at Trey's face, unable to contain himself between his overwhelming lust and anger. Fighting breaks out between them, and I rush in a little late to try to break it up. As I do, I'm shoved backward, hard. My beer falls to the ground with a loud crack and my back hits the side of the balcony—and then I'm over it.

Falling.

Falling.

Falling.

Wings unfurl from my back with a loud snap, breaking up my screams. For a second I hover over the pool, black feathers flashing through the air, while everyone down below and on the balcony stares at me. Then I plummet toward the water again. The second I hit it, everything goes black.

Exactly as I planned.

Chapter Two

OLIVIA

I wake in a hospital room with no idea how I got there and jerk upright when I realize I'm not alone. It's an honest reaction. No one likes to wake up and find a stranger has been watching them sleep, even if I expected a scene like this.

"Who are you?" I ask as I sit up straighter. "What's going on? Where am I?"

"You can call me Jo." The woman appears to be in her mid-30s with pale skin, shoulder-length honey blond hair, a sensible white blouse, and a black pencil skirt. Everything about her is professional, from her shiny nails to her closed-toe pumps to her black briefcase, but there's something about her that makes her stand apart from an average businesswoman. The symmetrical perfection of her face. The lustrous shine of her hair. The way the sunlight streaming through the window seems to gather around her. "Do you remember how you got here?"

"Not really." I place my hand on my forehead, trying to

ease the ache there. I'm wearing a hospital gown, there's an IV in my arm, and my head is pounding. I stare at the IV and my jaw falls open. "Why am I in a hospital? What happened to me?"

"That's what I'd like to find out." She crosses her legs, her skirt swishing as she moves. "I'm here to ask you a few questions about what happened at the party tonight. Don't even bother trying to lie to me—it won't work. As long as you speak the truth, we'll both get along just fine."

I reach up to touch the necklace around my neck, relieved it's still there even though my clothes are missing. It's gold and heavy, with ornate curls and a big aquamarine gem that changes color depending on the light. As soon as I realize what I'm doing, I drop my hand, but she's already seen it. I swallow and begin talking. "I was at a party and a fight broke out. We were on the balcony and I got knocked over, I think. I fell?" My eyes widen. "There were...wings. Feathers?" I shake my head. "No, that can't be real. Was my drink spiked or something?"

"Your drink wasn't spiked, and I can assure you that what you remember was real."

Fun fact: my drink *was* spiked. How do I know? Because I spiked it myself when Chester handed it to me. I needed to pass out, and I knew the drug would be out of my system by the time anyone tested me thanks to my angel-demon metabolism. But Jo doesn't need to know that.

"No, it's not possible," I say, getting increasingly upset for her benefit. "I fell from the balcony, but I'm not injured. And the wings. Oh shit, the wings..." I press my palms against my eyes. "I must be dreaming. Either that or I've totally lost my mind."

Her perfect ankles cross as she leans forward. "You're not dreaming, and I believe your mind is perfectly intact, though you may be in shock."

"Who are you?" I sit up a little straighter in bed so that I'm fully upright. "What are you doing here?"

"You were brought to the hospital after you passed out. I was sent to find you after a video was uploaded to YouTube of a girl falling off the balcony and suddenly sprouting wings." She scowls a little. "This video was seen by no less than three thousand people online, not to mention all the people who witnessed it happen in person. We were able to get the video taken down without much trouble, but the partygoers are more of a problem. My team is still trying to track down everyone who was there so I can wipe their memories. You've caused quite a bit of work for us all."

Wipe their memories? Shit, this isn't just any angel, this is Archangel Jophiel, the only one with that power. I'm going to have to be extra careful with what I say to her.

"Not that it's your fault of course," she continues, "and we've certainly dealt with worse incidents before, though not many. Most people grow up knowing what they are." She pauses to study me. "Do you really not know? Remember, it's impossible to lie to me."

I stare back at her and reply without hesitation. "What do you mean? Know what?"

She considers me for a moment and buys my lies. "Olivia, you're an angel."

"A what?" I blink at her. "Like in the Bible?"

"Not exactly." She waves a hand. "They got some things right, and other religions are correct about different things. But you get the basic idea, anyway."

I let out a slightly insane laugh. "This is a joke, right? Angels don't exist. And if they did, I'm definitely not one of them."

She sighs. "Who are your parents? Are they...different?"

"Different how? My mom died when I was a kid, and no one knows who my father is." The lies roll smoothly off my tongue, and Jophiel never even reacts. I nearly touch my necklace again, but this time I restrain myself. *Thank you, Mother.* "I grew up in foster care."

Jophiel gives a terse nod. "As I thought. Your father must be one of us, but it's unlikely he will come forward. It's forbidden for our kind to breed with humans."

"Our kind?" I ask.

A rush of air sweeps through the hospital room as her copper-colored wings suddenly flare out from her shoulders. I let out a small scream and recoil against the bed, giving it my all as the wings spread wide, taking up the entire wall. There's no denying what she is now. With her wings out she glows with an inner light, and everything about her is a little too perfect. You might even call it *divine.*

"Angel," I whisper while clutching at the bedsheets as if they'll protect me. "It's true."

"Indeed." Her wings disappear back into her shoulders as if they never existed. "Now, let's talk about your future."

I blink at her with big eyes like I've just seen a ghost. I'm really playing up the naïve half-human part, and Jophiel seems to be drinking it all in. "My future?"

"Now that you've Emerged, your other powers will be manifesting soon."

My jaw falls open. "Other powers?"

"Of course." A touch of pity crosses her face. "We all get

our wings and angelic gifts at twenty-one years of age, but most grow up among other angels and are well prepared for their Emergence. Since you had no idea what you are, it's no wonder you were a bit shocked."

"That's an understatement," I mutter as I drag a hand over my face, trying to pull myself together. "Sorry, this is a lot to take in."

"I'm sure it is, but now that we've found you, we'll take care of everything. Starting with your education. Every angel is sent to Seraphim Academy for Angelic Studies at around twenty-one or so, usually after they finish their human university studies. I've already informed the headmaster you'll be attending."

I hold up a hand. "Wait. I'm confused. I'm going to a school...for angels?"

"Yes. It's imperative that you attend Seraphim Academy and learn to control your powers and how to hide what you are from humans. It's a three-year program, and once you're done, we can help you find a suitable career for your skills."

"Three years," I say slowly. "That's a long time."

"It will fly by, I promise. No pun intended." She smooths her skirt as she stands. "It's fortunate for you that Seraphim Academy's next term starts in a few days, although that gives you less than a week before you need to arrive there. We will handle all travel accommodations and email you everything you need to know about the school."

Time to play reluctant. "Wait. A week? I need some time to think over this first, and—"

Jo shakes her head. "I'm afraid that isn't an option. If you don't learn to control your powers you will be a danger to yourself and others. Attendance is mandatory for all angels."

"But what about my plans for the future? And how will I afford this? I'm not exactly making a ton of money at the bar I work at."

She waves a dismissive hand. "Your plans for the future are irrelevant now that you know what you are, and you don't need to worry about the financial details. My company, Aerie Industries, covers tuition for all students, along with a small allowance for supplies." She offers me a clipped smile. "As you'll see, angels take care of our own. Even the ones who are half human."

I stare out the window with a frown. "I guess I don't have a choice, do I?"

"That's correct." She moves to the door, but then turns back. "One last thing. Where did you get that necklace?"

"Oh, this?" I touch it again. "It was my mother's." This is one of the first things I've told her that isn't a lie.

"I see." She looks skeptical, but lets it go. "As I said, everything will be emailed to you. All you have to do is show up at the school next week. If all goes well, I'll see you in three years when you come work for Aerie Industries."

She walks out of the room, and I finally drop the clueless act. I lean back on my pillows as a satisfied smile spreads across my lips. I did it. I got into Seraphim Academy, and they have no clue what I really am or who my parents are. My fists tighten around the sheets in my lap as I'm filled with resolve. *I'll find you, Jonah. I promise.*

———

*W*hen I get back to my apartment, Father is waiting for me. Of course.

I close the door. "I should have known you'd be here."

"This is a real mess you've gotten yourself into," Father says as he stands in the middle of my miniscule studio apartment between my bed and my TV, looking completely out of place. He's wearing a perfectly tailored gray suit with a crisp white shirt that stretches across his muscled chest and broad shoulders. "One I'm not sure I can get you out of."

"I don't want out of it." I drop my bag beside the bed. It didn't take much convincing to let me leave the hospital since I was physically fine, but traffic was so bad it took me forever to get home and now all I want to do is collapse.

Father pinches the bridge of his nose. If anyone saw us together, they would never think we were related. His hair is soft brown, his eyes are bright blue, and his face is smooth and impossibly handsome in a way that makes you want to trust him immediately. He looks thirty, thirty-five max. He's much, much older. "Why exactly are you doing this?"

I head into the small area that barely qualifies as a kitchen and pour myself some coffee, then heat it in the microwave. It's a day old, but coffee is coffee, and this addict needs her fix. "I'm going to find Jonah, and I need to attend Seraphim Academy to do that."

He follows me across the room. "I want to find your brother as much as you do, but this isn't the way. I've already got my best angels looking for him. Let me handle it."

I turn back and meet his eyes. "And where has that gotten

you so far? It's been three months, Jonah is still missing, and we're no closer to finding him."

He crosses his arms and sets his jaw. "What makes you think you can succeed where I have failed?" His tone challenges me, but I do things my own way. What can I say? Stubbornness runs in the family.

"I have a different set of skills. The ones Mother taught me." A sinful little smile crosses my lips. "You know how persuasive she can be."

"Don't remind me." He sighs, and for a second the weight of an immortal life rests on his shoulders before it's gone again. "Going to Seraphim Academy is a bad idea. It's too dangerous for you. Your mother and I have worked hard to keep you hidden from our world for all these years. I know it's been tough sometimes, but you were safe. Now you're throwing all of that away."

I suck down the rest of my coffee and refill my mug before popping it back in the microwave. It's hot pink and reads, *I'm a fucking angel.* Jonah got it for me for my twenty-first birthday, and it makes Father's eye twitch every time he sees it. "I'll be fine."

His eyes narrow. "I'm not sure you understand the implications. There's no turning back from this. Now that the angels know you exist, you have no choice but to attend Seraphim Academy for all three years. Unless they find out the truth about you, they'll make sure you attend each term. And if anyone finds out what you really are..." He trails off wearily. "I don't want you hurt."

"Don't worry. I plan to keep it hidden. As far as they know, I'm half human." When he still looks concerned and unwavering, I add, "I won't tell them who my father is either, if that's what you're worried about."

"No, of course not," he says, although there's a slight hesitation that I can't help but catch. I'm his biggest shame, and though he cares for me in his own detached way, I'll never be the child he wanted. Jonah is, and now he's gone. He clears his throat and straightens his tie, obviously uncomfortable. "Although it's probably best if you did keep that information to yourself."

"You got it." I give him a mock salute with my mug. "Anything else I should keep in mind?"

"Just be careful." He rests a hand on my shoulder, and I'm filled with a comforting warmth at his touch. Sunlight streams through the window nearby, hitting his slightly curling hair and framing his silhouette, and in that instant, I can almost see the outline of his silver wings. I'm awash with a wave of his power that feels like basking in the glow of the sun. I can't help but crave more of it, along with his approval, but then he takes his hand away. "Promise me."

"I'll be careful. I promise."

After giving me a long look, he disappears in a flash of light. One second there, the next gone, leaving me feeling like the conversation was only half finished. Teleportation seems like overkill when you can fly too, but that's one of the perks of being an Archangel—they have powers the rest of us don't.

I glance around my apartment. I still have a lot to do, but everything is going exactly as planned. I've dreamed of attending Seraphim Academy ever since Jonah told me about it, and soon I'll be there. I just wish he could be there with me too.

Jonah is my half-brother and a year older than me. He

should have been starting his second year at Seraphim Academy next week, but he disappeared at the end of last year's term and no one knows why. Father's been searching, but he hasn't found any leads. If there's something going down at that university, only another student will be able to uncover the truth. That's why I have to infiltrate the school and find out what happened to Jonah. Luckily, I can be very persuasive. And if I have to, I'll tear the place down with my bare hands to find my brother.

I just have to make sure no one finds out what I really am. Angels and demons have lived in an uneasy truce ever since the Earth Accords, but my very existence breaks all the rules. If anyone learns my true identity, I won't just get kicked out of Seraphim Academy—I'll be killed.

Chapter Three
OLIVIA

"What's it like at Seraphim Academy?" I asked, trying not to let my jealousy show. Jonah started at the school a month earlier and wasn't visiting me as much ever since. I missed him already. I hadn't seen Mother in two years and Father wasn't exactly a common visitor those days either. I was pretty sure they both wished I didn't exist. Jonah was my last connection to the non-human world...and my only real family.

He lounged on my bed beside me while he threw a baseball in the air and caught it. He had our father's light brown hair, and at that moment it was a little long and curling up around his ears. He was handsome in that guy-next-door way, with the kind of face that made random strangers spill their entire life story. "It's like a normal college but everyone has wings."

"Smart ass." I rolled my eyes. "I wish I could go."

"It wouldn't be safe for you."

I sighed. "I know. It's just frustrating that everyone else can attend, while I have to pretend I'm human and hide what I am.

I want to learn to use my powers too. I'd even settle for going to Hellspawn Academy."

He snorted. "You'd be in even more danger there with the demons."

"Maybe. At least I could feed openly there."

Jonah gave me a warm grin. "Yes, but at Seraphim Academy you'd have a big brother to look after you."

"Ugh, I don't need looking after."

"Sure you don't." He chuckled softly. "But it really is a shame you can't go to the academy too. I could introduce you to all my friends. I think you'd like them. Especially my roommate."

I sat up a little and arched an eyebrow. "Why's that?"

"He's something of a lady's man. A new girl every week. You two have a lot in common."

"Sure, except he does it for fun, and I do it for survival. And if he knew what I was, he would probably try to kill me."

Jonah wrapped an arm around my shoulders. "I'd never let anyone hurt you, sis. Never."

I punched him in the arm. "Don't get all corny on me."

He laughed and sat back. "Sorry, I know you hate that shit."

I didn't though, not really. I wish I'd let him know how much it meant to me that he was the one person I could be completely myself with—who knew what I was and loved me anyway. Especially since I only saw him two more times before he disappeared, and then it was too late.

———

*I*t's four days later, and I'm on my way. I've given up my job, my apartment, and most of my meager possessions, but it feels good to start fresh, without the weight of my past holding me down. Just about everything I need should be provided by the school anyway, or so I've been told.

It's a long drive from Los Angeles to the northern-most part of California, but I follow the directions that were emailed to me and head into the mountains, then take an unmarked road that leads higher and higher. The trees grow taller and older as I climb toward the sun, and the road becomes narrower and more treacherous. I nearly turn back—I'll admit I'm not the best driver—but the thought of my brother keeps me going, and I finally make it to my destination.

Seraphim Academy sits at the top of a tall mountain, isolated from the rest of the world by its location and a large stone wall covered in ivy. I stop in front of a black wrought iron gate with a winged logo and the letters S and A. The gate opens, and I take a deep breath. All my planning has led me to this moment. After months of waiting for Jonah to appear or be found, I'm taking matters into my own hands.

I park next to a pretentious-as-hell red convertible and nearly ding it—oops—then look for the print-out of the map I was sent...and can't find it. Of course. I try to load it on my phone and get no signal. Seriously? No cell service up here in the mountains? How do people survive? I'll have to ask someone for directions to the dorms so I can find my room and get settled in. I don't have much, just a few boxes in the trunk and backseat of my car with my clothes and a few other things I couldn't leave behind, like my mug from Jonah.

I climb out of my car and take in the school grounds. Seraphim Academy is beautiful, with a lush green lawn, tall redwood trees, and white stone buildings beside a lake that sparkles under an endless blue sky. We're surrounded by thick forest on every side and so high up that the sun feels a little closer and the air is crisp and warm. Angels get their powers from light, and the introductory email explained that this area in Northern California is one of the sunniest places in the world.

A few other students walk toward the stone buildings or the lake, and it all looks so perfectly normal you'd forget this is a school for angels—until someone flies overhead, blocking the sun for a second with their large, outspread wings.

After taking a deep breath, I head toward an imposing building that looks like a gothic church made of pure white stone. It's got the arches, the buttresses, the towers, the works. All it's missing are the crosses or other religious symbolism, although a huge stained-glass window depicts an angel with shining wings and light emitting from his palms. Above it, the roof forms a point over a steepled bell tower—where three large, muscular men stand on the edge and stare down at me, as if unaware of the dangers of falling such a great distance.

Angels love to be up high, looking down at everyone else like the arrogant creatures they are. And I'm pretty sure those three men up there are the worst of them all, because they're the sons of the Archangels.

They're also my brother's best friends.

And my main targets.

Chapter Four

CALLAN

I cross my arms and gaze across the campus grounds like a king overlooking his domain. I can see everything clearly from up here in the bell tower, from the lake to the headmaster's house to the parking lot. A few angels dart across the sky, but most of the students hurry across the lawn while carrying books, boxes, and other assorted things to the dorms. You can always tell the newbies because they're scared to pull out their wings.

Our second year at Seraphim Academy is about to start, but this time it's all wrong—because one of us isn't here.

I turn back to Bastien and Marcus with a scowl. "It's been months. Jonah should be back by now."

Marcus raises a shoulder in a shrug, his body lazily draped over the black leather couch. "Maybe he doesn't want to come back."

I shake my head. "Don't be ridiculous. He wouldn't miss the start of the new school year. Something's gone wrong. Have you foreseen anything, Bastien?"

"As I said the last three times you asked, no, I haven't," he replies dryly from the armchair he's sitting in, without looking up from the old book he's reading on fae magic. "None of my contacts have heard anything either."

I let out a growl as I start pacing on the stone floor. "Demons must have found out what he was doing and taken him. It's the only explanation."

"Let's not jump to conclusions," Bastien says. "There is no evidence of that."

"There's no evidence of anything! Jonah is one of *us*. The fourth member of our group. Practically a brother. Why am I the only one upset by this?"

Marcus runs a hand through his dark hair. "We're all upset. You think I want to go back to my dorm and see his empty bedroom? No, I really don't. But I have faith he'll be back soon, or we'll find a clue as to why he's been gone so long."

"Statistically speaking, the chance of finding anything at this point is low," Bastien says. "It's been three months. The case has gone cold."

Marcus reaches over to punch Bastien in the arm. "You're not helping."

I turn away from them and pinch my forehead. As much as I hate to admit it, Bastien is right. We've spent the last few months waiting for Jonah to return, or at least send us a message letting us know he's okay, but it's like he completely vanished. The Archangels have been looking for him too, without any success. Something must have gone wrong and stopped him from completing his mission and returning. I fear we might have lost him forever.

Through the open window, I spot a car I don't recognize as

it enters the parking lot. It's a silver Honda Civic so ancient I'm impressed it's still running, with no less than three dents that I can see from this distance. The driver is a woman, though I can't make out too many details from this angle, and she drives slowly as she searches for a spot. She finds one— next to my car. Where no one else dares to park. I cringe as she barely misses my bumper, and she pulls into the space so crookedly I'm sure she'll fix it, but she doesn't. Whoever that woman is, she definitely needs to be kept far, far away from my car. Or off the road entirely.

She gets out of the car and shakes out dark brown hair that cascades down her shoulders in thick waves. I can't see her face, but she's wearing tight black jeans with an ass so fine I almost forgive her for her terrible parking job.

She grabs a messenger bag and shuts the door, then glances around the campus like she isn't sure where to go next. Another first year, no doubt. After a few seconds she begins walking toward the lawn with a confident step, but as she gets closer and her features come into focus, every muscle in my body tenses up. She's easily the most beautiful woman I've ever seen, but that's not the problem.

The problem is that I recognize her.

"It's her."

"Who?" Marcus gets up and moves to my side. His gaze follows mine out the window and he lets out a low whistle at the sight of the woman. She's nearly below us now, on her way to the building we're on top of, and we've got a clear view of her cleavage from the low V of her tight red shirt. She definitely knows how to wear clothes to accentuate those curves, and it's hard to look away.

"The woman in the photo." I take out my wallet and pluck

the photo out. Bastien is on the other side of me now too, and he glances between the photo and the woman. She's younger in the photo, but there's no doubt it's her. Same wavy dark brown hair. Same intriguing green eyes full of secrets. Same red lips begging for a kiss.

"Are you sure?" Marcus asks.

"I'm sure." I shove the photo back in my wallet. "She's the one Jonah warned us about."

Bastien peers down at her. "That's the new half-human. She just Emerged last week. How is she connected to Jonah?"

"I don't know," Marcus says. "What are we going to do about her?"

I clench my jaw. "We're going to do what Jonah told us to do."

Marcus frowns. "Do we have to? It seems extreme."

I give him a stern look. "She can't be here at Seraphim Academy."

Bastien strokes his chin as he looks down at her. "We'll have to make her leave."

"How will we do that?" Marcus asks.

The woman catches sight of us, three large men standing at the edge of a bell tower looking down at her. She stops in her tracks to stare up at us and something in her eyes feels like a challenge. Now I'm even more intrigued.

"We'll do whatever it takes," I say.

Bastien nods. "Even if it means making her miserable."

"I don't like it," Marcus says. "It's a shame to make someone that hot leave so soon."

I give him a sharp look. "Quit thinking with your dick for once and remember our promise to Jonah."

Marcus lets out a dramatic sigh. "Fine."

"We have to do this." I step onto the ledge and let my wings unfurl with a harsh smile. "Now let's welcome her to Seraphim Academy."

I hear the snap of the other men's wings flaring wide, and then we descend upon the unsuspecting woman.

The poor thing. She has no idea what's coming for her.

Chapter Five
OLIVIA

The angels stretch their shining wings out and catch the sunlight, practically blinding me—and then they descend. They hit the ground in a rush, landing in a triangle around me, so close that the rush of air makes my hair fly back. I'm suddenly surrounded by three of the most gorgeous men to ever walk the Earth, and you'd think that would make it my lucky day, except none of them are smiling.

The one in front of me is the biggest, with muscles Thor would be jealous of and the strong jaw and golden hair of Captain America. His wings are pure white and edged in gold, and everything about him is large and imposing and all male. He gives me a look that tells me he's the boss here, and he's used to getting his way. His alpha male attitude is a major turn on, I'll admit.

Until he opens his mouth, that is.

"You don't belong here."

Does he know who I am? Has Jonah told him about me?

Time to find out. I prop my hands on my hips and face him down. "Is that so?"

"Leave now, and it won't be a problem," his voice commands. I'm not sure he has any other way of speaking. He's obviously used to telling people what to do. Unfortunately for him I've never been one for following orders.

"Hmm," I pretend to think about it with my head cocked. "How about no."

I start to brush past him, but one of the other muscular men stretches out a bronze and white wing to block my path. This guy's got olive skin, dark brown hair with a hint of a curl, and a sensual mouth I'd love to kiss. He stands with a deceptively casual pose and has a cocky tilt to his chin, like he knows how good-looking he is and knows that you know it too. He could be Latino, Middle Eastern, or something else—he's got one of those faces that could pass for just about anything. A lot of angels do, actually. Probably because they're not from Earth originally.

"We're not done speaking with you," he says.

"Listen to us," the third angel adds in a sharp voice. He's beautiful, as all angels are, but in an unconventional way. More interesting-looking than handsome, with strong cheekbones, a sharp jaw, and cold eyes radiating intelligence and arrogance in equal measure. He's tall and lanky, and with his shiny black hair he reminds me of a raven, even though his wings are dark gray with silver streaks. If he were in a superhero movie, he'd be the sexy villain you love to hate. "If we say you don't belong here, then you don't."

I let out a huff. "Is this because I'm half human?"

Their leader nods. "Exactly. We don't want your kind here."

"It's for your own good," the bronze-winged angel says. "You shouldn't be at this school."

"I think I know what's best for me, thanks." The sarcasm drips off me like sweat. This is not how I planned this first interaction with my brother's friends. Nope, my plan involved a lot more flirting and seduction and convincing them to reveal their secrets after a round or two of hot sex. That's definitely not in the cards now that I've seen what overbearing assholes they are. I'm going to have to come up with a Plan B to get information from them. "I'm not leaving, so you might as well put those flashy wings away and let me pass. Or better yet, tell me where I can find the dorms to put my stuff."

"I can help you with that," a female voice says behind me. She moves to my side while frowning at the men. "Really, you three. I expected better of you."

She takes my arm and leads me away while they scowl at us. She has strawberry blond hair, pale skin, and big, warm eyes with a hint of sadness that I nearly miss. I recognize her immediately from a photo I saw on my brother's phone.

"Thanks, but I was handling it." My blood is still burning after interacting with those jerks, even as it sings with desire too. I wanted those men, all three of them. One at a time or all-together, I'm not picky. Being a succubus is such a pain sometimes.

Except I'm not the only one experiencing the lust. A steady trickle of it gives me a little boost of energy, and I realize all three men are not only looking at me with disgust, but with desire too. *Thanks for the snack, boys.*

"I'm sure you were, but women should stick up for each other, especially when men are involved." She gives me a kind smile. "Besides, you seem a little lost. I can show you around. I'm Grace, by the way."

I can't believe my luck. First, I run into my brother's friends, and even though they turned out to be grade-A jerks, the encounter saved me from having to track them down. Now Jonah's girlfriend is befriending me. I can definitely work with this.

I give her a friendly smile, turning on the innocent, naïve act I gave Jophiel. "You're right, I could use some help, thanks. I'm Olivia, but call me Liv." I glance back at the men. They've returned to the bell tower and are glaring down at me through a large window, although they've put away their wings. "Is everyone here so rude?"

"Not everyone. Those are the Princes, as they're called here, and they think they can boss everyone around." She shakes her head. "I suggest you avoid them, if you can."

Following the path, we curl around the bell tower but not out of their sight, unfortunately. "Why are they called the Princes?"

"They're basically angel royalty. All of them have at least one Archangel for a parent." When I look confused, she explains, "Archangels are the oldest and most powerful of all angels, and the seven of them form the council that rules over us—which means those three men basically rule the school. They can do anything they want and get away with it."

I'm tempted to look back at the men again, but I restrain myself, even though I can feel the weight of their gazes upon me still. "Are they really so bad?"

"They didn't used to be. I was once close with them." Her eyes drop and her smile falls. "But something happened at the end of last term and everything changed." She takes a breath. "As I said, it's best you avoid them."

"I'll try." Except avoiding them isn't in the cards. They must know something about my brother's disappearance, and I'm going to find out what it is. "Do they always perch up there like crows?"

"Most of the time. They've claimed the bell tower as their own. That building they're in is the main hall, where most of your classes will be. Anything that requires sitting at a desk will be in there. I can show you around the rest of the campus too if you'd like."

I give her a warm smile. "That would be great."

She leads me down a path next to the large green lawn, toward the lake and other buildings in the distance. Students sit together on the grass or stretch out under the sun with their eyes closed, wings out and fluttering in the breeze as they enjoy a peaceful moment before classes begin. For a moment, I envy them. They don't have to lie about who they are or hide their true nature from everyone around them. They don't have to worry about what will happen if they get caught.

"That's the gym over there," Grace says, breaking me out of my thoughts. She's pointing at a large building beside a big field near the lake. "Combat Training classes are all held in there or on the field. You'll also be taking Flight classes there or at the lake."

I let out a nervous laugh. "Combat? Flight? Shit. I am totally unprepared for these classes. I've never fought anyone before, and I'm scared of heights."

"Don't worry, many people arrive here not knowing how to fly or fight. You'll get the hang of it all soon enough. What other classes do you have?"

I pull out my class schedule. "Angelic History and Demon Studies."

She nods as we continue down the path. "Every year you'll take Angelic History and Combat Training, and each year you'll have to take a Supernatural Studies course, but the order you take them in doesn't matter. Most of us take Demon Studies first so we know what we're up against."

I hold up a hand to stop her. "Hang on. Demons are real?"

She blinks at me. "Of course they are."

"Wow. Okay." I suck in a breath. "Sorry, this is all new to me. A week ago, I thought the world was full of humans and that was it, and now I learn there are not only angels, but demons too."

"And fae," Grace added. "Although they prefer to stay in their own realm, so you probably won't ever encounter one. Don't worry about them for now."

"Good idea. My head is spinning enough as it is." The lie is easy, always so easy, especially with Mother's necklace on. I can hear her voice in my head now. *"One of the best ways to seduce someone—or deceive them—is to pretend you're not very smart or capable. People are always quick to believe someone is dumber than they are, especially when you're a woman. You can use that to your advantage."*

Grace gives me a smile that is almost pitying. "I'm sure this must be very overwhelming for you. Oh, you should also have a class based on your Choir." She glances over at my schedule. "That's odd. It says, 'to be determined.' Do you have any idea what type of angel you are?"

"Um, I didn't even know there *were* types of angels."

"There are four Choirs, and all angels belong to one of them depending on how they control light," she explains with the patience of a saint. "Erelim create a burning light that can injure others, sort of like a laser. Malakim use light to heal the body and mind and can make plants grow too. Ishim, like me, manipulate light to make themselves and other objects invisible. And Ofanim use the light of truth to sense lies, see through illusions and glamour, and some of them can even see the future on rare occasions."

"How would I know which one I am?" I ask as we continue down the path.

"It's genetic, so people take after one of their parents."

"No luck there. I grew up in foster care. They told me my father was an angel, but I never met him, and my mother was human."

"That could make this more challenging. Have you noticed any magic since getting your wings? Anything unusual?"

"Nope. Nothing." Lies, lies, lies. They're just rolling off my tongue now.

She shrugs. "Sometimes it takes longer. You don't need to worry. The professors here will help you figure it out."

I sigh. "Or maybe since I'm half-human I won't have any of these powers."

"I doubt that, but I don't know much about it, sorry. Headmaster Uriel might be able to tell you more." She stops outside another building, this one with an outdoor patio. "This is the cafeteria. It's a buffet, so you can turn up whenever you're hungry and get as much food as you want. You can also get food to go if you want to eat in your room or by the lake."

"Is it expensive?"

She laughs softly. "No, it's free for students. Pretty much everything here is."

My eyes widen. "Wow. That's really generous of the school."

"Aerie Industries funds the academy, and they take good care of us. As they should, since most of us work for them when we're done here."

My tour with Grace continues, and over the next few minutes she shows me the headmaster's house, the library, the student store, and then she leads me down a short path toward a four-story stone building. "That's the dorm. You should have been assigned a suite already, which you'll share with another First Year student."

"Dorms, huh? I've never stayed in one of those."

"Did you go to college?"

"Just a local community college for two years." I shrug. "What about you? Do angels go to college?"

"Some of us do. We grow up in angel communities around the world, but since we don't get our wings until we're twenty-one, it gives us time to get a degree first if we want. I went to Stanford, for example. Seraphim Academy is sort of like a graduate school in that sense. Of course, sometimes it still feels like high school."

Her dark eyes catch on a group of women walking past us as she says this. They're beautiful, even for angels, and they hold their heads high and walk confidently, like they're used to people leaping out of their way. Every single one of them has an athletic figure and identical straw-colored hair. The one in front has her hair tied back in a perky little ponytail and she meets my eyes and sneers, before they turn as a group and head toward the dorms. The one in the back bumps me hard with her bag before she walks inside.

SERAPHIM ACADEMY 1: WICKED WINGS

It's difficult not to call her out as she passes. "I see what you mean. Who are they?"

"Seraphim Academy's resident mean girls. They're all descended from Valkyries and think they're better than everyone else because of it. That one in the front was Tanwen, their new leader, even though she's also a First Year."

"Wait, Valkyries? I thought that was Norse mythology. You're saying *they're* real too?"

"They are. As you'll see in Angelic History, any sort of winged being in mythology or religion can probably be traced back to us." She waves a hand dismissively. "Anyway, I suggest staying out of their way as best you can. It's better if you don't get their attention."

"So, avoid the angel royalty and avoid the mean girls. Is there anyone I *don't* have to avoid?"

"Everyone else should be fine, I hope. Although we don't get many half-humans here, so some people might be rude to you about it."

"Just what I need," I mumble.

"I don't *think* anyone will bother you," she says with a smile. "If you ever need anything or have any questions, just let me know."

I give her a genuine smile in return. She's nice when she didn't have to be. I appreciate it. "I will. Thanks."

Grace seems like a kind and caring person, which makes me almost feel bad for deceiving and using her. *Almost.*

Chapter Six

OLIVIA

Grace and I split up outside the dorms, and I head inside to check out my new home and meet my new roommate. This building is done in the same white stone and gothic design as the rest of the buildings on campus. There's a small lobby with an elevator and some vending machines, and a guy sitting behind a temporary desk with a clipboard. His nametag reads *Blake,* and he's got ashy blond hair and way too tan skin. Someone has been spending a lot of time in the sun.

"Checking in?" he asks. "Name?"

"Olivia Monroe."

His lip curls. "Oh, you're the half-human. Sign in here."

I sign the line, and he pulls a key from a drawer in the desk. I knew pretending to be part human would make me an outsider, but I had no idea it'd be this bad. It stings a little, even if I'm not actually half-human.

"You're in room 302 with Araceli." He snorts. "That's fitting."

I grab the key. "What do you mean?"

His lip curl turns into a full-on sneer. "No one wants that pointy-eared freak here either."

I roll my eyes. That's enough of that. "I can't speak for her, but I'm not going anywhere, so you might as well climb off your high horse already."

He leans back and shrugs, and I pocket my key and stomp off. Looking for Jonah here might be harder than I thought if everyone is a total prick to me. Then again, they'd treat me a lot worse if they knew I was actually part demon. Breeding with a human is forbidden, but breeding with a *demon*? It's so taboo, it's unthinkable.

I peek inside the common room, which has leather couches, heavy wood tables, and chairs with thick arms. There's a large-screen TV on one end, but it's turned off. Floor to ceiling windows let in tons of light, and sliding doors lead to an outdoor patio with tables and chairs. A few students are lounging around reading books, using their laptops, or chatting with each other while eating snacks. One of them spots me and nudges her friend, and then the room goes quiet as the entire place stops to stare at me.

I give an awkward wave before stepping back from the door. So much for getting through this year without much notice. It's clear that everyone knows who I am, and they have a lot of feelings about it already. I don't really care what these people think, especially since everything they know about me is a lie, but I need to find information on Jonah, and it would be a lot easier if people would talk to me like a normal person.

I hop in the elevator and head up to the third floor. As the door opens, I step out and nearly bump into someone getting on. It's the sneering Valkyrie from before, who Grace said was named Tanwen. Her blue eyes narrow when she sees my face. "Get out of my way, human trash."

My eyebrows dart up. "What did you call me?"

"You heard me." She crosses her arms and looks at me like she's daring me to fight her.

The elevator door shuts before I can come up with a smart reply. What a bitch. I'm more angry than offended, especially since if Valkyrie girl knew I was actually a succubus, she'd probably piss herself.

I shake it off. I don't have time for petty shit, I have a mission to accomplish, and to do that, I need to get my base of operations set up.

There's another small lounge area here in front of the elevator, and on the other side is room 302. My key unlocks it, and I step inside a small living room with a mini-kitchen and a bathroom. Two doors on either side lead to the bedrooms, and I'm relieved to see I won't be sharing a bedroom with someone else. I'll still have a roommate, but we each have a little privacy —a really good thing when you need to feed on sex to survive. Not that I expect to be doing much feeding here. That would be far too dangerous. But hey, you never know.

There are two women chatting in one of the bedrooms, so I head for the empty one before they see me. I dump my bag on the double bed and look around the small space. It's got a desk, a closet, and a window overlooking the lake. It's not much, but it's not bad either. Everything looks clean and well-maintained, although it's sparse enough for us to add our own touches. Reminds me a lot of some of the places where I lived while in foster care, and it feels just as lonely. Yes, I really did grow up in foster care, since neither one of my parents could raise me safely, and loneliness was my best friend—until Jonah.

There's also access to a balcony, which extends the length of the dorm suite, with two chairs and a table. It's big enough an angel could extend their wings and take off. That could come in handy.

I head back out to get the rest of my stuff, but I'm stopped by the two women. They look like they could be sisters, with the same soulful brown eyes, except one has a purple streak in her brown hair. The other stands with the confidence and grace of someone who has lived for hundreds of years, even though she looks no older than thirty.

"Oh honey, this must be your roommate," the older angel says.

"Hey, I'm Araceli," the purple-streak girl says, offering me her hand. "Nice to meet you."

"Liv," I say, as I shake it. "Short for Olivia."

"I'm her mother, Muriel." She gives me a big smile, then looks back at her daughter. "Do you need anything else? Should I stay and make you some dinner? Do you need help organizing your closet?"

"No, Mom," Araceli says with a groan. "I'm fine. Really. You can go now."

"Are you sure? Liv, do you need any help getting settled?" Muriel asks.

"I'm good, thanks."

Araceli's tone grows exasperated. "Mom. Please."

"All right, I'm going. Although I think your bathroom could be organized a little better..."

"Mom!" Araceli practically stomps her foot.

"Sorry, sorry." Muriel leans over and gives Araceli a kiss on her forehead. "I just can't believe my baby is already grown up and attending Seraphim Academy. I'm so proud."

Araceli rolls her eyes, but she hugs her mother. "Thanks for your help, Mom."

"Of course, honey. You call me if you need anything at all and I'll be right over. Liv, it was a pleasure to meet you." She gives me a warm smile before moving to the door. She hesitates again like she doesn't want to leave, but finally she gives a little wave and shuts the door behind her.

Araceli lets out a huge sigh and collapses on the couch as soon as her mother is gone. "Finally. I thought she would never leave!"

I glance at the door wistfully. "I thought it was cute. She obviously loves you a lot. You're lucky."

The words slip out, and I regret them immediately, but it's hard not to be jealous when Father is currently pretending I don't exist, and I haven't heard from Mother in three years.

She takes a closer look at me. "You're the half-human girl. I guess they stuck both the outcasts together in one suite. Strength in numbers or something."

"You're an outcast too?" Maybe I'll have one friend. Not that it'll help me since she's brand new, too.

"Yep." She pushes her purple streak aside and shows me one of her ears, which are slightly pointed at the top. "I have fae blood from my father's side, so I'm seen as a pariah among angels, even though I grew up among them and don't know my fae side at all. I'm sure you've noticed they're not the most welcoming group to anyone who is different."

"No kidding. I've already been told to go home by multiple people today."

She props her lime green combat boots up on the arm of the couch. "Just ignore them. Some people think angels should remain pure, or whatever." She rolls her eyes. "Did you really not know you were part angel until your Emergence?"

Perching beside her on the sofa, I decide to take any friend I can get at this point. "I didn't. This has all been a total shock. What's an Emergence?"

"That's what we call it when angels get their wings. For most of us, it's a joyous occasion."

I snort. "Mine was anything but."

"So I've heard."

My eyebrows dart up. "You know about it?"

She lets out a short laugh. "The angel community is small and tight-knit. *Everyone* knows about it. We've all seen the video of you falling into that pool. Even an outcast like me."

I swallow. "Great. No wonder everyone has been staring at me."

"Don't worry. We'll stick together and give the middle finger to anyone who gives us shit. Hey, what classes do you have?"

I like this girl already. I pull my schedule from my back pocket, and she looks it over quickly.

"Awesome, we have Combat Training and Flight together." She frowns as she stares at something on the page. "So you don't know what your Choir is?"

"Nope. I'm clueless about everything. What about you?"

"I'm a Malakim, or a healer, like my mother."

"Have you done much healing yet?"

"Not really. I tried practicing on some plants and a sick dog, but I don't really know what I'm doing yet. Before this I went to nursing school, so I have some idea how to help sick or injured people, but using magic is totally different from practicing medicine." She gives me a thoughtful look. "I don't get a Malakim vibe from you. You feel more like an Ofanim or something."

Crossing my legs, I settle in. Araceli is easy to talk to. "Maybe. I really have no idea. About anything. I've been pretty lost ever since I got the invitation to this school." I feel bad for lying to Araceli since she seems so genuine and open, and as a First Year student she isn't on my list of people to investigate, but I have to keep my ruse up as long as I'm here.

She gives me a wide grin. "Well, it's a good thing you got stuck with me as your roommate. I can help you figure this all out, and I know a bit what it's like to be an outcast in the angel community."

"That would be great, thanks."

She helps me bring up the rest of my things, and then we each head into our own bedrooms to finish unpacking and get settled in before orientation tomorrow morning. Except when I close my bedroom door, I notice something on the bed that wasn't there before. A square box wrapped in brown paper and gold ribbon.

I open it up carefully, in case this is some kind of trick, but I'm even more confused when I pull out a white, hooded robe and a plain white mask that completely covers the entire face except for the eyes. Underneath it is a card printed on thick paper with letters embossed in gold script. There's an image of a golden throne taking up most of the page, and below it is a date, a time, and coordinates. Along the bottom are the words: "Attend at your own risk. Secrecy is mandatory. Loyalty is paramount."

I nearly run out and ask Araceli if she got one also, but then I run my finger along those bottom words again. What if she didn't get an invitation? I could already be breaking the rules by even telling her about the invite. But what exactly have I been invited to attend?

*O*nce we're settled in, Araceli and I head over to the cafeteria for dinner. Like the dorms, the cafeteria has floor-to-ceiling windows that let in a lot of light during the day. White tables and chairs are set up across the wide space, and along the sides are buffet stations with all sorts of different foods, ranging from tacos to lasagna to roast beef.

At first, all I can do is gaze around the room and take it all in. It's hard to believe all of this food is free. My birth parents made sure none of my foster homes were too terrible, so I was never worried about food—but money was another story. Neither of my parents could have any ties to me, because according to them it was too dangerous to have anything connecting the three of us. That meant no support from them either. Everything I had—my car, my apartment, my education —I had to work for myself. Meanwhile, Jonah got everything he could ever want, grew up in a damn mansion, and was adored by everyone around him for being the son of two

Archangels. Not that I'm jealous or anything. I love Jonah. But still.

The angels here take it all for granted as they walk around the buffet and get whatever they want, just like they do everything else at this school. None of them know what it's like to grow up with practically nothing.

I grab some fish tacos plus a salad, and then make my way to the table where Araceli is already sitting. Someone bumps into me hard and my tray hits the ground, spilling my food everywhere and making a loud enough noise that everyone in the cafeteria turns to look.

"Oops," Tanwen says with a smile that is anything but sorry. "Might want to watch where you're going next time, clumsy human."

"*You* bumped into me!" I reply, but she's already moved on, and her Valkyrie friends just snicker as they follow behind her. As I stare at their backs I wonder if they dyed their hair to match, or if they're all basically clones of each other.

I let out a huff and begin cleaning up the mess. One of the cafeteria workers comes to take over, and I apologize profusely for making their job harder before going to get another tray of food. I know what it's like to have to clean up after someone else.

By the time I get back, Araceli has almost finished her food. "I see you've already met the Valkyries," she says, as I sit down.

I throw a dirty look at the group of women, who have taken over a large corner table. "Lucky me."

Grace walks up to our table holding a tray and gives us a smile. Beside her is a curly-haired guy wearing a purple polo shirt and those hipster jeans that are just a tiny bit too short. "Can we sit with you?"

"Sure." I scoot over a little so they can both join us at the table. I'm happy to see them. Grace knows my brother, so hopefully the guy does too.

Araceli looks surprised by our new guests, but smiles. "The more the merrier."

"This is Cyrus," Grace says, gesturing to her friend. "He's a Second Year like me, and an Ofanim."

"Nice to meet you," I say.

"Good to see you again," Araceli says.

"How do you all know each other?" I asked.

Araceli leans back and pushes her empty plate away. "We all grew up in the same community in Arizona, near Yuma. Lots of sun there. How do you know Grace?"

"She was kind enough to save me from the Princes this afternoon, and she showed me around campus."

Araceli's dark eyebrows shoot up. "What do you mean, she saved you?"

"Shh, there they are now," Cyrus says, and we each turn to look.

All three men walk into the cafeteria like they own the place, and people practically leap out of their way as they move toward the buffet. The big, muscular blond guy is at the front, charging forward like he's on a life or death mission to get food. I don't think he does anything by half. The tall, black-haired one is just behind him, shooting daggers with his cold eyes at anyone who dares look at them. The third guy, with the olive skin and sexy mouth, walks more casually and flashes a smile to the crowd, like he's trying to reassure everyone they're not really so bad.

As I watch, the leader spots me and his eyes narrow. He stares at me with open hostility, and the two other men follow his gaze. Great, now everyone in the cafeteria is staring at me too, probably wondering why I've caught the interest of the Princes. At first I'm annoyed, until the lust and desire gives me a little boost. Even angels can't resist the allure of a succubus—including the Princes.

It's an eternity before the three men turn away to get their food, but the damage is done. I can already hear the hushed whispers going around the room, no doubt talking about me. If anyone in the school didn't know about me before, they most certainly do now.

"What was that about?" Cyrus asks.

"The three of them surrounded me when I arrived and told me I don't belong here," I say.

"Wow, I had no idea they hated half-humans so much," Araceli says. "They're even worse than I heard."

"I never thought they did either," Grace says with a sigh. "But people change."

Cyrus leans forward and says in a loud whisper, "She should know, she used to date one of them."

"Really?" I ask. "Which one?"

Cyrus waves a hand. "Not one of those three. There was a fourth Prince last year."

Grace's head drops and the sadness in her eyes returns. "His name is Jonah. He disappeared at the end of last term."

I'm thrilled the conversation has already come around to my brother. "Really? What happened to him?" I ask, as though this is the first time I'm hearing about Jonah, like it doesn't rip my heart out every time I think of him missing.

"No one knows," Cyrus says. "He vanished without a

trace, and no one has been able to find him. Some people think he ran off, and others think demons took him."

"Do you think the Princes had anything to do with his disappearance?" I ask.

"No, they were like brothers," Grace says, as she picks at her food without really eating it. "But they changed after Jonah disappeared. They're harder now. Meaner."

We quiet down as the Princes finish getting their food, cast me one last hostile look, and then walk out of the cafeteria with it. The room seems to collectively relax as soon as they're gone.

"Well, one thing hasn't changed—they still never eat with us commoners," Cyrus says.

"What else can you tell me about them?" I ask.

Cyrus grins, and I can tell he loves to gossip. "The blond one is Callan, and he's the son of Archangel Jophiel and Archangel Michael. He's an Erelim and basically the leader of the Princes, just like Michael was the leader of the Archangels, and he doesn't let anyone forget it."

My eyebrows shoot up. "*Was* the leader?"

"Michael was killed two years ago by Lucifer. It nearly ended the truce between angels and demons, but no one could prove it was actually Lucifer who did it. He had an alibi, but we all know it was him."

"Of course." It sounds like something I should agree with. I have no idea if Lucifer killed Michael or not, but it's not really relevant to my search for Jonah, so I move on. "What about the others?"

Cyrus leans forward, clearly enjoying this. "The one with black hair is Bastian, and he's an Ofanim and a cold, unfeeling jerk. He's Headmaster Uriel's son, which is why the Princes get so many perks."

"What kind of perks?"

"For one thing, they get the entire bell tower to themselves, which they use as some kind of private lounge. They're always up there, and no one else is allowed inside unless invited by them. But you've been there, right Grace?"

"I have." She's focused on her food, obviously having a hard time with this conversation. She's either a very good actor or she really is upset over my brother's disappearance.

"I've seen them up there," I say. "They watch over the school like they own it or something."

"They pretty much do," Cyrus continues. "The third one is Marcus, and he's one of Archangel Raphael's many sons. He's a Malakim and he was Jonah's roommate last year. I heard he doesn't have a roommate this year, because Headmaster Uriel is hoping Jonah will come back to school any day now. They even left all of his stuff in there."

Grace shakes her head. "He won't come back, because he didn't run away. He would never do something like that, not without telling anyone where he was going, or taking anything with him." Her voice chokes up a little and she grabs a napkin and dabs at her eyes. "I'm sorry, I just really miss him, and I'm so worried about him."

Me too. I shove a bite of taco in my mouth to keep from talking.

"Someone will find him," Araceli says. "All the Archangels are looking for him. He'll be back soon."

Grace sniffs. "I hope so."

He will be, at least if I have anything to say about it. And now I know exactly where to start looking: Marcus's dorm.

Callan is pacing again. He's been doing it a lot ever since Jonah vanished. Back and forth along the edge of the bell tower, his footsteps so predictable on the stone I could write a song to the beat.

"We need a plan," he says.

I stretch my legs out on the couch and fold my arms behind my head. "A plan for what?"

"To get rid of that woman in Jonah's photo."

"Her name is Olivia Monroe," Bastien says in his matter-of-fact voice. "I did a little research on her after our encounter. Unfortunately there's not much in her files."

Callan finally stops pacing. "What did you learn?"

"She grew up around Southern California in various foster homes. Her mother died when she was six due to a drug over-dose, and her father is unknown, although no doubt an angel. Until recently, she was working in a hotel bar near LAX."

"Choir?" Callan asks.

"Unknown."

"What's her connection with Jonah?"

"Also unknown."

"He never mentioned her to me," I say, with a trace of bitterness. I'm still annoyed Jonah gave Callan the photo instead of me. I was his roommate and his best friend, but apparently he trusted Callan more.

Callan pulls out the photo again and smooths his thumb over it. "He gave me this only hours before he left. It was obviously important to him, and we made a promise to him."

"We need to learn everything we can about her," Bastien says. "Find out how she's connected to Jonah. Maybe she'll know why he hasn't returned."

"We *need* to get her as far away from this school as possible," Callan growls.

"How?" I ask. "She didn't seem very intimidated by us."

"Not yet, perhaps. We'll have to take more drastic measures."

"Like what?"

"We'll start by making her life miserable. If that doesn't convince her to leave, we'll take it up another notch."

The whole thing feels off. I shake my head. "I'm not comfortable with this. And I'm not sure Jonah would approve either."

I think back on that moment at the end of last term.

"Are you sure you want to do this?" Bastien asked.

"Yes, and we all know it has to be me," Jonah said. He wore his baseball uniform, and would be playing against the fae in the championship game in only an hour. And after that...I couldn't even think about that. "Don't worry. I'll be fine, seriously. But I need to ask you guys for a favor before I go."

"Anything," I said.

Jonah pulled out the photo and handed it to Callan. "If this girl ever shows up at Seraphim Academy, you need to make her leave, however you can. It isn't safe for her here."

"What are you talking about?" I learned over to look at the photo. I was immediately struck by the girl's beauty and intrigued by her.

"Who is she?" Bastien asked.

"I can't tell you that," Jonah said.

I raised an eyebrow. "New girlfriend maybe? Should Grace be worried?"

Jonah shook his head. "Just promise me you'll do whatever it takes to get her away from this place—for her own good."

I realized then how serious Jonah was, and how worried he looked. He must care about this girl. I thumped him on the back, trying to make him feel better and bring some levity to the situation. "Hey man, we promise."

"Thanks. I knew I could count on you guys."

"We made a promise to him," Callan says, bringing me back to the present. "We said we'd do whatever it takes, and we will."

I stand up and let my wings unfurl. "Yes, we did, but that doesn't mean I agree with your methods. But fine, bully her into leaving if you think that will work. Bastien can try to uncover all her dark secrets. I'll handle her my own way."

"Yeah, we all know how you handle women," Callan snarls.

I give him a wry grin. "Then you know I'm damn good at it."

I leap off the edge of the bell tower and spread my wings, letting the cool night air filter through them and lift me up. It's a short flight to the dorms, and though I could fly directly into my room through the balcony door, I decide to land on the ground and walk into the common area first. Maybe the woman in question—Olivia—will be there, and I can figure out what to do about her.

I pass by the common room and flash a dazzling smile at a few ladies I pass by, but none of them is the one I'm looking for tonight. A few of them give me seductive glances, and I could probably take one of them up to my room if I wanted, but I'm not feeling it. Truth is, I haven't been all that interested in women since that incident with Grace after Jonah disappeared. Until now. One glance at Olivia changed all of that.

On the other hand, it'll be rough heading back to that empty suite tonight. I hadn't realized how hard it would be until we returned for this term and I saw Jonah's door wide open, with all his things still inside. Bringing someone back to my room suddenly sounds like a good plan after all. But then the guilt comes back and the desire fades. I step into the elevator and resign myself to a long night alone.

Olivia appears in the doorway and slips inside just as the elevator shuts. Her eyes slide over me for a moment and then she turns away, like she's pretending I don't exist. Fine, I probably deserve that. I wasn't exactly friendly to her earlier. Quite the opposite.

The elevator is old and slow, and my eyes can't help but roam over her. She meets my gaze and a spark of desire passes between us. We're alone in a small elevator and suddenly it feels very intimate. I can't look away, and I have the strongest desire to touch her, though I keep my hands to myself.

"About earlier." I clear my throat. "I really don't have anything against half-humans, you know."

She slowly turns those green eyes on me, which are not

giving me any leeway. "Sure. That's why you and your friends told me to leave the school."

"It's for your own good, that's all. We're trying to help you."

She snorts. "Thanks, but I don't need your kind of help."

The elevator doors open to the fourth floor, and I get out and head to my room. She gets off the elevator too, but heads in the opposite direction, down the hall. I fumble for my key as she walks away, and she glances back just as I get the door open. Our eyes connect, and that same desire sparks between us. She quickly tucks back a piece of her dark hair and looks away.

I enter my room and close the door. She must have felt it too, this attraction between us. I've never been very good at denying myself anything once I want it—and she is definitely very tempting.

The guys have their own methods, and I have mine. They may not like it, but I'm going to use them. I'll get close to her, make her trust me, and then find out how she's connected to Jonah—and then I'll use that to fulfill my promise to him and get her far away from this school.

Chapter Nine

OLIVIA

My new plan is in motion.

My original plan was to befriend Grace and seduce the Princes, but only one part of that plan is working out so far. The four of them are at the top of my suspect list—okay, at the moment they're the *only* ones on my suspect list—but I need to look beyond the obvious too. If it were that easy, my father would've found Jonah by now.

Hence, the new plan. Last night I waited for Marcus to return to the dorms, and then I followed him back to his room. Now I know which one is his, and I'll break inside sometime when he isn't there so I can search my brother's room. I'm going to find out everything I can about Jonah's time here at Seraphim Academy so I can figure out what happened to him, and then I'll find him. I refuse to believe he's dead or gone forever. And if he is? Then I'm going to find the bastards who took his life and make them pay.

In the morning, Araceli and I head to orientation in the auditorium, which Grace showed me briefly during our tour yesterday. We find a spot in the middle of the rows of plush gray seats, and a few other angels look at us and whisper, or nudge their friends. Araceli gives them an overly large wave, making it obvious we know they're staring at us, and the students quickly turn back around. She turns to me and rolls her eyes. "Think they'll ever get tired of gawking at us?"

"One can only hope." I glance around while the other seats quickly fill up. I spot Tanwen and the rest of the Valkyries in the front with their identical straw-colored hair, and catch a glimpse of the Princes in the corner, glancing at the crowd like kings surveying their minions.

After everyone has sat down, a very tall, thin man with black hair steps onto the stage and moves to the podium. The entire room quiets immediately, and I sit up with interest because he looks a lot like Bastien, except this man radiates the power and magnetism of an Archangel. This must be the Headmaster.

As Uriel's eyes move across the auditorium he seems to focus on each one of us in turn, and many students squirm under his gaze. Uriel is an Ofanim, which gives him the power to detect truth, and probably other powers too since he's an Archangel. I shiver a little as that intense gaze falls on me and lingers there. The hair on my arm stands up, and in his eyes I'm faced with a vast, unknowable intelligence from centuries of living. I have the sense that Uriel can see into my very soul, and I'm terrified of what he might find. My necklace should protect me, but I can't help but clutch it and silently pray it's working, until Uriel finally moves his gaze to the next student. Only then can I breathe again, but I'm still rattled by the brief encounter.

"Welcome to Seraphim Academy," Uriel says, his voice

reaching across the room even without a microphone. It's not loud or commanding, yet somehow we can all hear it perfectly as though we're in an intimate conversation with him. Archangels and their tricks. "I am Headmaster Uriel and it's my privilege to oversee Seraphim Academy as another term begins. I welcome both our new students and our returning students, and I'd like to go over a few things before you begin classes tomorrow.

"First, let me tell you a little about the school, for those of you who are new. Seraphim Academy was originally established in 1921, when many angels fled Heaven for Earth. This was the first mass exodus of angels, and there were very few angels who attended the school then—fourteen to be exact. Yet the school continued to grow as more and more angels fled the devastating war in Heaven, which of course culminated in the Earth Accords thirty-two years ago. At that point the school expanded dramatically, and every year it grows as more angels are born on Earth. This year we've set a new record with four hundred twelve students from all around the world, and we've added a few new professors to our roster as a result. I'd like to ask them to join us on stage so I can introduce them to you now."

He turns to the side as four people walk onto the stage. My gaze skims across the line of professors until my eyes stumble and trip over a man near the end. He's devastatingly handsome, with almost-black hair, dark stubble trailing down his jaw, and piercing green eyes. He's far too good-looking for any teacher to reasonably be, with a mouth made for kissing and a strong body that begs to be touched. I should know.

My breath catches in my throat as he gazes across the audience, and I sink down a little in my seat so he won't see me. At first I tell myself it can't be him. There's no way my luck is this bad, but there's no denying it. It's *him*.

I start to get up without realizing what I'm doing, and only Araceli's hand on my arm stops me. "What are you doing?" she whispers.

I shake my head, not really sure *what* I'm doing, only that my heart is pounding out of my chest, and I need to get out of here as fast as I possibly can, except doing so will only draw more attention to myself, and that's the absolute last thing I want at this moment. Shit.

I slump back down. It's fine. Maybe I can avoid him, and nothing bad will happen. There are lots of professors here, and I only have four classes, or maybe five if they figure out what type of angel I am. What's the chance that he'll be my professor?

Uriel gestures at the man I can't take my eyes off of. "I'd like to introduce Professor Kassiel, who will be teaching Angelic History at Seraphim Academy for all First Years."

Shit, shit, shit. There's no way I can get out of him being my teacher. This is bad, really bad.

Because I know him.

Intimately.

And worst of all, he knows me too.

He knows my secret.

He knows what I really am.

I'm screwed.

Chapter Ten

OLIVIA

our months ago

*T*he bar is dead tonight, and I'm starting to think I might go to bed alone and hungry, until a man walks in who makes me suck in my breath. I would have taken anyone at this point, man or woman, no matter what they looked like, but an attractive person definitely makes what I have to do easier. And this guy? *Damn.* I lick my lips in anticipation as he approaches the bar.

He's wearing a black three-piece suit that I bet cost more than my monthly rent—which isn't cheap, since this is Los Angeles and all—and it fits him like it was tailored for his body. And wow, what a body it is. Broad shoulders. Tall but not too tall. A tapered waist that makes me think he's got a six pack under there. I'm planning to find out soon enough.

He removes his jacket and folds it neatly over the back of the bar chair. Now in only his white shirt and charcoal tie, he rolls up his sleeves to his elbows slowly, revealing masculine wrists and strong, sexy forearms. Why is it guys are so much sexier when they roll up their sleeves like that? I nearly leap over the bar and jump him right there. He's one of the most gorgeous men I've ever seen, and trust me, I've known plenty of gorgeous men...intimately. This guy puts them all to shame, and I can't even put my finger on why. There's something about him that draws me in like no one else has done before.

His hair is short, thick, and a brown so dark it looks black until the light hits it. He has matching stubble across his face, but it's his eyes that really get me. They're green, a lot like mine actually, and there's something about him that feels familiar and makes him irresistible.

He's exactly what I need.

Our eyes hold for a little longer than normal, and I wonder if he feels this strange connection too. Sexual tension simmers between us without even a word spoken. For a second I wonder if he's like me, but then I dismiss that thought. I wouldn't be able to feed on another Lilim, and I can already feel a trickle of his delicious lust giving me a touch of strength.

He breaks my gaze and clears his throat. As he folds his hands on the marble counter, I realize I've been polishing a glass this entire time so hard it'll probably have permanent streaks. This isn't like me to fall apart all over a guy. I pull myself together and give him a lazy, seductive smile. "What can I get you?"

"A scotch, neat."

Well that's just unfair. He has a British accent, as If he wasn't hot enough already. I bet women fall all over themselves to be around him wherever he works. I've known him one second and I'm drooling all over the bar already.

I pour his drink, taking my time. I've got this routine down, and all I need to do is stick to it. First, you slowly fill their order, letting them get a good look at you from every angle. Some drinks are sexier than others to make. This one is too boring and simple to do many of my tricks, like shaking the drink in a way to draw attention to my breasts, but his eyes linger on me anyway. It helps there's not much else to look at in here, unless he turns around to stare out the floor-to-ceiling windows at the view of Los Angeles at night or the airplanes flying in to LAX. This rooftop hotel bar is dark, with low inoffensive music playing in the background, and everything is glass, metal, and marble. High quality furnishings and expensive alcohol for a more refined traveler—my favorite target.

Hotel bars near large airports are prime hunting ground, second only to strip clubs. Mother taught me that, and she should know—she's been doing this for centuries. Of course, she prefers staying at the hotels during her endless travels across the world, whereas I work at one. I need a way to make money, and Jonah would never approve of me working at a strip club. Not that I see him much anymore these days. Besides, at strip clubs you get regulars, and that only leads to trouble. Feeding on travelers is much safer.

Unfortunately for me, it's Tuesday night, which is always the slowest travel night. LAX is dead, which means this hotel bar is dead too. Before this guy walked in I was gazing wistfully across the empty tables while my hunger grew. The strip club life was starting to look better every day—I'd never go hungry there, and I'd probably make more money too.

It's a good thing this guy arrived in time.

I set his drink on the counter. "What brings you to L.A.?"

"I'm here to see my father." His voice makes it clear he's not excited about the prospect. He takes the scotch and downs it quickly.

I chuckle as his empty glass hits the counter, and I grab the bottle for a refill. "That bad, eh?"

His mouth twists. "He's not bad, not exactly, but he's definitely challenging. Our relationship is...complicated."

"Trust me, I know all about that." My smile is genuine because I can actually relate this time. "I'm not sure who is harder to deal with—my mother or my father."

He glances down at his drink with a frown and I sense I've hit a nerve. This isn't going well. Normally by now I'd have the target begging me to go back to his or her room already.

I try again. "Where are you visiting from?"

"I just moved to Northern California."

"And what do you do there?"

"I'm a history professor."

"Really?" I raise my eyebrows.

"Why is that so surprising?"

"The way you're dressed. I pegged you for a rich corporate type. A finance guy. CEO, maybe."

"You can blame my father for that. He has impeccable style." He picks at the shining button on his shirt sleeve. "The devil's in the details, after all."

"So they say." The saying is a little too close to home. I need to regain control of this situation. I lean forward on the counter, showing off my ample cleavage. "There's nothing better than a good-looking man in a well-fitting suit."

"My father would agree with you." His eyes dance down

my body. "Although I'd argue a beautiful woman in a little black dress is even better."

And just like that, I'm back in the game.

I reach out and caress his wrist lightly, using a tiny bit of my powers to ignite the desire in him. "I have a break in twenty minutes."

At my touch, a flicker of confusion passes over his face for the briefest moment, so fast I nearly miss it. Then he gives me an alluring smile. "Is that so?"

Thirty minutes later, I'm knocking on his door. He throws it open and at first we can only stare as the sexual tension rises —then we reach for each other without a word. Our lips meet, and the kiss is carnal and intense. I've never tasted anything like him before, and I need more, more, more.

My back hits the wall, and his hands are on my bare thighs, pushing my black dress higher. I grab the front of his shirt and yank it open, and yep, there's the six pack I was hoping for. His chest is lean and strong, and I run my hands down his hard skin, enjoying the feel of him under my fingertips. Then I reach for the front of his trousers.

"What's the rush?" he asks, as I pull the zipper down.

"I have to go back to work soon."

He lets out a sexy growl as he yanks me against him and hefts my thigh up. "Fine, but when your shift is over you're coming back for round two, and I'm going to take my time with you."

I wish that could happen, but for his own safety I can only sleep with him once. It's a shame, because I actually feel a connection with this guy, even though we've just met and have only shared a handful of words. If it were up to me, I'd spend

all night in his bed. We'd wake up beside each other and have
room service for breakfast. Maybe it would even turn into
something more after that. Something I've never had—a relationship.

It's impossible. Succubi and incubi—known collectively as
the Lilim—are doomed to live a life with many lovers but no
real love. We can't get close to humans without killing them,
and angels, demons, and fae are not much better off. We can
sleep with supernaturals more than once without killing them
at least, but over time we still drain them dry. It would require
a group of very strong supernaturals to withstand the insatiable
hunger of a succubus, and finding that is damn near impossible. If my mother, who has lived for thousands of years, hasn't
found lasting love, I have no hope of it either.

But then he's shoving my panties aside, and I forget all of
that. The only thing that matters is this moment with him right
now, with his mouth on my neck and his cock sliding inside
me. He thrusts hard, filling me up, caging me between him and
the wall. Every time his hips rock into mine, I feel his delicious
lust giving me power and strength, temporarily sating my
hunger. I lean my head back and close my eyes, partly because
it feels too good, and partly so he won't notice my eyes have
turned black—a side effect of a succubus feeding.

He lifts me up and wraps my legs around him, and his
mouth finds mine again, claiming it with every touch of his lips
and stroke of his tongue. I normally feel nothing when I have
sex with random strangers, but right now I can't *stop* feeling.
Sex with this stranger in a suit is unlike anything I've experi-
enced before, and it's intoxicating.

As he pounds harder, he hits me in just the right spot, and
I'm close, so close. He takes my chin in his hand and captures

my mouth again, sending me over the edge. I cling to his body as the climax hits me, and I feel him join me in release only moments later. I'm hit with a wave of power so strong it would knock me off my feet if I wasn't already wrapped around this man. His energy is so much stronger than anything I've encountered before, and I feel like I've fed on ten men instead of just one.

I don't know what he is—but I can tell he's not human.

He breaks the kiss and looks at me in surprise. "You're a succubus."

He knows.

I push him away from me, my heart pounding, my eyes wide. They're still black from feeding, confirming what he just said.

There are only three people in the world who know what I am. Until now.

I've made a huge mistake.

I throw open the door and run out of his hotel room as fast as I can. He shouts, "Wait!" but I'm already around the corner and banging on the elevator call button like my life depends on it, while simultaneously yanking down my dress. The elevator opens immediately and I rush inside, then press the Door Close button. He makes it to the elevator just as the door shuts.

I collapse against the mirrored wall, trying to catch my breath. How did he know? I made sure to keep my eyes shut, which means he must have sensed it when I fed on him. Shit, shit, shit. I should have known a guy that hot wasn't human, but I was hungry and reckless, and ignored everything my parents taught me. They will lock me up forever if they hear about what just happened.

I'll have to put in my resignation at the bar immediately. I might even need to leave the city. But he doesn't know my name or anything about me other than that I work at this hotel, and he doesn't live in Los Angeles. I won't ever see him again. I hope.

Chapter Eleven

OLIVIA

"And as a reminder," Uriel says, "flying is allowed over the campus, the surrounding forest, and to the nearby town of Angel Peak, but nowhere else. Thank you, and have a wonderful year at Seraphim Academy."

Other students stand up, and I blink rapidly as the world comes back into focus. Orientation is over, and I have no idea what happened after Professor Kassiel was introduced and my mind went back to that night we met. He told me he just moved to Northern California. He said he was a history professor. He obviously wasn't human. Dammit, I should have made the connection. Except Jonah went missing only a few weeks later, and I completely forgot about the encounter. Until now.

How am I going to get through this year when one of my professors knows what I really am?

Everyone starts to file out, and I hope I can slip out in the crowd without Kassiel seeing me. As I follow Araceli into the aisle, a tall, imposing man moves in front of me. Bastien's eyes narrow as he blocks my path. "Headmaster Uriel would like to speak with you in his office now."

I'm completely taken off-guard and dumbly ask, "He does?"

"That's what I said, isn't it? Follow me."

I cast one last look at Araceli, but there's no way she can save me. Why would Headmaster Uriel want to see me? What does he know?

People move out of the way like Bastien is a snake who might bite them, and we're outside the auditorium quickly, putting me out of sight of Kassiel at least. Bastien walks down the path and I walk beside him, my movements stiff. He doesn't say a thing, even though I keep glancing over at him. I can't help it. There's something about him I find so intriguing. I want to peel off his hard shell and arrogant layers and see what's lurking underneath.

He takes me to a two-story Victorian house that seems out of place on campus, and leads me inside the front door. "This is the Headmaster's house," Bastien explains in a clipped voice. There's an ornate staircase made of dark wood, and a blue and gold Persian rug under us, but the home feels cold and unwelcoming.

"Do you live here also?" I ask.

"Of course not. I live in the dorms now, like all other students."

"But you did before?"

His tone grows sharper with every question. "Yes, I grew up here."

I'm so curious about what it was like to grow up as Head-master Uriel's son, living here on campus as a child. And what about his mother? Is she in the picture? But Bastien's glare makes me keep my mouth shut.

He stops outside a dark wooden door. "This is the Headmaster's office. Please wait inside, my father will be with you shortly."

"Will do." I hesitate at the door. Okay, just one more question. "Are you his assistant or something?"

He scowls at me. "I am, yes."

He turns on his heel and leaves me there. I'm so tempted to sneak around the house and poke through Uriel's things, or even better, find Bastien's childhood room, but I've heard rumors about Uriel, and I worry he'd know what I was doing, even with my necklace on. Probably a bad idea—I don't want to get kicked out on my first day of school. Or killed.

I step into the office and sit in one of the black leather wingback chairs in front of his thick mahogany desk. He has a bookcase with ancient-looking books on it bound in leather, some of the titles so faded I can barely read them. Old relics are scattered around the room—an antique globe on the corner of his desk, a silver sword with a sapphire in the hilt hanging on the wall, and a glass case with a single feather inside that seems to be made of darkness itself.

The door opens and Uriel steps inside. I stand up quickly, my heart skipping a beat. He's even more unnerving up close. He has the same subtle radiance as Father, except he's like the sun on a cold, winter day—it may be bright, but it's not exactly warm.

"Thank you for meeting with me." He moves behind his desk and takes a seat. "You may be seated."

I sit down again. "Bastien said you wanted to speak with me?"

"Indeed. I've been informed that you didn't know you were half-angel, and that you don't know who your father was. You also haven't had any indication as to what Choir you belong to. Is that correct?"

"Yes. This is all new to me, and I'm still not entirely sure I belong here." Keeping my face neutral under his scrutiny isn't easy.

His cold smile makes me shiver a little. "You do. Of that, I have no doubt. However, it might take some time for your powers to emerge like your wings did, especially if you have unconsciously been suppressing them. I'd like you to spend some time with Bastien privately so he can better assess you."

I nearly groan, but manage to keep it silent. "Assess me? How?"

"He'll use his powers as an Ofanim to detect truth, plus he'll run some tests and ask you some questions." Uriel holds up a hand in a gesture of placation. "Nothing too extreme or invasive, I promise."

I try not to squirm in my seat, but the thought of being alone with Bastien while he studies me like a lab rat makes my skin crawl. On the other hand, this might be the perfect chance for me to do a little assessing of my own to find out what he knows about Jonah's disappearance. "If you think it will help, I'm okay with it."

"Excellent." Uriel hands me a piece of paper with my new schedule on it. Where it read *to be determined* before, it now has instructions for meeting with Bastien at the library at the end of each school day. "With Bastien's help, I believe we'll be able to learn more about you, starting with your Choir."

"Great," I manage to squeak out. Except I already know which Choir I belong to, I don't need any help awakening my powers, and I definitely don't want anyone knowing more about me. Especially Uriel.

Except every time he stares at me I feel he like already knows every one of my secrets. A chill runs down my spine as his gaze falls to my chest. "That's an interesting necklace."

I drop my hand quickly as I realize I've been playing with the necklace for the last few minutes. It's a nervous habit of mine, and one I need to quickly squash if I'm going to stay here at Seraphim Academy. "Thank you."

"Such a unique design. Gold with an alexandrite gem, is it not? It reminds me of something I saw long ago. A fae relic." He arches an eyebrow. "I don't suppose you know anything about that, now do you?"

"I don't even know what a fae is, really." I shrug, and it takes all of my acting skills to remain calm. "I think it's just costume jewelry, but it was my Mom's so it has sentimental value."

"Of course," he says, although I'm not sure he's convinced. He closes the file he had open—my file?—and rests his hands on the table. "I hope you enjoy your time here at Seraphim Academy and find everything you're searching for. Should you ever need any assistance or have any questions, please visit my office any time."

Everything I'm searching for... Does he know why I'm really here? I can't tell if he's just being polite or if there's a hidden meaning behind his words, but the way he's looking at me is creeping me out, and I quickly jump up. "Thanks," I croak out, before I rush through the door.

I nearly crash into Bastien on my way out of the house, and he gives me a withering look. "Running away, are we?"

I turn around, gather my inner strength, and straighten up.

I won't let these jerks intimidate or bully me. I'm not leaving the school, not until I figure out what happened to my brother, and they'll just have to deal with it. "Hardly. In fact, I'll see you tomorrow at the library."

A flicker of confusion crosses his face, and then he scowls and rushes back into the house. Uriel didn't tell him. A slow smile spreads across my face.

Day. Made.

Chapter Twelve

BASTIEN

I storm out of the house, my hands balled into fists at my side. It's just like my father to do this without asking me first, or even telling me his plans. It's probably another one of his experiments, which you'd think I would be used to after twenty-two years of them, but he always manages to surprise me. The most ridiculous part is that he can probably discern the half-human's Choir much easier and quicker than I can, but he claims this is a training exercise for me. Another test to see if I am worthy of taking his place someday.

Uriel only had me in the first place because of necessity. When the Archangels saw how quickly other angels were breeding now that we lived on Earth, they worried they would lose power without any children of their own to potentially take their place someday, thus they all made a pact to have at least one child. Archangel Raphael had already had plenty at that point, but he sired Marcus anyway as part of the deal, and two more children since. My father agreed to the plan reluctantly, and chose another Ofanim to ensure that his child would have be of the same Choir. My mother, Dina, was a very well-respected prophet, but she had no love for my father and no desire to raise a child. She did it out of duty, and as part of the deal she gave me up when I was a small child to be raised by Uriel. I've only seen her a few times since she left.

Thus the Princes came about—five male children sired from the Archangels. Azrael's son Ekariel was the first, but he was killed when he was a child, presumably by demons, but no one can confirm that. Marcus and I were born next, followed by Callan and Jonah, who were sired by not one but two Archangels each, which means they face high expectations from the entire angel community. That's one reason it was even more of a shock when Jonah went missing. Of course, he didn't actually disappear—a few of us know where he went. But he should have returned by now, and it's troubling that we haven't heard from him at all.

I'm thinking about Jonah and our promise to him when I walk into the student store, which is a misnomer since nothing in here costs money. I still need to pick up my books for my second year at Seraphim Academy, and when I step inside it looks like many other students are in the same situation. The student store is filled with books, gym uniforms, and anything else we might need for our classes. It also has some snacks and things for our dorms, such as sheets, towels, and so forth. There are also a few items of clothing, ranging from important things like emergency underwear to sweatshirts with the Seraphim Academy logo on it. Everything in here is provided by the school at no charge, although students are expected to only take what they need. If someone is caught being excessive or greedy, they may have their privileges revoked at the student store and the cafeteria. It works as a good deterrent because no one wants to be that person who isn't allowed a meal, or who has to use their own money to buy something. The angel community is small and tightknit, and the potential shame keeps people in line.

I head for the textbook section and pick up the one for Human Studies, and when I turn I spot the half-human walking down the aisle while checking a piece of paper. There is no avoiding her.

Olivia stops beside me and grabs the Demon Studies textbook off the shelf. She cocks her head. "Are you following me?"

"Hardly. I have to get books too, just like every other student."

"Except you're not just like every other student, are you?"

"What does that mean?"

She gives a little shrug, drawing my eyes to her bare shoulders and her smooth skin. "I'm told you get certain perks like your own private lounge in the bell tower. I'm sure there are other things I don't even know about too."

"You don't know what you're talking about." My voice is even colder than usual, but she doesn't react at all. Any other student in the school would be running for the hills with the look I'm giving her, but she seems immune to intimidation.

"Why don't you instruct me then? Or is that what you'll be doing in our sessions?" Her dark eyebrows lift up and her words sound dirty, although that might just be her voice. Everything she says sounds sensual. The woman is dripping sex appeal, and even though she's very much not my type, it's impossible not to notice it.

I scowl at her. "In our sessions I will be studying you to determine what your Choir is. Nothing more. With luck, we will uncover your powers quickly so I can stop wasting my time on you."

She shrugs. "Suit yourself."

She turns and moves on to the next shelf to find another book. As she grabs it, I stare at her and try to sense something, anything, about her Choir. Most people's Choirs are obvious. Her roommate, for example, has an aura that screams in your face that she is a healer, a Malakim. The Valkyries are also obviously warriors, Erelim, and were practically born shooting burning light from their fingertips. But this half-human is a mystery. I can't read her aura at all, which worries me. I've never met anyone like that before. Is it because of her human side? Perhaps she doesn't have any powers. I'll need to do some research on other half-humans to better know what to expect.

I'm not looking forward to the sessions with Olivia, but it will give me a chance to study her better. Callan wants the girl gone as quickly as possible, and doesn't care what he has to do to achieve that goal. He's always been the type to set his eyes on something and make it happen, no matter who he has to shove out of the way to get it done. Marcus, on the other hand, thinks we should get to know her in order to learn about her connection with Jonah. But Marcus always thinks with his dick, and it's clear he wants to fuck the half-human too. He's not exactly picky, after all.

And me? My eyes narrow as Olivia saunters away, her hips swaying enticingly as she grabs some gym clothes in her size. I want to study her until I uncover her secrets. I'll tear down every wall she's hiding behind, until her past is laid bare and all of her truths are naked and on display. Then I'll know what to do with her.

Chapter Thirteen

OLIVIA

The next morning, I wake with a hard pit in my stomach. Classes start today, and my gut churns at the thought of attending Angelic History. There's nothing I can do about it other than leave the school, which I'm definitely not going to do. I'll just have to hope that Professor Kassiel doesn't recognize me. It's been four months. Maybe he's forgotten me entirely. I doubt it, but I don't know what else to do. If he does bring up that night, I'll deny everything—although I can't imagine he'd want the Headmaster to know he slept with a student either, especially not when he's just started working here.

It takes me a while to get ready because I have to work around Araceli. I haven't lived with another person since I turned eighteen and got out of foster care, and I forgot what a pain it is to share a bathroom. Demons get their powers at eighteen, and when you have a new guy or girl in your bed all the time it's a lot easier to deal with when you live alone. On the other hand, it's also a lot less lonely with Araceli around, and trust me, it's hard to forget she's there. She's constantly singing to herself, dancing around the place, and generally filling the suite with her presence. I can see this getting annoying fast, especially because angels are all morning people and I am definitely *not*, but at the moment I find it somewhat charming.

I chug a ton of coffee, we grab a quick bite to eat in the cafeteria, and then we head to our first class, Combat Training. Araceli and I are both wearing our gym clothes, which have the Seraphim Academy logo on a white t-shirt above dove gray shorts. Araceli is practically bouncing as we head to the gym, while the morning sunlight shines down on her skin, making it glow a little. She's got her brown and purple hair tied back, and I can see the slightly pointed tips of her ears from her fae heritage. She must not feel the need to hide that side of herself, which I admire.

"I can't wait for Combat Training," she says. "Mom taught me a little, but she's a healer and not a fighter, so her skills are a bit rusty."

As we walk, I tie my hair back in a quick, messy bun. The morning sun warms the back of my neck, and my angelic side drinks it in. "You'll do better than me. My skills are nonexistent."

"The humans didn't teach you any form of combat?"

"Not really. I took a self-defense course once, but somehow I don't think that's the kind of fighting we're going to do now."

"Probably not. Professor Hilda is a Valkyrie and a former member of the Angelic Army. I heard she's tough as nails."

"What are the Valkyrie exactly?" I ask. "Everyone talks about them like they're a big deal, but all I know about them is from mythology. I never imagined they'd be real."

"Valkyries are a division of the Angelic Army with all

female warriors, known for their fighting skills and for being damn near impossible to kill. They once served directly under Archangel Michael, before his death anyway. Now I suppose they serve under Michael's replacement, Zadkiel. And speaking of Zadkiel, I see Tanwen is in our class also."

I groan at the sight of the blond girl walking into the gym ahead of us. "Just what I need. I'm sure she'll remind me many times that I don't belong here thanks to my human half."

Araceli holds the door open for me. "Tanwen is a total bitch, but to be fair, she does have more reason than most to hate humans. Her mother was the leader of the Valkyries, but she was killed by human hunters when Tanwen was a kid. Those are people who search for any sort of supernatural and wipe them out."

"I didn't realize there were humans who did that sort of thing. But that doesn't mean she should hate anyone with their blood."

"No, it doesn't. I think she just gets off on being the meanest girl around, and she'll use whatever makes you different or lesser to bully you. I've known her my whole life, and have gotten pretty good at avoiding her or ignoring her. Unfortunately her father is Zadkiel, and now that he's taken the empty spot on the Archangel Council, she's going to be insufferable. She's the only daughter of Archangel, even if he wasn't one when she was born."

Except, she isn't the only one, and my father's been an Archangel from the beginning. But I'll keep that little secret to myself.

We head into the gym, which looks like every other gym in every school I've been to, except there are old-fashioned weapons hanging on one wall and armor on another. Professor

Hilda stands in the center of the room with her arms crossed as she watches the students file in. She's a large woman, built like a Viking with broad shoulders and wide hips, and has white-blond hair cropped close around her head.

The students stand around and chat, and Araceli and I make our way to the back wall to wait for class to start. That's when an angel I don't expect to see walks into the room. Callan doesn't look like he belongs in a combat training class for beginners. No, he looks like he should be out there on a battlefield swinging a broadsword and cutting down his enemy. Maybe that's why he walks to Hilda and begins talking to her quietly.

I nudge Araceli and nod at Callan. "What's he doing here?"

"I'm not sure. He should be in the Second Year class, not this one."

A handsome guy in front of us with dark skin and friendly eyes turns around and grins. "I heard he's so advanced in combat that he tested out of even the Third Year class. All that training from Michael, I guess. But they need him to do something, so he's working as Hilda's assistant during the combat classes."

Well, that's just great. There'll be no escaping him now. I thought since the Princes were all Second Years we might not have any of the same classes, but no matter where I go or what I do, one of them always seems to be in my face. But hey, at least I have a chance to beat Callan up in this class. Okay, who am I kidding? Look at the muscles on his arms, and the six-pack straining against his gym shirt. Even his thighs are impressive, from what I can see under those shorts. There's no way I can beat him up. If I do manage to land a punch, he'll probably laugh it off.

Hilda claps her hands, and when she speaks she has a strong accent that sounds German. "Welcome to Combat Training, First Years. I am Professor Hilda, and this is my assistant, Callan. We'll skip the part where I explain my history and why I'm qualified to teach this class and get right to the point. You're here to learn to fight, because even if the Great War is over, it's never going to be safe for us. There are still demon attacks we must defend against, and the humans grow bolder every day as they try to hunt us down. And who knows, maybe the fae will decide they want Earth next. We must be vigilant at all times." She slams a fist into her hand, and some of the students jump. Yep, this is definitely a lot more intense than my self-defense class.

"First, I need to see what I'm working with here," Professor Hilda says. "Some of you have had combat training before, and some of your parents have sorely neglected this vital part of your education, but no worries, I'll get you all up to speed in the next three years. When you graduate, you'll be ready to enter the Angelic Army, should you so choose. That is my guarantee."

Callan crosses his arms and surveys the students with an impassive, hard look on his face. When his blue eyes land on me, his jaw clenches. I wait for him to look away, but he doesn't. He just keeps staring, and I refuse to look away either and instead narrow my eyes in an open challenge. Heat spreads through my body to my core as we face off across the gym, and everything else around me fades away. It's just me and him, and the arousal growing between us. The staring turns from hostile to something else, something that makes my inner succubus hungry. Does he feel it too?

I can't help it, I lick my lips. Only then does he frown and look away. One point for me.

"When I call out your name, step forward and you'll be assigned a partner," Hilda says. She begins going through her list, and Araceli is paired off with the friendly guy in front of us, whose name is Darel. He gives her a big smile and seems like a nice enough guy, which has been rare so far at the school.

As Araceli walks to the front, someone mutters, "Glad I'm not paired with pointy-ears there."

Araceli's smile falters and she touches the hair by her ears self-consciously, but then she keeps going like we didn't all hear that line. I find myself angry on her behalf, even though I barely know her. Maybe because I can relate to what she's going through. I shoot a glare at the Valkyrie who said it, but she ignores me.

Hilda calls Tanwen's name, and the blond saunters to the front of the class with an arrogant smirk on her face. As the daughter of a Valkyrie, she's obviously had plenty of combat training and is ready to show it off.

"Your partner is Olivia," Hilda calls out.

My stomach stinks. Seriously, me and Tanwen as partners. Did Hilda do this on purpose? She must know Tanwen, and she must know about my situation. Why would she pair us up if not to humiliate me?

Once the entire class is paired up, Hilda moves to the side and crosses her arms. "Try to take down your opponent however you can so I can see what I'm dealing with here. Once they hit the floor, it's over. And remember, you may not use any of your angelic powers. That means you, Erelim. Don't make me send anyone to the healing room."

We spread out around the room and I face off against Tanwen, whose blue eyes take me in with disdain. My parents gave me a tiny bit of combat training, but not much. Just enough to get me out of a tight situation so I can escape and hide. I have a feeling that won't be good enough here.

A whistle sounds, and my back hits the floor of the gym, while Tanwen's pretty face sneers down at me. It happens so fast I don't even have time to react.

This does not bode well for me.

As pain courses through my back, Tanwen shakes her head. "That wasn't even a challenge. Surely you can do better than that."

I pick myself up off the ground, already sore in numerous places. It's a good thing angels and demons heal quickly, although it still hurts like hell when we get our asses handed to us.

Which happens to me, over and over. Tanwen is intense, and taking me down isn't even a challenge for her. Meanwhile Araceli and Darel are giggling as they roll around on the mat, and I don't even need to be a succubus to feel the lust between them. I try not to pout, but why can't I be paired up with a hot guy, instead of being a Valkyrie punching bag?

Callan walks over as I hit the floor again, this time with a kick that sweeps out my feet from under me. I hit my side this time and Tanwen just shakes her head.

"I see you're putting the half-human through the ringer," Callan says, as he towers over me. From this angle I have a nice view of his very firm legs, at least.

"Of course I am," Tanwen says, flipping back her ponytail. "How else is she going to learn?"

"True, although I'm not sure she can get a blow in," Callan says.

Tanwen shrugs. "I'm not trying to teach her combat skills. I'm trying to show her she doesn't belong here."

I drag myself back to my feet. "That's what everyone keeps telling me, but I'm still here."

"This is only the first day," Callan says. "It'll be a miracle if you survive the week."

If I thought I might get any help from Callan in his role as assistant, I was wrong. He turns back to Tanwen and nods. "Impressive form. I can see you've been practicing."

"Always," she practically purrs. She's giving him a flirtatious smile and some fuck-me eyes. "How are you doing, anyway? It's been way too long since we hung out. We should get dinner sometime. Now that I'm a student here we can catch up."

"Catching up would be good," he says, but then he looks at me, and I know he doesn't want her, not like she wants him. Nope, as hard as he might deny it, his lust is directed at me and not her. It's enough to heal my aches and take the pain away, and I stretch my arms and neck with relief.

He walks away, and Tanwen looks like a cat who just caught a mouse as she grins at me. "Ready for another go? Since I'm in such a good mood, I might even let you get a blow in."

Spoiler alert: she doesn't.

*T*here's a short break to rest and lick our wounds, and then it's time for my next class, which is Flight. We stay in the same gym uniforms but head outside by the lake, and I'm so exhausted from Tanwen beating me up that I don't have to pretend very hard that I don't know how to fly. This first day is mostly an introduction to the idea of flight, where the professor makes sure we all know how to extend and retract our wings without a problem. Most of the class doesn't have a problem with this, although I put up a good show that I'm having trouble, and Tanwen rolls her eyes and whispers to her friends about me. I ignore their catty looks. I want everyone to underestimate me, even if it's frustrating some-times. At least there are no Princes in this class.

After Flight ends, we have a longer break to catch lunch, and I change into some fresh clothes after taking a shower. I eat a sandwich, chug some coffee from my *I'm a fucking angel* mug, and then I head off to Demon Studies.

This class is held on the second floor of the main hall, and as I enter the large gothic church-like building I can't forget my first day here when the Princes swooped down on me from the bell tower. None of them do that this time, presumably because they're all in class, which is a relief.

I notice the looks and the whispers as I head up the stairs, and wonder how long they will last. I keep my head high as I walk along the white stone floors, but when I enter the room I stop in my tracks—because Marcus is inside, sitting at one of the desks. And worst of all, the only open seat is directly behind him. So much for avoiding the Princes.

I refuse to let them intimidate me, so I walk toward the desk with outward confidence, even if I'm faltering a little inside. I remind myself that I need to get information from them, so maybe it won't be too bad having them in my classes after all, and Marcus seems like the most tolerable one. He gives me a little nod as I pass him, which I ignore. His dark hair is especially wild today, and as I sit behind him I can't help but notice how rich and luscious it looks. He's got hair a girl could envy. Or daydream about running her fingers through. Not that I'm doing that. Nope.

The professor walks in, and he's wearing a bowtie covered with tiny lightning bolts, making me think of Harry Potter. He's got on a dapper little suit to match it in off-white, and I wouldn't be surprised if his wings were the same color. He has a kind smile and bright blue eyes, with salt and pepper hair.

"Welcome to Demon Studies," he says. "I assume you're all here for Demon Studies anyway. If you're not, then you should hurry and find your actual class before it's too late. You definitely don't want to be late on your first day of class, after all!" He claps his hands together. "Now, as long as we're all in the right place I'd like to go over a little of what you can expect here. This is one of the only classes that has students from all three years in it, just like the other Supernatural Studies courses. Some of you I recognize from last year's Fae Studies course, and it's good to see you again." He does a little wave. "To the rest of you, I am Professor Raziel, and it is my pleasure to meet you all. I can't wait to help you learn about demons, our ancient enemy." He makes it sound like he's talking about teaching us to make a pie, and not about the denizens from Hell that angels have been fighting for thousands of years.

Marcus casually whispers over his shoulder, "Overly cheerful, isn't he?" He gives me a quick grin and then turns around again. If Raziel notices or hears him, he doesn't react. I bet the Princes get away with all sorts of things in class.

"This year we're going to learn all about the various kinds of demons, because just like angels there are many types. In fact there are seven types, which align with the infamous Seven Deadly Sins. I'm sure you've all heard about those before, and you may have heard things about demons from your parents or from other angels you know, but in this class we're going to try to stick to facts and not stereotypes or opinions. Some of what you've learned so far might be wrong, so I'd like you to keep an open mind. Demons are not our enemy anymore, not like they once were. Ever since the Earth Accords, we've been in an uneasy truce with them, and it's important to learn about them so we can understand them better."

"And so if they break the truce we can defeat them," Blake, that douchebag who gave me my dorm key, says.

Raziel looks flustered, but he nods quickly. "Yes, yes, of course, we must be prepared to fight them should it come to that. As I was saying, we're going to go over all the different types of demons, from imps to Fallen, and everything in between."

"And succubi, right?" a guy sitting next to Blake asks.

My hair stands on the back of my neck and I worry maybe someone here knows something, but the guy who asked is just grinning and nudging Blake like he said something funny, and I realize it's because he's a horndog who just wants to talk about sex demons.

"Yes, we will talk about the two different types of Lilim later this year." Raziel lets out an exasperated sigh like he's heard that question a dozen times before. "But first, let's discuss how angels and demons are similar and different. Like angels, demons have limited immortality, meaning they don't age after a certain point, but they can still be killed. They also have superior strength and speed, and heal faster than humans, just like we do. Another similarity? Due to their immortality, they found it difficult to have children in Hell, as we did in Heaven, but on Earth it is much easier for all of us to procreate. No one is entirely sure why, but it means ever since the Earth Accords there's been a boom in both angel and demon populations."

He continues on, but I tune him out, and find myself staring at the back of Marcus instead. The man is far too hot for his own good, and he knows it. You can tell from the way he smiles, like everything has come easily for him his entire life, and he just expects to be worshipped. He turns and gives me that lazy smile now and I scowl at him, even as my heart beats a little faster. Damn succubus blood.

I try to focus on what Raziel is saying, but it's difficult. As Marcus runs a hand through his hair, I get a sexy whiff of sandalwood, and my hunger stirs. I bite my pen and concentrate harder on the class.

"Now, let's discuss differences," Raziel says. "Whereas angels get their powers at twenty-one, demons get their powers earlier, at eighteen."

So far everything he's said has been true. I can only hope his class will be fair and grounded and contain some actual knowledge. And hey, at least I should ace this course, right?

Assuming I don't get too distracted by Marcus, anyway.

Chapter Fifteen
OLIVIA

*N*ext on the schedule I have the class I've been dreading, Angelic History. It's also in the main hall, but on the third floor, and it feels like I'm marching to my doom as I walk down the long hallway. I try to think of a way to get out of taking this course, but if I reveal that I've been well-versed in both angelic and demonic history, I'll ruin my cover and expose what I am. I have to keep up my clueless half-human act, and that means I need this class.

Professor Kassiel is already inside, sitting at his corner desk with a book in his hand, but he doesn't look up when I enter. I let out a relieved breath and stick to the far wall as I hurry to the back of the class, keeping my head down and trying to draw as little attention to myself as possible. I find a seat in the back behind a tall angel and slouch down in my chair. So far so good. Now I just need to make it through the next few months without him noticing me.

Fat chance.

More First Year students file into the class, and I see a few familiar faces from my other classes, but no one I know by name. I'm sad Araceli is in a different Angelic History period, but not sad that Tanwen isn't here.

When the clock strikes the hour, Kassiel rises from his desk and moves to the center of the room. He's wearing another impeccable, perfectly tailored suit that obviously cost a fortune, and I can't take my eyes off him.

"My name is Professor Kassiel and I'll be teaching you Angelic History 101 this year. We're going to be covering the basics, and while some of you might think you know this stuff, you might be surprised by what you learn once we get into the details."

His voice is exactly as sensual as I remember with the lilting British accent, and it's impossible not to stare at his striking green eyes. I'm not the only one who notices. The desire in the air is palpable, and I shift in my seat uncomfortably, suddenly starving—and not for food. I knew being a succubus at an angel school might be a problem, but I didn't realize just how much until now. I bet the Lilim at Hellspawn Academy don't have this issue.

Kassiel clasps his hands behind his back as he begins pacing in front of the classroom, cutting a sharp profile. "History is important both to know where we came from and to learn from the past so that we don't repeat it. Unless you know what we've done, you won't know how to do better in the future. It also gives insight into the present and why the world is the way it is at the moment."

I can barely concentrate on what he's saying. All I can think about is how he tasted and felt under my hands. I cross my legs and shift in my seat, trying to ignore the growing ache between my legs.

"Let's begin with a quick overview, as I'm told at least one person in this class grew up in the human world."

Oh crap. That would be me. I sink a little lower in my seat, even as people glance at me and make it obvious I'm the one he means.

Luckily Kassiel keeps talking and doesn't notice. "There are four known worlds—Earth, Heaven, Hell, and Faerie. The one we're in is obviously Earth and is the world of humans. Angels all originally came from Heaven, while demons came from Hell, and fae from Faerie. Thousands of years ago, the fae learned how to open gateways between the worlds, and they shared this magic with angels and demons. This one action had many long-lasting consequences, including many wars, and the fae came to regret sharing that magic—but that's something for your Fae Studies course, perhaps. All we need to know right now is that it allowed angels and demons to visit Earth.

"Angels kept their gateways heavily regulated so only a few people came to Earth at any one time, and at first they sent people like Sandalphon and Metatron, who we will discuss in detail in a few weeks. Others later visited different parts of the world, bringing knowledge from the more civilized and advanced society in Heaven. Meanwhile, demons and fae also began to influence Earth, and humans started to worship our three races as gods. Many scholars have wondered why there are so many winged gods and goddesses in mythology, both good and bad—Valkyries, Harpies, Cupid, Isis, and so forth. Those are all angels, while some of the other gods, like the half-animal ones such as Horus and Pan, are demons. Many of the elemental and nature gods are based on the fae. As you can see, angels, demons, and fae have been impacting the human world for as long as we have recorded history, and we're going to learn more about that this year."

I know all of this already, but it's fascinating to hear it from his mouth. There's something about the way he talks that makes me want to prop my hand under my chin and watch him talk about history—never one of my favorite subjects —for hours.

"For most of history, angels, demons, and fae all lived in their own worlds, with a few exceptions. Angels were always very strict about who they let travel to Earth, and the gateways were controlled by the Archangel Council. Demons, on the other hand, allowed anyone to go through as they please, and many demons decided to live on Earth instead of in Hell, creating bloodlines that go back centuries. The fae rarely go to Earth and prefer to stay in their own world—and don't like people going to it either, especially after the Faerie Wars, which we'll cover next year. This year we'll be going in depth about the long war between angels and demons, which I'm sure you all know came to an end thirty-two years ago, when Michael and Lucifer signed the Earth Accords. Does anyone know why they did this?"

A girl in front raises her hand and seems a little flustered when he nods at her. "We'd lost so many angels that the council was worried we might be wiped out."

"That is a part of it, yes. Demons had the same problem. After thousands of years of war, with very few new angels and demons being born every year, both races were at risk of extinction. What else?"

"Heaven and Hell were both destroyed," a guy on the right calls out.

"Correct. Due to the war, both worlds were in ruins.

They'd become desolate battlefields, with empty cities and burned fields. Both the Archangel Council and the Archdemons realized that in order to keep both our kinds alive, our future was on Earth. They called for a truce, and after many weeks of negotiations, they ended the war with the signing of the Earth Accords. Working together, Michael and Lucifer used a magical item created by the fae known as the Staff of Eternity to send every last angel and demon to Earth and seal off Heaven and Hell for all time. As part of the truce, there is to be no fighting or breeding between angels and demons, and we must keep our existence a secret from humankind."

"But what about demon attacks?" another girl asks. "They keep happening, even with the truce."

"Yeah, and what about Michael?" the tall angel in front of me chimes in.

"Demon attacks do still occur, but they're pretty rare, just as angel attacks on demons are also rare. When they do happen, the perpetrators are punished swiftly and decisively, so they are not seen as the beginning of a new war or a threat to the truce. Both angel and demon leadership take these attacks very seriously. As for Michael's death..."

He turns toward the student who asked the question, but then his eyes land on me. Shit. I was so intrigued by his words I forgot to slouch, and now it's too late. He does a double-take, his words forgotten, and his jaw falls open as his eyes rake over me. Everything that happened four months ago is laid bare before us, and I know he remembers it all, just as I did. Any hope that he's forgotten me or that I could stay under the radar is out the window.

I can see it in his eyes—he knows what I am.

He tries to recover from his shock and turns back to the board, but stares at it like he's completely forgotten where he is and what he's doing. Great, I broke our professor.

He glances at me one more time, while the other students send each other quizzical looks, and then he runs a hand over his face and takes a moment to recover.

"As I was saying," he begins. "Michael's death is a mystery, and since Lucifer had an alibi, at this time no one can prove it was demons who did it."

"Bullshit," someone mutters under their breath.

Kassiel clears his throat. "The investigation is ongoing. What we do know is that in the last thirty-two years both sides have tried to make peace, but it hasn't always been easy, and many people on both sides wish to start the war again. Old hatreds die hard, especially among immortals who were at war for thousands of years. But others hope that this younger generation, all born on Earth, will be different and can learn to live among both humans and demons peacefully."

His eyes meet mine again and my heart skips a beat as our gazes lock. Is he saying he won't turn me in, or that he accepts me even though I'm half-demon? That he doesn't hate demons as much as some others might? Or am I reading too much into his words?

What I'm not reading too much into is the sexual tension between us. Even across a classroom with a dozen other students around us, the heat is there. I know he can feel it too, and my inner succubus wants to leap over the desks, push him against that chalkboard, and wrap my legs around him until we're both gasping with pleasure. I tear my eyes away before I start drooling, and squeeze my thighs together. *Not now*, I tell the hunger. I'm definitely going to have to feed soon, or I'll never make it through the week.

He keeps talking, and I somehow manage to get through class without ripping off my clothes or Kassiel's, despite his many heated looks. It's a huge relief when class is over. I grab my bag and start to hurry out with the other students, but then his voice stops me.

"Olivia, may I speak to you for a moment?"

Shit. This can't be good.

I stay to the side until everyone has left the room and then I approach Kassiel slowly, where he perches against the side of his desk. He watches me come closer with a heavy, unreadable gaze.

I draw in a breath. "If this is about that night, neither of us knew who the other was, and—"

"That's what I need to speak to you about." He furrows his brow and I know he's going to bring up the succubus thing.

I interject quickly to stop him. "Don't worry, I won't tell anyone about what happened. In fact, the less we speak about that night the better, I think."

He frowns as he studies me, and I desperately want to know what he's thinking. "Of course."

"Is it a problem for me to be in class? Because we could ask Uriel to move me to another professor."

He stands up straighter. "No, it's not a problem. Our relationship will remain completely professional. Student-professor relationships are strictly forbidden, and I don't think either of us wants to jeopardize our position here."

I nod. "Agreed."

Except knowing it's forbidden? That only makes me want it more.

Chapter Sixteen

KASSIEL

I can only stare at Olivia as she leaves the room. How can it be?

I never forgot her after that night in Los Angeles. She ran away once I realized she was a succubus, and after that I did a little digging, but no one knew who she was, and eventually I let it go. There are many demons who don't wish to be found, and it was obvious she was one of those by her reaction. But what is she doing here now? How can a succubus attend Seraphim Academy? Is it some kind of mistake?

And the biggest question of all, does she know my secret too?

I pack up my things and leave the classroom, since I'm done teaching for the day. I walk across campus to the professors' building, which has all of our offices and a lounge area. It also acts as a dorm for those professors who live on campus, like me.

I head into the professors' lounge and grab one of the sandwiches there, then lean against the counter. Hilda and Raziel are in here, each doing their own thing at separate tables. Hilda is wolfing down a sandwich like she hasn't eaten in days, while Raziel is reading a newspaper. I haven't talked to either of them much since arriving at the school, but they've both been friendly so far.

"What do you know about that student, Olivia Monroe?" I ask, trying to keep my voice casual. I've heard the other professors gossip about their students before, so hopefully my question won't seem too odd.

"The half-human?" Hilda snorts. "She's going to need a lot of help if I'm going to get her into fighting shape."

Half...human? That can't be right. "Are they sure she's part human? How do they know?"

Raziel folds up his newspaper. "Her mother was a human."

"And her father?" I ask.

"No one knows who is he is," Raziel says.

"Coward," Hilda says. "He should step forward and own up to his mistake, for his daughter's sake. It's the right thing to do."

"Yes, it is," I say. "But how do they know she's an angel and not Fallen?"

Raziel's head tilts. "Well, she has wings, although they are black, which is a bit unusual I'll admit. But she can create light, so she's definitely not Fallen."

"There's a video of her Emergence, and it's pretty clear she's an angel from that," Hilda adds. "It should be in her files, although it was taken down from the internet by Aerie Industries."

My eyebrows dart up. "A video?"

Hilda nods. "Yeah, she got her wings at a party when she

fell off the balcony. You should watch the video, it's pretty shocking."

"It must've given those angels at Aerie a lot of cleanup work," Raziel adds.

"Thanks," I say. "I'll check it out."

I grab another sandwich and head to my office. Once I'm inside, I pull up the school file on Olivia, which is only accessible to Headmaster Uriel and professors. I read through what little they know of her, including information on her mother's death, and feel even more confused. When I met her in the bar, Olivia mentioned she had a complicated relationship with her mother and father. She was either lying then or she's lying now. I have a suspicion I know which it is.

I hit play on the video. Someone caught the incident on their camera phone, and at first they're filming someone doing shots by the pool at a St. Patrick's Day party. There's a scream and the camera pans up to catch a girl flying above the pool, with black wings spread and light glowing from her entire body. She hovers there for a moment and then she falls into the water, where her wings vanish along with the light. Things turn into total chaos next as a bunch of people dive into the water to rescue her, and when they pull her out, she's unconscious. That's where the video ends.

I lean back with a frown. She's definitely an angel. Was I wrong about her being a succubus? No, I know what they feel like, and I recognized that black glow in her eyes after she fed on me. But she clearly has wings too, and I might have believed she was a Fallen except for the glowing light. Unless that was all fake, but Aerie Industries would have investigated her thoroughly after this incident.

Which means she's something that should be impossible.

98 ELIZABETH BRIGGS

Something so forbidden it's never spoken about. Something that could change everything if people knew.

She's half angel and half demon.

No wonder she looked so nervous when our eyes met. And now that I know the truth about her, I'm not sure what to do with it.

I know her secret, but does she know mine? Did I say anything that night about my past? I wrack my memory trying to remember our conversation. We spoke of my father, and I mentioned I was a history professor, but little else. I don't think she knows anything about me, just as I know nothing about her.

Does Uriel know what she truly is? He must. He knows everything that happens at this school. If so, there's no reason for me to bring it up. She's obviously keeping that side of herself a secret, but what is she doing here? She must know it isn't safe, although I doubt the demon school would be any safer for her.

I stare at her photo on my screen, gazing into those mysterious green eyes. I'll keep her secret as long as she doesn't interfere with my own plans. I'll be her professor and nothing more, no matter how much my blood sings when she's near. It will be torture having her in my class, but I've survived worse before. If anyone can resist a succubus, it's me.

But damn, it's going to be a long year.

Chapter Seventeen
OLIVIA

*J*ust when I think my first day of class can't get any worse, I remember I have to meet with Bastien.

I head to the library, which is on the other side of the lake and set back against the forest. The front of the building is covered in mosaics depicting angels fighting demons, and a grand door leads me inside.

Bastien is waiting by the front desk, and he gives me a sharp look as I enter. "You're three minutes late."

"Sorry, Professor Kassiel needed to speak with me after class."

Bastien's eyes narrow a little, but then he turns on his heel. "Follow me. I've reserved a private room for us to begin our testing."

He leads me through the library, which has tall shelves completely filled with books both new and old. I catch glimpses of ancient texts on demons combined with new texts on biology. Father told me that when angels had to leave Heaven they only had a week to gather the most important things to take with them. Most libraries had been destroyed in the war already, but the few texts that were saved were sent to this library. It's a strange feeling, knowing that most of angelic literature and knowledge is contained within these walls, going back thousands of years. Maybe that's not so impressive to immortals with such a long memory, but it is to me.

On the far side of the library are private rooms for studying, and Bastien leads me to one of those. He flips the lights on and takes a seat on one side of the table, his back straight and his posture perfect. I take a seat across from him much more slowly.

"By now you should know about the four Choirs," he starts. "I am one of the Ofanim, who can detect lies and see the truth, among other things."

"Have you detected any lies from me?" I ask.

His eyes narrow. "Not so far, but we'll see what happens during this session."

"I have no reason to lie," I lie. I nearly touch my necklace, but I have it tucked away inside the collar of my shirt today. I don't need anyone else noticing it and becoming suspicious, and I have to trust that it will keep me safe. Mother wouldn't have given it to me unless she thought it could handle even the strongest Ofanim.

"We'll see about that. I'm going to use the light of truth upon you now, which should reveal more about you to me."

He holds his hands close together and a glowing white light appears between his palms. He lets it get bigger and bigger until it's almost the size of his torso, and then he releases it toward me. I cringe as the light surrounds me and feel a little tingle, but nothing else happens. His scowl deepens and I know the necklace is working.

"Do you see anything?" I ask, trying to look and sound innocent.

"No. Very unusual. I should be able to detect something, but with you I get absolutely nothing. It's almost like there is some type of magic blocking it. You wouldn't know anything about that, would you?"

"No. I don't know a thing about magic."

He leans forward with determination in his gray eyes. "I'll try again."

He continues casting different truth spells on me, but still doesn't get any of the information he so desperately desires. A sense of satisfaction forms in my chest when I see how much trouble he's having, and it gives me confidence that I might actually be able to pull this deception off long enough to find Jonah.

"Has anyone tested your blood?" he asks.

I stiffen a little at the thought. Would they be able to detect demon blood in me? Probably. I shoot him a look of confusion to show I'm just a simple-minded human. "No, and I don't think I'm okay with that."

"Very well," he grumbles. He'd obviously love to stick me with all sorts of sharp objects, and maybe even that one in his pants from the way he looks at me sometimes and the little buzz of lust I detect from him. I can't decide if he wants me, hates me, or just sees me as one big puzzle. Maybe all of the above. I think that's how I'm going to get to him. If he sees me as some mystery he can solve, then he might be more inclined to open up to me about Jonah. If any of the Princes will know about his disappearance, it's Bastien.

He steeples his fingers on the table. "There are other ways to tell what Choir you belong to. We'll go through a list of questions. First of all, have you felt anything when someone has lied to you recently? Like a strong sense of wrongness?"

"No, I haven't felt anything like that. But maybe no one has lied to me."

"I doubt that, but let's try it now. The sky is orange. Anything?"

"Nope. Nothing."

"Hm. I do find it unlikely you are an Ofanim. Perhaps a Malakim? Have you ever touched an injured person or animal, or even a plant that was dying, and had it heal or come back to life?"

The questions continue on for the next hour and I answer in the negative for every single one. When our time is up, he's more frustrated than ever and no closer to getting any answers. He instructs me to meet him again at the same time and place tomorrow so he can run more tests, ask me more questions, and generally get even more frustrated.

The game is afoot, and I find myself quite liking it. I've always enjoyed a good game of deception, and if he can help me find my brother, I'll do whatever it takes, and I'll be whoever I need to be...as long as I win.

———

*T*hat night, after finishing dinner in the cafeteria, I tell Araceli I'm turning in early when we head back to our dorm. I wait until I'm sure she's in her own room, and then I quietly slip out onto the balcony wearing all black, with my hair tied back. I let my black wings unfurl, and carefully float down to the ground without making a sound. I haven't mastered flight yet, but I can at least land carefully.

My wings disappear, and I pad across the grass quietly, sticking to the darkest parts of the campus. At night, the grounds are pretty empty. Angels prefer daytime, while the night is for demons. My time.

At first, I don't see anyone outside. This is almost too easy. Then I hear some giggling and some hushed whispers and spot a small beam of light behind a tree. A man and a woman together, doing something that only increases my hunger. The succubus inside me is tempted to go over and feed off of them, but the angel in me sneaks past without them noticing.

When I reach the main hall, I hide in the shadows, watching the light from the bell tower. The Princes are up there, as I hoped they'd be. Every now and then I spot a glimpse of Callan pacing through the tall windows, but I can't get a better look at what they're doing without flying up there, and they might see or hear me if I do that. I wait, and wait, and just when I think I might need to return tomorrow night, Marcus walks past the window. That's all the confirmation I need.

I sneak back to the dorms and go up to the fourth floor. Thanks to Father, I have the gift of invisibility, like every other Ishim. I use it now by bending light around myself to hide from view as I pick the lock on Marcus's door—something Mother taught me. It takes me a few minutes, and I keep glancing around, worried someone will spot me even with my necklace and my powers, but the hallway is quiet and empty, and finally the lock picks do their job and the door clicks open.

I don't bother turning on a light as I quietly slip inside. I don't need it, thanks to my demon vision. The living room area is a lot like the one I share with Araceli, although this one has more personal touches in it, like some pictures on the walls.

There's also a much bigger TV. I don't spend much time snooping around in here, and instead head for one of the bedrooms.

This one has the covers thrown back, along with clothes hanging over the back of the desk chair, and a red guitar tucked in the corner. This must be Marcus's room. I catch a glimpse of a photo on his desk with Marcus, Archangel Raphael, and a ton of other guys who look similar to them, but I leave the room. I have no idea when Marcus will be back and I need to hurry. As much as I'd like to go through all of his things—in the name of finding my brother, of course—I don't have time.

The other bedroom is completely the opposite. The bed is made, and everything is tidy, like it hasn't been touched in months. The sheets are a dark hunter green, Jonah's favorite color, and on the nightstand there's a picture of him and Grace by the lake. I touch his pillow, where I can almost see him lying in bed while reading one of the horror novels he loved so much. I run my hand along the desk, disturbing a light coating of dust, and imagine Jonah sitting here doing his work. I palm the worn baseball sitting in the corner and picture him throwing it in the air. My heart squeezes, my chest tightens, and I close my eyes as worry for my brother takes over.

I shake it off and go through his desk, but all I find are flyers for a pizza place in Angel Peak, some pens and pencils, and a few dusty paper clips. Nothing exciting. I was hoping to find a laptop or his smartphone, but I'm sure someone else got to them first.

Next I open his closet door. His clothes are hanging inside, and I rifle through them. I spot his baseball uniform and another pang of longing hits my chest. I check the rest of the closet, and I'm about to give up when I find a garbage bag on the floor in the back. Inside is a long gold robe and a matching mask, exactly like the one I got, except for the color.

I don't know what it means, but it's the only lead I have. Now I definitely have to attend that meeting—or whatever it is —this weekend.

I hear the front door open and shove the robe back in the bag and in the closet. Going invisible again, I stay still as I hear Marcus's footsteps move through the dorm. He pauses at the doorway to Jonah's room, and I realize I left the door open. He frowns, turns on the light, and then stares at the bed. I hold my breath as the seconds tick by, and I think for sure my cover is blown. I can't help but stare at the grief on Marcus's face, but I see something else in his eyes too—guilt maybe? Or am I imagining that because I just want to see it there?

He closes the door, and as soon as he's gone I can breathe again. I wait until he moves into his own room, and then I quietly sneak out onto the balcony and escape. That was close.

And now I'm one step closer to finding out what happened to Jonah.

Chapter Eighteen

OLIVIA

My second day of classes go about as well as the first. This time in Combat Training we're not paired up at least, so Tanwen doesn't get to beat me up today. Instead, we go through some basic stretching and martial arts poses to help us build our balance and practice getting in different positions. It's a nice break after yesterday's beat down, and since I've been doing yoga for years, I'm actually not too bad at this. Araceli and Darel make googly eyes at each other during the entire class, while Callan stands in the corner with his arms crossed, shooting daggers at me with his eyes as I stretch, emphasizing my assets to drive him a bit mad.

In Flight, we practice taking off by jumping from a ledge on to a soft padded area in the gym. I make a show like I'm still learning and fall a few times, and the mean girl posse nudges each other and laughs every time. You'd think grown-ass women would be above this stuff, but I guess some things never change.

In Demon Studies, I'm forced to sit behind Marcus again,

and he gives me another of his charming smiles that no doubt makes most girls melt. If he keeps it up, it might work on me too, but for now I'm holding strong. That might change depending on how hungry I get.

Professor Raziel walks in wearing a white suit with a bowtie with green polka dots. "Hello class! Today we're going to discuss one type of demon, the Fallen. This is probably the demon you've heard the most about, so it seems fitting to start here since there are many misconceptions about them, and about their leader, Lucifer. What can you tell me about the King of Hell?"

"He was once an angel," Marcus pipes up. "All the Fallen were."

Raziel nods. "Yes, and what you might not know is that Lucifer was actually an Archangel. What else?"

"He left and went to Hell," Blake says.

"That's right, he did, although many people debate the exact reason why. Some say it was because he wanted more power. Some say it was because he disagreed with the way the Archangels were running things. Some say he saw an opportunity and took it. Maybe all of these things are true. Who knows? What we do know is that he left Heaven, the land of light, for Hell, the realm of darkness. There were already many different types of demons living there, but they were all separate tribes who sometimes fought against each other. When Lucifer became the King of Hell, he united these different groups and turned them into one organized Legion under his rule. Many angels followed him, mainly those who were also disillusioned with the Archangels, and others who were simply loyal to him. These angels all changed as they adjusted to Hell, and they started to feed on darkness and control it, much like we do with light. They became the Fallen, and their Deadly Sin is pride."

As he goes on about the Fallen, I wonder how this class would be taught by the other side. The Seven Deadly Sins are an angel creation—demons don't talk about themselves like that. And I notice Raziel doesn't mention that the Fallen represent the sin of pride because angels are so damn prideful already.

Also, demons tell a different story as to why Lucifer fell. According to them, he left for freedom. Not just for himself and for those who followed him, but freedom for humankind. Lucifer disagreed with the angels' belief that humans need to be guided, or as demons call it, "controlled." Demons believe freedom is the most important value, sometimes even to the point of anarchy and chaos. As such, Lucifer left the angels and banded together the demons to enact his own plans on Earth. That's not to say he didn't also do it so he could gain power and have his own people to rule. There are multiple sides to every story, and a little bit of truth in all of them.

Before we leave the class, Raziel says, "Oh, I almost forgot to mention. I'm going to pair you up with another student, and together you'll do an in-depth report on one type of demon, which I'll assign to you. I'd like you to focus on finding historical, religious, and mythological figures from Earth who are known to be that type of demon, and write an essay on them. This will be due at the end of the year and will count as your final exam. Now, let's see here..."

He begins to pair people up, and I already know I'll be paired with Marcus because that's just my luck. All I can hope for is that we won't be assigned the Lilim to study—that would be way too close to home.

"Marcus and Olivia," Raziel says, as I expected. I think even the professors have something against me. "You'll be studying imps."

Well, at least there's that.

———

*A*fter another awkward Angelic History class with Kassiel, and an unproductive session with Bastien, it's a relief to head back to my room to relax. Although there won't be much relaxing, because my succubus hunger is strong, and I need to do something about it before it gets so bad I'm giving fuck-me eyes at every angel I see. That'll lead to doing something that can blow my cover. Nope, I need to nip this problem in the bud fast, but first I need a cup of coffee and a few minutes to chill after a long day.

I exit the elevator and pull out my key, but then I freeze. Spray-painted on my door are the words *YOU DON'T BELONG HERE* in long black letters. It's a shock to see something like that, and for a long moment I can only stare at it. Then I glance around, but there's no one else around. Even if there was, I doubt anyone would be sympathetic, or tell me who did it. Not that I can't guess. I'm sure it was Tanwen, and I grit my teeth as I unlock the door and step inside. She can bully me all she wants, but it's not going to work. I'm here to stay.

Chapter Nineteen

OLIVIA

After spending so much time around so many tempting men, I need to feed sooner than I expected. Most succubi need to feed on a human once a week, and before I got my angelic powers I was the same. After I turned twenty-one, I learned I can feed on light the same way angels do, although it doesn't completely sustain me. I still need to feed my succubus side once every few weeks. Sex with Kassiel lasted me longer though, and Mother said that would be the case if I fed off of supernatural beings, especially powerful ones.

Only problem is I can't feed at the school, because it's way too risky. I've never fed on an angel before except for that time with Kassiel, and we all know how that went. I have to assume some of the other angels might be able to recognize me as a succubus too, which means I'm going to have to go somewhere off campus, and not to Angel Peak either. There's a small town on the main road at the bottom of the mountain, and I should be able to find what I'm looking for there.

I wait until Araceli is asleep, which is easy because she

snores, and then I sneak out and head for the parking lot. I hop in my car and drive off, narrowly missing what Araceli told me is Callan's convertible. I'm tempted to nick it, since it wouldn't be more than he deserves, but I leave it be this time.

No one stops me on my way out, but I feel a keen sense that someone is watching me as I drive out of the gate. No doubt there are cameras recording me, but why should I care? This isn't a prison, and I can come and go as I please.

It feels like an even longer drive down the mountain, especially in the dark. I take it extra slow around some of the sharp turns near steep cliffs. By the time I reach the bottom of the mountain, I'm seriously regretting not flying. I'll have to make this quick if I want to get back in time to actually get some sleep before class tomorrow.

I stop at a dive bar with several trucks and cars outside, and figure this is probably my best bet for tonight. I check my makeup and smooth my hair in my rearview mirror, and then I get out of the car. I'm wearing a tight little red dress and some fuck-me heels that always get attention, especially with my curvy legs and hips. I'm not vain, but I am a succubus after all, and we're pretty damn good-looking. It's part of my nature to use my looks to my advantage to feed.

The bar is dark inside, with tacky neon beer signs, clichéd sayings framed on the wall, and sawdust on the floor. The pickings tonight are slim, but I survey the bar, taking everyone in. My eyes immediately hone in on a hot guy sitting against the wall with dark hair, a short beard, and no wedding ring. Perfect.

His head turns my way, and when our eyes lock, I give him a come-hither smile and put a little of my power into it. Not that I really need to, but I'd like to make this quick so I can head to bed. I have more classes in the morning, and I need to be alert in case I'm paired with Tanwen again for Combat Training.

A slow grin spreads across my mark's lips, and I think, *wow this is too easy,* as I start walking toward him. He stands and heads in my direction, and I worry maybe I used a little too much power on him already, but then he says, "Excuse me," and brushes right past me. My mouth falls open as he leaves the bar.

Damn, are my skills rusty, or what?

I smooth down my dress, brush off my ego, and charge forward. There are four other guys in the bar, and two of them have wedding rings, which knocks them out of the running. I might be able to seduce them, but I won't. I don't mess with married people. I may be a sex demon, but I have some principles. Maybe that's from my angelic side.

That leaves two guys, and one is at least sixty with a huge bald patch, while the other looks like he hasn't showered in a week. The only other people without wedding rings are in groups or pairs, and those would take a lot more time to work on. There's also the bartender, but I don't want to do anything with her in case I need to come back again. That leaves these two men. When I get close, the stench from no-shower guy makes this an easy decision. I sit next to the older man, trying not to get weirded out by the fact that he could be my dad, if my dad was human. The irony is that Father looks about half this guy's age, but is thousands of years older. That's immortality for you.

I could ease into this slowly, but the hunger is intense, and I just want to get this over with. I place my hand on the guy's arm and lean in close. "Need some company?"

SERAPHIM ACADEMY 1: WICKED WINGS

I put some magic into my touch, and he responds immediately to me, looking at me with unveiled desire. His eyes go straight to my boobs, and I nearly roll my eyes, but I keep the smile plastered on. Sometimes it really bothers me that I have to do this, even though it's necessary for me to live. But seriously, feeding on only light or darkness would be a whole lot easier.

"Hell, yeah," he says, tipping the lip of his trucker's hat.

Yes, Hell indeed.

It doesn't take much work before we're in the front of his truck and I'm riding him with my eyes squeezed shut while his meaty hands cup my ass. The succubus in me is going *yes yes yes* while the rest of me is trying not to gag. I have no other choice, I remind myself. I have to do this to survive. But I still hate it.

The only way to make it better is to picture Kassiel's hands on my body instead. I remember his lips on my neck and the way he filled me up. I moan softly and my nameless partner moves faster, but it's the memory of Kassiel that is turning me on, not this trucker.

But then it's not Kassiel I'm riding, but Bastien. He stares at me with those intense, intelligent eyes and presses that sensual mouth to mine. I turn my head and now it's Marcus kissing me instead, and I weave my fingers in his thick brown hair as he lightly nips my neck. Then it's Callan, wrapping those big muscular arms around me and holding me close as he pounds into me.

With the four of them on my mind, I make it through the encounter quickly, and my eyes turn black as I feed off the man. Succubi—and the male version, incubi—can feed off of sex, or even lust and desire, in many ways. Having lust or desire directed at us is like a little snack, while sex is a meal—and orgasms are the perfect dessert. And sex with Kassiel? That was like an all-you-can-eat buffet that kept me full for a month. I can only assume that's because he wasn't human, but I haven't been able to test that theory on any other angels or demons since.

When we're done I say, "Thanks," and practically leap off him. I clean myself up with some tissues from my purse, and then head back to my car. The trucker calls after me in a haze. Humans get hit hard when we feed off them and get addicted to us fast, even though we can only sleep with them once without killing them. The feeling will pass soon, and he'll be fine after he sleeps it off, leaving him with a story he can tell his friends about how some hot woman screwed him in the front of his truck.

And me? I'm full enough for a little while. The all-consuming hunger for sex is at bay, for the time being. I just wish encounters like this didn't leave me feeling so damn empty.

Chapter Twenty
BASTIEN

"I'm telling you, there's something suspicious about her," I say, while idly tapping on the keyboard and staring at the computer screen. I've already scoured Olivia's files, hoping they might have something that will help us unravel her secrets, but they proved to be worthless.

Father must know the truth of who and what she is, but he's keeping quiet on the subject so far. I'm on duty this afternoon while he's at some Archangel meeting. All I have to do is sit in his office and answer the phone. Easy enough...and extremely boring. Which is the only reason my mind wandered back to Olivia and what I saw last night, and why I called Callan and Marcus in here. The *only* reason.

Marcus twirls in an office chair with his head back, his hair wild. "You think there's something suspicious about everyone."

"He may be right this time." Callan looks out over the grounds through the large window, his arms crossed and his shoulders squared. "She's important to Jonah in some way. We need to find out how they know each other."

I shake my head. "It's not only that. Last night when we went back to the dorm, I noticed her car was gone."

Callan turns away from the window. "Where do you think she went?"

"I don't know, but we should find out." *As soon as possible.*

Marcus shrugs. "Lots of people leave campus at odd hours. There's no rule preventing them from doing so."

I shake my head. "But by car instead of flying? And at such a late hour? No, we owe it to Jonah to figure this out. If it's nothing, then we won't worry about it and move on. But if it is something, we should uncover it sooner than later." With her being connected to Jonah, we can't afford to leave any stone unturned. "I'm going to check the security cameras."

"Isn't that unethical?" Marcus asks.

My fingers are already flying across the keyboard. "Father has given me access to them so I can monitor the school for any threats. I think this qualifies."

"She's hardly a threat," Callan mutters, but he also stands over my shoulder so he can watch. Marcus scoots closer too.

It only takes a few minutes to find the footage of the parking lot from last night. I fast forward until it catches Olivia walking to her car wearing tall heels and a dress that accentuates every curve. She isn't carrying anything other than her purse.

Marcus whistles softly. "Where's she going in that outfit? On a date?"

I raise my hand to silence him as the footage continues. Callan winces as we watch Olivia nearly take out his car again, and then I switch to the gates as she drives away. We follow her on a few other cameras set up outside the grounds, but lose her down the hill.

A little over an hour later, she returns. She parks, and we use the cameras to follow her as she walks straight to the dorms, carrying only her purse again. Her hair looks a little mussed, but that's nothing that couldn't be explained by the wind. She walks a little slower, like there's something weighing her down, but it could simply be tiredness. She returns to her dorm room and disappears.

"Nothing," I mutter. Dammit.

Callan rubs his jaw. "Definitely suspicious though. We'll keep an eye on her, and when she next goes on one of those late-night excursions, we'll follow her. Meanwhile, keep putting pressure on her to leave the school. Remember, it's for her own good."

I nod. "Yes, and we might be able to use what we find to get her expelled."

"If she's doing anything wrong," Marcus points out, as he begins his spin in my chair again. "Have you learned anything from your one-on-one sessions?"

We've only had a couple, but they were frustrating, to say the least. "Not yet. But I'll uncover something soon. There is some sort of magic blocking me from discovering anything about her powers. Could she have fae magic and us not be able to sense it?"

Marcus pauses his spin. "How would she get that kind of magic? Do you think she's part fae?"

"Could she have a fae-made object?" Callan asks. "Like the Staff of Eternity, the one my dear old dad used to close Heaven with." The bitterness in his voice creeps in, like it sometimes does when we're alone and he talks about Michael. Only when we're alone though.

The office phone rings, and I hold up a finger and answer

it. It's the mom of a Third Year student named Blake who hasn't been able to get ahold of her precious baby in days. I assure her I saw her son earlier, and I'll have him call her as soon as possible. After hanging up, I pull out my phone and text him. He's an idiot, someone I'd never associate with normally, but I keep everyone's numbers in my phone for just such reasons. **Your mother contacted the school worried about you. Call her. Now.**

He replies in seconds. **I'll call her immediately. Sorry about the trouble.** I didn't expect him to do anything less than call her that moment. When one of us tells someone to do something, they always do it. Except Olivia.

As I put my phone away, I answer Callan and Marcus's questions. "I haven't seen anything indicating she's part fae or possesses one of their objects, but it's too early to know for sure."

"I've been trying to put pressure on her to leave the school, but nothing seems to be working so far," Callan says. "She's very stubborn. I'm going to have to try harder."

"What you have in mind?" I ask.

"I'm not sure yet, but I might ask Tanwen. She's good at this sort of thing."

"Are you going to get back together with her?" Marcus asks.

Callan snorts. "Definitely not."

Marcus chuckles. "That's not what she's been saying. Careful, or she might get the wrong idea."

"I'll make it clear."

I fade out their conversation as my mind goes back to Olivia. I pull up the live security cameras and switch through them until I find her walking out of the dorm. She tucks a piece of dark hair behind her ear as the wind picks up, as it often does at this altitude. My eyes narrow as I watch her move out of view. *I'm going to uncover your secrets, whatever it takes. You can't hide the truth from me.*

Chapter Twenty-One

OLIVIA

The rest of the week passes quickly in a blur of classes while avoiding the Princes and Valkyries as much as possible, and I'm just glad I make it to the weekend without any problems. Saturday night I'm supposed to attend that secret society meeting, or whatever it is, and I'll hopefully be one step closer to finding my brother then.

As Saturday morning arrives, Araceli busts into my room at the crack of dawn. She throws open the curtains and declares, "We're going shopping!"

Freaking angels. They're all such morning people. Me, I was looking forward to staying in bed until noon. I'm still used to a bartender schedule. Or a demon one.

I eye the window, through which I can see a gray sky and trees blowing hard in the wind. It's the kind of day you can just tell is going to be chilly and miserable.

"Today? It's way too cold." I pull the covers up to my nose and hide.

Angels absolutely hate the cold, so I have to pretend I do also. It's why Seraphim Academy's school year runs spring to fall, with winter off. Demons, meanwhile, dislike heat. The whole thing about Hell being fire and brimstone? Yeah, that's angel propaganda. It's more like a perpetual realm of night, according to my Mother, anyway.

Araceli peers outside. "Can we take your car? It's got a heater, right?"

"Yeah, sure." I don't love the idea since my car is such a piece of crap, but I have to keep up the ruse, and I'm not the greatest at flying yet. "But I'm warning you in advance, I'm not the best driver."

"Aw, we'll be fine." She waves her hand. "Flying would be torture this morning, and I want to go."

"All right, but give me a few minutes to get dressed and down some coffee. You know I can't function without it."

She rolls her eyes but says, "Fine, fine."

I take a quick shower, chug my coffee, and we're out the door in an hour. When the cold air smacks us in the face as we exit the dorms, I reconsider flying. With both demon and angel blood, I don't have a strong hatred or preference for cold or heat, but it's actually pretty damn cold out today, especially for the end of March.

We walk toward the parking lot, but then I spot the Princes prowling around. I yank Araceli back to hide behind the brick building of the main hall.

"Hang on." I have not had nearly enough coffee to deal with their shit this morning.

"What?" She looks around in alarm. "What is it?"

"The Princes." I peer around the wall, watching as they

saunter toward Callan's car. Araceli ducks down to look under my arm, and another student walks by and gives us an odd look. I picture what fools we must look like, hiding behind the building, and I straighten up. "Come on."

"Why?" Araceli follows me toward the parking lot, but she's more hesitant than I am. "I don't want to deal with them, either."

"If we hide from them, they win." Even though I believe what I'm saying, I can't help but let out a little sigh of relief when Callan's car drives away without them seeing us.

After they're gone, we hurry to my car. The sooner we get it started, the sooner it warms up. I waste no time pulling out of the parking lot, and it's only a short drive to Angel Peak, with Araceli giving me directions since my phone's GPS doesn't work well up here. Nope, that would be too easy.

We make our way into the tiny town, which has only enough shops to keep us from needing to go to a bigger town. It's the quaintest thing I've ever seen. Each storefront looks like it's been teleported straight out of the 1950's, all done in pastel colors with decorative trim. I find a parking spot and as we get out I look around while trying not to let my chin drag the ground. A cobbler, seamstress, office supplies. There's even an ice cream shop.

I turn in a slow circle. "Wow."

"It's a trip, isn't it?" Araceli grins at me. "My aunt lives here, so I spent a lot of my childhood visiting."

I can't help the envy that trickles through me at hearing that. Even the half-fae outcast had a happier childhood than I did. Pushing those thoughts away, I try to suppress the negative emotions toward the person that has been nicest to me since coming to Seraphim Academy. She doesn't deserve them.

"We should be able to get some fun stuff for our dorm here," Araceli says.

"Okay, but I don't have a lot of money," I say.

Araceli looks up from her purse. "Didn't they give you your allowance? I know it's not a lot, but it should be enough."

"No, although I remember being told that I'd receive some sort of stipend. I wasn't sure how to get access to it." And wasn't sure I wanted to either. Nothing in life is free. I learned that lesson early on.

"Come on." She grabs my elbow and pulls me down the street. "We'll go to the bank first. I bet it's there."

"There's an angel bank?" That's something I didn't know.

"Yep. In the human world it passes as a credit union for employees of Aerie Industries, and it only has branches in angel communities. Lots of angels have accounts at other banks as well, but this one is just for us, and run by angels. The town is enchanted to ward off humans anyway, so it'd be nearly impossible for one to open an account even if they did find the branch."

The bank is at the end of the street in a building that looks like an old Victorian house, painted pastel blue. We step onto the front porch and the planks under our feet creak with age. I arch an eyebrow at them, wondering if they'll hold.

Araceli grins. "Quaint."

Quaint isn't a strong enough word. We step inside, and Araceli walks straight to one of the tellers waiting for customers in a little booth.

"Hello," the lady says in a bright voice. "How may we help you?"

"I need to make a withdrawal from my account, and so does my friend, Liv."

"I'm not sure if I have an account at all." I give a little finger wave and an apologetic look. "If you could check, I'd really appreciate it. Olivia Monroe, please."

"Of course." The redhead taps away at her computer. "Do you have any ID?"

I hand her my driver's license and watch her check it. This experience has been such an odd mix of human and angel procedures.

"Everything seems to be in order, Ms. Monroe." She hands me my license and looks at me with her perfectly manicured eyebrows raised. "How much would you like to withdraw?"

"How much is there?" I ask.

"A thousand." The redhead's bland smile is unsettling. To her, a thousand dollars is no big deal. To me, it's a lot.

I stumble over my words. I have an account that I didn't open or ask for, with a bunch of money inside. Aerie Industries is paying me a thousand dollars just to attend school. For a second I almost feel bad for deceiving everyone, but then I get over it. I'm here on a mission. The angels can't find my brother, so they can damn well pay me for doing their job for them.

"Is that for the school year?" I ask. I do some quick math in my head. I have a couple hundred dollars saved up from my job at the bar. I should be able to make it work for the next year even without a job, considering I can get a lot of things free, and since I'm not paying for an apartment anymore. I'll need gas in the car, which is paid off at least, plus money for insurance and my phone, even though it doesn't get service up here.

"No, just the month," Araceli says as she looks at some paper in her purse. "It's pro-rated since we're only here some of March. You'll get two thousand next month."

My jaw drops. What in the world am I expected to spend two grand a month on?

Nothing, that's what. That shit is going in my dorm in case I need to make a quick escape. I might hide some off campus too. If anyone finds out I'm part demon, I'll need to be ready for anything.

"I'll take it all, please." I try to sound confident, like a cool thousand for half a month doesn't make me want to crap my pants.

The clerk, who I'm suddenly very fond of, hands me ten one-hundred-dollar bills, counting them out into my hand. I fold nine of them three times and tuck them into a tiny pocket in my black jeans. The other one I put in my wallet to spend today. I've never carried this much money in my life before, and it makes my head spin.

Araceli withdraws some money too, and then we head out again. "I've had this account since I was little. There's a branch of this bank in Arizona as well." As we walk out into the cold, her face brightens. "There's Grace and Cyrus. They flew."

They land on the sidewalk and Grace gives us one of her warm smiles. "Going shopping? Can we join you?"

"Of course," I say, as I eye them in their short-sleeve shirts. Araceli and I are bundled up like we're going out into the snow. "How do you stand the cold?"

"It's something we learned this week in Light Control, which you'll take next year," Cyrus says with a grin.

"Just gather a bit of sunlight around you, like this," Grace says. She focuses, and a glow wraps around her and then vanishes again. "It keeps you toasty warm."

Grace and Cyrus head into the bank, and while we wait

Araceli works on pulling light around herself like a warm winter coat. I want to try it also, but doing so would reveal that I can use my angelic magic, and I can't have that. So instead, I just shiver, while she makes herself toasty warm.

"You'll figure it out," Araceli says while rubbing my shoulder, and I feel another pang of guilt for deceiving her. "Soon all this angel stuff will make sense, I promise."

"Thanks," I say.

"Araceli!" Darel practically skips along the street toward us. "What are you doing here on this lovely morning?"

"We're going shopping," she says with a laugh. "Care to join us?"

"I'd love to escort such beautiful ladies." He gives her a wink and then takes her arm like a gentleman. The two of them stroll off down the road, forgetting about me completely. It's tough to ignore a succubus, but love will do that, even the first stirrings of it. I'm not mad, though. I hope it works out for them. Plus, I enjoy the taste of their lust growing too.

Grace and Cyrus walk out, and they chuckle when they see Araceli has ditched us. "I guess that's going to be a thing," Cyrus says, delighted by this new gossip.

"Seems that way," I say.

"They're cute together," Grace says.

"We can hear you," Araceli calls back.

We all burst into giggles, and for a second I feel something rare: happiness. It's easy to pretend with these people. They're friendly and open with me, accepting me into their fold even though they've only known me for a week. I wish it all wasn't a lie.

As we walk down the street and admire the cute little shops, I chat and laugh with the others, but I also remind myself I'm here for a reason. When Cyrus and Darel slip inside a clothing shop for men, I use the opportunity to grill Grace and Araceli some more. I need to get all the information I can.

After we get a coffee at a little stand on the corner, I ask them, "Hey, have you heard any rumors about a secret society on campus?"

"A secret society?" Araceli asks with a little laugh. It sounds forced, and her eyes dart side to side. "At Seraphim? No way."

Grace waves her hand dismissively. "Those are just rumors. They go around every year, and everyone speculates on who got invited to join and who didn't, but then they die down again because there's nothing to them." She shrugs. "Sorry. It'd be pretty cool if the school did have one though."

I take a little sip of my coffee. "I figured it was just a crazy conspiracy theory."

It's hard to tell if they know anything or not, although Araceli definitely reacted oddly. Was she invited to the meeting tonight? Or Darel, I wonder, as he walks out of the men's shop empty-handed and heads straight for my roommate?

Cyrus appears at my side carrying a shopping bag. "Where to next?"

We wander through town for the rest of the day, and even though I tell myself I'll only spend a tiny bit, the prices are higher here than in Los Angeles. After buying a pretty day planner to keep track of my assignments, some pictures to hang in our dorm room, plus a pair of jeans I spied through a window, my wallet is a lot lighter. I guess angels can afford a premium price so they can have a place where they don't have to hide their wings or their magic. It's common here to see someone flying overhead, or glowing softly as they pass by, and everyone seems to know everyone else. Except me, of course. I still get the weird looks and the hurried whispers, although with friends at my side, they don't bother me quite as much.

Chapter Twenty-Two

OLIVIA

That night, I silently move through the forest toward the location on the invitation, wearing the white mask and robes. It's pitch black out here, with no moon to light my way, but it doesn't bother me. Here on top of the mountain it's so clear it's like I can see every single constellation in the sky—very different from where I grew up in Southern California.

Soon I come upon a small clearing where two people in white robes and masks are already waiting. I can't tell who they are, but they must be first years like me. One of them is probably Tanwen, knowing my luck. Both robed figures give me a nervous glance as I take a spot in the clearing a little distance away from them. We all stand around awkwardly as a few more people walk in, until there are fourteen of us total. I'm not surprised—seven is a sacred number for angels, just like six is for demons.

People in gold robes and masks suddenly emerge from all sides of the forest, surrounding us in the clearing, and it's hard to tell how many of them there are. One of them has a gold crown over his or her mask, and when they speak, the voice is unidentifiable. "Congratulations. You have been chosen from all of the angels at this school to possibly join the Order of the Golden Throne, the most ancient secret society in this world. Created three thousand years ago, the Order has been working from the shadows to guide humanity and angels on Earth for all of history. We recruit directly from the academy from both students and professors, and when you leave this school you will go on to become leaders of angel society." The leader pauses and glances among the people in white robes. "However, just because you received an invitation to tonight's gathering does not mean you have been accepted into the Order. No, at the moment you are initiates only, and to join the Order you must pass three tests. Only then will you become a full-fledged member at the end of the school year."

If this secret society went back that far, then my parents gave me a seriously lacking education. I've been starting to figure that out over the last week, but it's a lot worse than I realized, and there's so much I don't know. This secret society stuff sounds like more of the "angels are holier than thou" philosophy I can't stand, but I'm pretty sure my brother was a member, and this is the only clue I have so far. Which means I have to pass whatever tests they're going to throw at me.

"Before we give you the first test, we want to talk about our core values," the leader continues. "We believe angels are superior beings, and our purpose is to control Earth from the shadows to guide humanity to a brighter future. We believe demons are evil and must be eradicated from Earth to protect humanity. And finally, we believe that loyalty to the Order is paramount, along with discretion. You must not talk about the

Order or this meeting with anyone, even if you do not become a member. We will find out if you break this rule, and there will be consequences."

Oops, guess I already broke that rule. I wonder what these dire consequences will be?

The person to my right snorts, and he must be thinking something along the same lines. All of the golden masks turn toward him at once, and he visibly stiffens. There is nothing more unnerving than a dozen or more people in masks all staring at you.

"Do you find this amusing?" the leader asks, in their unnatural voice. "Initiate?"

The person—who I assume is a man based on their body type, though I could be wrong—adjusts their mask. "No, it's just that everybody already knows about the Order. People talk." Like the leader, this person's voice is masked somehow, just like their face.

"See that you are not one of them," the leader orders. "Now, you may wonder why we have chosen you to become initiates. We have been watching you for some time, and at least one of our members has nominated you because we believe you have the traits we are looking for. Some of you come from a well-respected angelic family, while others have shown a strong hatred for demons or a willingness to help guide humans toward the light. Do not question yourselves. If you received an invitation, then you deserve to be here—but keep in mind that only a few of you will make it to the final trial.

"For the first test, we ask you to demonstrate your utmost loyalty to the Order. To do so, you must steal an item from a professor, or even the headmaster, if you so dare. Make sure you don't get caught, as you will likely be suspended or fired for such an act. You have a month to procure this item, after which you'll receive another invitation to the next meeting, where you will present it to us. Make sure it's something good, or we might reject your offering. Should we accept it, you'll be given the second test. Good luck."

With those last words, the golden-robed people step back into the darkness of the forest and disappear, leaving those of us in the white robes standing around awkwardly. We glance at each other, but since we can't recognize anyone, we can't really size up our competition.

I can't help but wonder who nominated me. I don't meet any of their criteria, and I find it hard to believe they would invite the half-human with unknown parentage. Either someone knows who my father is, or I've been invited for some other reason. For all I know, it's a prank. Or maybe the invitation was meant for someone else, and it got put in my room by accident.

Whatever the reason, I'm taking advantage of it. I have no interest in actually becoming a member of the Order, or in any of the things they believe in, but I feel like I'm on the right path. My gut tells me this secret society is the key to finding Jonah, which means I'm going to pass whatever tests they throw at me. Bring it on.

———

*A*fter I return to my room, I find myself unable to sleep, and my mind drifts back to the night I met Jonah.

A noise outside my window got me out of my bed in a hurry. Father had just left, and Mother rarely came to see me, except in dreams sometimes. Whoever was out there couldn't mean anything good for me.

My current round of foster parents didn't pay much attention to me, so they hadn't noticed when I hid a baseball bat under my bed. I grabbed it and flattened myself against the wall, then peeked out the window with the braveness of a ten-year-old who was used to taking care of herself, but also knew there were definitely monsters out there that might get you.

To my surprise and relief, a gangly boy about my age pressed his face against the glass. I was on the second story, but his wings kept him hovering at my level. I gaped at him for a minute, and then I cracked open the window, raising my bat, just in case. "Who are you?"

"Jonah," he said, a little too loud. "Who are you?"

"Shhh! I'll ask the questions." My foster parents watched a few too many police shows on TV and they were rubbing off on me. "Why are you flying around outside my window?"

"I came to see why my dad was visiting you," the boy said. "I followed him here."

"Your dad?" I blinked at him and lowered my bat, then spoke without thinking. "He's my dad too."

"Really?" Jonah's face lit up.

Uh oh. I wasn't supposed to tell anyone about my real parents. Father was teaching me about my people, and he warned me many times that if they found me, they'd want to hurt me, but I was too excited at the prospect of meeting someone else like me. I opened the window all the way and waved Jonah inside.

"You have to be quiet." I sat on my bed and set the bat beside me. "I'm Olivia, but you can call me Liv."

Jonah didn't sit, and instead vibrated with excitement, his

wings still out. They were sparkling white with silver streaks, and I really wanted to touch them, but I knew that wasn't okay. "You're my sister?"

I nodded while biting my lip. His hair was dark blond and his bright smile looked nothing like my own, so it was hard to believe we could be related. His blue eyes were almost gray, while mine were a strange green that people usually commented on when first meeting me. "How can you fly? I thought angels don't get their wings until they're twenty-one."

"I got mine when I was seven," he said, as he looked around the room, checking everything out. There wasn't much there, since I'd only moved in a few weeks ago. "Mom says it's rare, but it happens sometimes."

"Who is your mom?" Could it be possible? Was there someone else like me?

"Archangel Ariel."

"Oh," I said, disappointed. He was a full angel, and I was...not.

All of a sudden, Father appeared in the room in a flash of light, and Jonah and I both let out a cry of surprise. He took us in, looking stern and scary. "Jonah, what are you doing here?"

Jonah looked up at his dad with defiance. "I wanted to know where you sneak off to sometimes. Why didn't you tell me I have a sister?"

"It was for Olivia's protection. No one is supposed to know about her. Not even you."

"You should have told us." I got a little warm glow in my chest for siding with Jonah. I had a brother. I wasn't totally alone anymore.

Father pinched the brow of his forehead with a sigh. "Perhaps you're right. But Olivia is safer if no one knows about her.

Jonah, I'm going to have to get Jophiel to wipe your memories. I'm sorry."

"No!" we both cried out.

I grabbed onto Father's sleeve and looked up at him with eyes on the brink of tears. "Please, Father. I don't have anyone. Don't take Jonah away too."

He stared at me, and for once, his hard demeanor melted. He touched my head gently in a rare act of tenderness. "All right. But you both need to promise me you will never tell anyone about each other. That goes especially for you, Jonah. None of your friends can ever know about Olivia."

"And if I promise, I can come back and visit Liv?" Jonah asked.

"Yes, whenever you want," Father said.

"Then I promise!"

"Me too!" I chimed in.

Father grabbed us both in a hug, and as he held us there, I felt something rare...belonging. I had a family. I wasn't alone.

From that night on, Jonah came to visit me regularly, and we kept our promise. He didn't care that I was half-demon, because I was his sister. He told me all about the angel world, and his visits were the highlight of my life. And then he disappeared, and I remembered what it felt like to be completely alone in the world again—and I swore I'd do anything to find him.

Chapter Twenty-Three
OLIVIA

On Monday, Bastien, Callan, and Marcus walk into the cafeteria as Araceli and I head out after breakfast. Stiffening, I try to sidestep them, but they plant their big selves in my way.

Of course.

Marcus gives me a suave smile, but it has a bit of a predatory gleam. "In a hurry?"

"I hope so," Callan growls. He's my least favorite of the Princes, by far.

This time I'm not going to hide from them like a coward. I refuse to budge, and just cross my arms and glare at them until they huff and pass around me. *Another point for Liv.* For anyone else I would've politely sidestepped, but not these jerks. They can get out of my way.

With a small grin, I stroll out of the cafeteria, with Araceli gawking at my side. "That was great," she says as she glances behind us, like she's worried they might come after us. "As soon as I saw them, I ducked out of the way without thinking, but you stood up to them."

I shrug a little. "It's no big deal. I just don't think they have the right to waltz around like they run the school."

"You and me both, but I'm not crazy enough to challenge them. You're brave, girl."

My good mood lasts me precisely until it's time for Combat Training to start, and I'm faced with Tanwen kicking my ass again. Surprisingly, she doesn't. Not surprisingly, she's so busy kissing up to Callan that she forgets to bother me. I spend the time sparring with Araceli and Darel, while getting little snacks from their lustful energy, along with Callan. Because even though Tanwen wants him, he wants me.

I keep my guard up for the rest of the day, but it passes without any major complications. Marcus and I ignore each other in Demon Studies, where Professor Raziel is still teaching us about the Fallen. In Angelic History, Professor Kassiel tries to pretend I don't exist and fails, and I squirm the entire time listening to his sexy voice. While he lectures, I stare at the stubble on his neck and daydream of running my tongue along it. If I want to pass that class, I need to get control of myself. Afterwards, Bastien spends our time together grilling me about my childhood. It sounds more like he's looking for loopholes in my story than a way to figure out what my Choir is. The session only makes him grumpier.

At dinner, I grab some pizza and sit at our normal table with Araceli, Grace, and Cyrus. Darel, who Araceli is already half in love with and fully in lust with, joins us too. It's nice to have a group of friends, even if I know our friendships can't last. They'll never stay friends with me if they find out what I really am, or that I've been deceiving them, but for now it's nice.

"What are these flyers I'm seeing around campus for a football game against demons?" I ask.

"It happens every year," Cyrus says. "We have games against the demon school, Hellspawn Academy, and with the fae school, Ethereal Academy, as part of a way to build connections with them in a friendly environment, or some shit like that."

Darel smirks. "I heard it's so we can go up against them without having any real consequences. Burn off some steam and let out that aggression, since it's illegal to actually fight them."

"So, there's a demon academy too?" I ask. "Is it seriously called Hellspawn Academy?"

"It really is," Cyrus says. "They don't consider it an insult, believe it or not."

"The games are pretty fun, even though no one is allowed to use their powers," Darel says. "No flying, no burning light, none of that. But we can still use our superior speed and strength since supernaturals all have those. It makes for a pretty fast-paced and intense game." He grins. "I made it onto the team this year, so you all need to come to the games."

Araceli flips her hair and smiles. "We wouldn't miss it."

Cyrus swallows a big bite of pizza. "The first game is here on campus against the demons. Then the fae and demons have a game at Hellspawn Academy, and we have a game with the fae. At the end of the year, two winning teams face off for the championship."

"Does the school have other sports teams too?" I ask.

"No, the sport rotates every year since we don't have

enough students for different teams. Last year it was baseball, and this year is football."

Baseball. Jonah's favorite. I'm sure he played on the team. I'll have to look up who else was on the team with him and see if they'd have any reason to do him harm.

I poke at my pizza and try to sound innocent. "Is it safe having demons and fae here on campus?"

Grace gives me a slightly pitying smile. "Pretty safe. There are plenty of professors and official people around to make sure nothing bad happens. Sometimes a fight breaks out, but nothing serious. You don't need to worry."

Cyrus glances at her quickly. "Well, I mean, Jonah did go missing after the last championship game against the fae, but that was probably a coincidence."

I glance up quickly, then shove a piece of pizza in my mouth to hide my surprise. This is news to me.

Grace's face grows pinched at the mention of my brother. "We don't know if it's connected or not. The Archangels cleared the fae of any involvement."

I don't know much about the fae, but it sounds like I need to learn more...and figure out what happened at that game.

Araceli and I finish up our dinner, say goodnight to our friends, and head out the door. When we step out into the cool night air, I spot Marcus leaning against the wall outside, looking deliciously sexy in a black leather jacket while the breeze teases his wavy hair. His dark eyes catch mine and lust flares between us, so strong I nearly tremble when it hits me.

"There you are," he says, straightening up. "I'd like to talk to you. Alone."

Araceli gives me a nervous glance, but I nod at her. "It's fine," I say. "I'll meet you back at the dorm."

"Okay." She hesitates, but then rubs her arms and darts away.

When we're alone, I ask, "Were you waiting for me?"

"I was," he says. "We need to set up a time to work on our project for Demon Studies."

"Is that all?" I let out a soft laugh. "You had me worried there when you said you wanted to speak alone."

He gives me the sexiest little grin. "I just wanted you all to myself."

I roll my eyes at the cheesy line. "I'm free at 4pm on Wednesday. Does that work?"

"Sounds good. Meet in the library?"

I nod. "See you then."

As I walk away, he calls out in a teasing voice, "We both know you wanted to be alone with me, too."

I pretend I don't hear him, but I hate how right he is. I do want him alone. In my bed. On a table. On the floor. Doesn't matter, as long as we're both naked. But that's not going to happen, so I swallow my desire and head back to my dorm...alone.

Chapter Twenty-Four

KASSIEL

At midnight, the campus is deathly quiet, especially out here by the lake. The moonlight glistens off the black water as it moves softly in the wind, and I take a deep breath and take it all in. After a long day of teaching, it helps me clear my head to have a moment alone to myself out here.

"I never imagined I'd see you out of your suit."

The sultry, familiar voice makes me jerk upright, and I turn to spot the owner of it walking toward me. "Olivia."

She's wearing a black hoodie, and she pushes it back as she approaches, then shakes out that beautiful mane of dark hair. "What are you doing out here?"

"I could ask the same of you."

"I couldn't sleep, so I thought I'd take a walk around the lake. I didn't expect to see anyone else out here."

"Sometimes I unwind out here after a long day of teaching." I should get up and say goodnight to her to avoid her as much as possible, but I find myself rooted to the bench I've been sitting on. Something in her eyes looks so vulnerable and lost I can't send her away. I pat the spot next to me on the stone bench. "Care to sit with me for a few minutes?"

She glances at her watch and nods her head. If she was half-human like everyone thought, she wouldn't have been able to see it in the meager moonlight. But she's not, and she just confirmed it for me without even realizing it. *Careful, my dear, or someone else will catch on soon too.*

"I guess I can spare a few more minutes." She perches on the edge of the bench and stares at the water, like she's purposefully trying not to look at me. Then it hits me...she's hungry. Lilim are always hungry, especially young ones like her. Since she's only half succubus, I'm not sure how often she needs to feed, but she can probably feel my own desire for her every time I look at her, and it probably makes it even worse.

I jerk my gaze away from her and try not to think about how much I want her. "How are you doing? With your... special diet?"

Her body visibly stiffens. "I don't know what you mean."

"Sure you don't." I lean over and pick up a rock, tossing it into the lake. With my superior strength, it skips all the way to the other side and out of view.

"Nice throw."

"I've had a lot of practice."

She arches an eyebrow. "How old are you? Or is that weird to ask an angel?"

I chuckle softly. "It's considered rude to ask, because the older you are, the more powerful, but it's fine. I'm only one hundred seventy-two years old."

"*Only?*" she asks, with a little laugh.

"In the supernatural world, that's practically a baby."

She shakes her head with an amused smile. "And in the

human world, it's old enough to be my great-great-grandfather or something like that."

"Time is different for those of us with immortal lifespans. Years will start to fly by, and you'll wonder where they went. Then you'll look up, and suddenly all the technology is obsolete, and you need to learn everything all over again."

"So what you're saying is, you're old," she says with a teasing grin.

I grin back at her. "Pretty much, yeah. Now get off my lawn, youngster."

"Not a chance." She tilts her head as she studies me, and I'm struck again with how lovely she is. "You definitely don't look old. Especially in jeans and a t-shirt. I thought you lived in those suits."

"Only when I'm in public. Like I told you before, my father ingrained in me that a man is only as good as his suit, and it's hard to get over that even after all these years. But then, you understand how complicated relationships with parents can be, don't you?"

It's a leading question, going back to what she said that night, and with it she instantly tenses again. "I don't know who my father is."

"Is that so?" I ask. "A pity. Maybe now that you're here, he'll claim you. What about your mother?"

"Dead."

"That's not what you told me back at the bar that night."

"You must have heard me wrong." She looks at the water and stands. "It's late. I should get back to my room."

She's falling back upon her lies then. I hoped she would be honest with me, but I understand her need for secrecy better than anyone. As she starts to walk away, I call out, "Olivia."

She turns and looks at me in the dark, easily meeting my eyes thanks to her demon blood. "Yes?"

"I won't expose you." I can't explain why, but I won't give her up. Not unless I'm forced to. "Your secret is safe with me, I swear it. And not just because I'm worried about an inquiry for sleeping with a student. So if you ever need to talk...I'll be here."

Her eyes lower to the ground for a few seconds. Then she meets my gaze again and gives a curt nod. "Good night."

As she walks away, I let out a long breath. Getting close to Olivia is dangerous for so many reasons. For one, it's forbidden for a teacher and a student to have a relationship. For another, she could find out what I am and expose me too. I can't afford to have my cover blown, especially not when I'm closer than ever.

And the most dangerous reason? When she's around, I feel more than I have in a century.

Chapter Twenty-Five

OLIVIA

*L*EAVE NOW BEFORE YOU GET HURT

Wadding up the paper, I stuff it deep into my bag before anyone else sees it. "Assholes."

The threatening note is the latest of a long line of them left in my bag, slipped under my dorm room door, or under the windshield wipers of my car. I even found one shoved in my bag after I shopped in the school store. Tanwen was nearby that day, so I'm sure she's behind the notes.

I just finished up my last session with Bastien, and after a long day of classes all I want to do is go to my room and take off my bra, but that's not in the cards today. I stop by the cafeteria to grab a coffee, and then head back to the library. I'm a few minutes early, but Marcus beats me there anyway, already waiting in one of the private rooms.

"Hey, gorgeous." He stands when he sees me and holds out my chair for me. "You ready for this?"

He's got several books on imps out already, which I don't need. Mother told me all about the other demon races, and I'm not sure I trust these books to be unbiased anyway. On the other hand, I thought I knew everything about angels too before coming to Seraphim Academy, and I've learned a lot in the last week. Maybe there will be something helpful in the books after all.

Marcus flips one of them open. "From what I've read so far, imps represent the Deadly Sin of envy and can create illusions. They feed on attention and awe, so they tend to have jobs like actors, musicians, and magicians. That should make this project easier."

"Do we have to do a presentation or just the paper?" I ask, as I grab one of the books.

"We have to do a 3D model of an imp using its powers." Marcus stares at me like I should've known this.

"You're joking." A 3D model? Out of what? Paper mâché? I don't think so. "That's a bit much, don't you think? And imps look just like humans, they just have the power of illusion."

Marcus bursts out laughing. "We don't have to make a 3D model. Just write a paper."

"Oh, I see how it is." I can't help the smile that spreads across my face as he laughs. His features, sharp and handsome, soften as he chuckles.

He opens his notebook and checks his messy handwriting. "We're supposed to find historical, religious, and mythological people who are imps and write a ten-page paper on them by the end of the year. We did a similar thing last year in Fae Studies."

"That shouldn't be too hard. There's Loki, Houdini..."

Marcus's eyebrows shoot up. "How do you know they're imps?"

Shit. Mother told me. I'm not supposed to know this stuff.

For a second I forgot. I give a little shrug and try to play it cool. "Grace told me. She took Demon Studies last year."

"Cool. We can definitely research those two. I think we need another person. Maybe a woman. Let's see what these books say."

We spend the next hour combing through the books Marcus brought while taking notes, and making an outline for what we need to research more. Though I originally pictured Marcus as more of a cute jock type, he's smarter than I expected.

"Hmm, there's a book we don't have." Marcus shuffles through the books on the table. "It's about the darkness of imps, and how they're seen as the more innocent of demons, but it outlines the atrocities some of them committed. I know I've seen it before."

"That could be useful."

He snaps his fingers. "I know! It's in Uriel's private library. I'll get it next time I'm there with Bastien, and I'll bring it next week when we meet again to finish up the research."

"Uriel has his own private library?" I ask as I help gather up the books on the table, keeping my voice casual. I still need to steal something for my first trial, and I have less than a month to do it. I remember seeing a bookshelf when I met with Uriel before, but I was pretty distracted and overwhelmed at the time.

"Yeah, in his office. Mostly stuff that's considered dangerous or not fit for students to read at their leisure. Dark magic kind of stuff. Old demonic tomes."

We put the books back on the shelf, and I peruse some of the other nearby books on demons. One of them looks interesting, and I pluck it off the shelf and flip through it.

"Same time again next week?" Marcus asks.

"Sounds good," I say, closing the book. I'm going to check it out and take it back to my room, because it has a section about Lilim that looks interesting. Surely I know all there is about my kind, but given what I've discovered I don't know about angels and demons, there might be something in the book I could learn too.

He leans against the bookshelf next to me and I catch a whiff of his scent. Sandalwood. "This was fun. We should hang out more."

My succubus side wakes up and purrs, and I'm tempted to bury my face in his chest and breathe him in. I clutch the book to my chest to stop myself. "I don't think your friends would approve."

"That's their problem. I want to get to know you better. Maybe over dinner sometime. What do you think?"

"I think that's a really bad idea." By now, my hunger has grown considerably and all the sexual tension with Marcus doesn't help in the least. "I'll see you in class."

I spin on my heel and start to head out. Why is Marcus suddenly being so nice to me? Is this some new angle to trick me into trusting him, then deceiving me? I've seen plenty of high school dramas on the CW, I know how this stuff works. Or am I being too suspicious? Maybe he actually...likes me? But that's a problem too. I can't have a boyfriend. Long term relationships are not possible for a succubus. I'm destined to be alone for the rest of my immortal days. Letting Marcus get close is only going to cause problems for both of us.

"Liv," he calls out. I turn to see him walking toward me with my planner in his hand. "You forgot this."

"Thanks." I hold out my hand, and Marcus places the

planner in it, his fingers brushing mine. Desire shoots through me, strong and potent. I haven't felt anything like this since the night with Kassiel. This is different, though. I'm not sure in what way, yet.

Sucking in a calming breath, I pull my hand away and put the planner in my bag. Walking away with my desire stoked and hunger gnawing at me is one of the most difficult things I've done in life.

———

J find Kassiel by the lake again that night. I'm not sure why I come back, except perhaps because I believed him when he said he wouldn't expose me. He must have figured out by now that I'm half demon and half angel, a creature forbidden to even exist, but it doesn't seem to bother him. It's a relief to be around someone who knows what I truly am. For the short time with him, I don't have to pretend.

I sit beside him in silence, unsure what exactly to say. By coming here, I'm acknowledging that I do want to talk with him and that he's right about me, but I won't admit it out loud either. There's also the unspoken tension between us as two people who once had mind-blowing sex together, but can't do it again...no matter how much we want to.

"What's your favorite class?" he asks. "And don't say mine, I've seen your eyes glaze over when I talk about things that happened thousands of years ago."

I laugh and relax a little on the bench. "Flight, obviously. Isn't that everyone's favorite?"

"Okay, other than that one."

"Probably Demon Studies."

He chuckles. "Because you're so well-versed in the subject already?"

Well, yes, but... "No, because Professor Raziel is funny. He wears the silliest bow ties."

"That he does. And I've never seen him wear the same one twice. He must have dozens of them."

"One for every day of the year, maybe?"

I find myself grinning as we talk about classes and professors until the moon is high, and we only stop when the air changes and the sky starts drizzling on us. We both laugh and stand up, holding our hands out to the tiny drops. While we've been sitting here a spring storm has gathered above us, and could unleash at any moment.

"I'm going to fly back before it starts pouring," Kassiel says, as he rises. "I suggest you do the same."

I nod. "Good idea."

"See you soon, Olivia."

His wings appear, as black as the night itself, and almost identical to mine. Except when he turns his back to me, I notice his feathers have shining silver tips, and when he extends his wings wide it's like looking at the night sky sparkling with stars. They're so beautiful they take my breath away as he launches into the air.

My own wings are shining black, so dark they look like ink, and I fly up beside Kassiel for a moment, enjoying the cool, damp air brushing against my face. We circle each other, a dance only for angels, and my chest tightens at how romantic it is to be flying with him. Then we move apart, me going to the dorms and him to the professor housing, and I remember that the two of us can never be.

Chapter Twenty-Six

OLIVIA

*W*eeks have passed since school began, and I'm finally starting to find my groove at Seraphim Academy. People still steer clear of me for the most part, but otherwise the bullying has mostly stopped, except for the annoying notes from Tanwen. The Princes are a problem, but I've gotten used to dealing with their haughty attitudes. Marcus and I meet every Wednesday to work on our paper, and he flirts with me shamelessly while I try not to let him wear down my armor entirely. Callan continues to toy with me during combat training, and Bastien still can't figure out what I am. Kassiel and I have met a few more times by the lake at night, and he tries to get me to confess what I am with pointed questions, all of which I dodge. On Sundays, I go to yoga class on the lawn, and even though Tanwen is there too, it helps keep my head clear and my body flexible. Two important things when you're part succubus.

Sometimes I almost forget why I'm really here. It's easy when the classes are interesting, and I have actual friends to hang out with for a change. But last night I found another invitation from the Order of The Golden Throne, and I realized it's been a month since the last meeting. I need to bring something to the trial tomorrow night, or I won't pass this first test. This secret society is the only lead I have, and I can't blow it.

I've done everything else I can think of to find Jonah. I watched a video of the championship game against the fae last year, but it was so boring I nearly fell asleep. Nothing happened that seemed suspicious, and no one I questioned saw anything odd that night. Another dead end. I checked out the other members of the baseball team, but none of them have any reason for hurting Jonah. And so far, neither Grace nor the Princes have given me any other leads, even though I've been getting closer to all of them and trying to subtly ask them questions about Jonah.

The Order of the Golden Throne is my only hope of finding him. Ever since Marcus told me about Uriel's private library, I've been observing the headmaster using my Ishim invisibility and Mother's necklace. He keeps a strict schedule, which isn't good for his security, but it's great for my need to steal something from his office. There must be something in there I can steal, and I purposefully waited until right before the next meeting to steal it. I don't want my stolen item anywhere near me if he notices it's missing and goes on a hunt for it.

Even with a plan in mind, I'm a bucket of nerves. I've skipped out on Angelic History, complaining to Kassiel that I have a headache, and he gave me a pointed look but nodded. He probably thinks I need to feed, which is true, but I've been surviving off of light and the lust I receive from him and the

Princes and I'm okay for now. I'll need to feed pretty soon though.

With my lock picks in my pocket and the light bent around me to make me invisible, I walk out of my dorm and make my way toward the Headmaster's house. Since the bell has rung and everyone is in fourth period, it's easy to move undetected across campus. At this time of day, I know the house will be empty because the Princes have class and Uriel uses the time to walk around the campus and meet with some of the workers.

I tiptoe onto the front porch of Uriel's home, but footsteps behind me make me freeze. Bastien walks up the path toward the house. Are you kidding me? They've followed the same pattern for a month, then on the day I'm breaking in, Bastien has to bring his sneaky ass here. Why isn't he in class?

I freeze, afraid if I move the wood under my feet might creak and he'll hear me. I stand to the right of the door, and there is just enough room for Bastien to use his key to unlock and open the door. If he moves a few inches to the right, he'll bump into me. I hold my breath.

As I wait and try not to move, silently urging him to go inside, he stiffens and breathes deep. He looks all around, and a white glow fills his eyes. He must suspect there is an Ishim hiding near him, but even his Ofanim magic can't get past my necklace. He sees nothing.

"Weird." He opens the door and strides in the house without bothering to make sure it closes behind him. I slip in on his heels and breathe a quiet sigh of relief when I make it without the door bumping into me.

I start to head for Uriel's office, where I visited on my second day here, but I want to scream in frustration when

Bastien goes straight for the room I need. But then, luck! He unlocks it with his own key, and doesn't close the door behind him. I sneak in and watch him sit at Uriel's large desk and turn on the computer. I creep behind his shoulder silently to watch what he's doing. The monitor lights up, showing views of all the cameras on campus. Bastien fiddles with the controls and brings up the parking lot, then rewinds through the entire freaking night. But he doesn't go at full speed, oh no. He goes slow enough that he can keep a close eye on any movement in the lot. Pausing a few times when he thinks he sees something, he continues backing up until yesterday evening comes on and the sun reappears.

This is taking forever. Bastien needs to leave so I can get a book off the shelves and get the fuck out of this house. If Bastien is still here when his father gets home, I might be busted. I still don't trust that my necklace is really working with Uriel, and I don't want to test it again.

Bastien hits a few buttons and looks at the live feed, scanning through the cameras like he's searching for something. "I'll catch you leaving again, Olivia. It's only a matter of time."

The sneaky asshole is looking for me. He knows I've been leaving campus at night. Damn it. That means I'll have to fly from now on. I'm getting better, and I can probably make it to the town, but I don't want to. The thought of soaring over all those trees makes me nervous. What if I get too tired to fly back? I've never gone long distances before.

Just when I think we'll be in here forever, Bastien stands and leaves the office, locking the door behind him. Good thing I brought my lock picks.

First thing's first. Find a book that's dark and scary enough to impress the Order of the Golden Throne. After searching

Uriel's bookshelf, I find what I need on the top shelf: *Daemon Death*, imprinted on a cover that looks suspiciously like skin. I shudder and put the book in a pouch slung cross-body just for this purpose.

The sound of footsteps have me flinging myself toward the window, praying it opens without a sound. Uriel must be back from his meetings. No time for lock picks, I need to get out *now*.

I dive out the window and tuck myself into a roll, landing on my feet and running toward the front of the house and around the corner. We learned that in Combat Training last week, and I silently thank Hilda for teaching it to us.

Once in front of the house, I dart down the path, praying Uriel isn't looking out a window and Bastien isn't about to jump out from behind a bush. I'm much more comfortable creeping around at night, even though my Ishim magic should protect me, but I feel a lot better when I near the cafeteria. I hide behind a tree, until I'm sure it's clear, and then I release the light bent around me, coming into view again.

Leaving the protection of the tree, I walk into the cafeteria like I would any other day of the week. Nothing strange to see here. Just a girl getting some food with a dark and dangerous book resting on her hip.

Chapter Twenty-Seven

OLIVIA

The meeting is in the same spot as last time, so I make it there with no problem, even in the dark. This time, my white mask and robes only match ten other people's. We stand for some time in a line, waiting for the meeting to begin. Without warning, the golden-robed figures emerge from the trees and surround us.

"Your numbers are considerably lowered," the leader says, standing in front with the crown on his or her head. "But it's as we expected."

Another robed figure steps forward, with a smaller build. Female, I think, though it's hard to tell in the robes and with the voice-altering masks. She holds out her hand at the person on the far left. "One at a time, bring your stolen objects forward."

The person walks forward and pulls a bracelet from under their white robes. "Professor Hilda's bracelet."

The leader nods and the mysterious voice speaks. "We accept your offering."

The white-robed person moves to their spot again with a sigh of relief. The next person steps forward. "One of Professor Raziel's bow ties."

The smaller person in gold takes the bow tie. Another golden-robed figure steps up and shakes his or her head. "This does not belong to Raziel. There is none of his essence on this." The masked figure tilts his or her head. "You bought this in a store and hoped to deceive us, didn't you?"

"Um, no, never..." sputters the person in white.

"Your offering is unacceptable," the leader says. "Leave this clearing and never speak of anything you've seen here."

"What?" the initiate asks. "You're wrong! I got it from his bedroom, I promise!"

"You think we can't see through your lies?" asks the second robed figure. Something about the way he speaks and moves reminds me of Bastien. Could it be him? "Fool."

People in golden robes suddenly surround the initiate, grabbing the person's arms, and dragging him or her out of the clearing. There's a lot of yelling, and then it goes eerily silent. After a few minutes, the masked figures return to their places among the trees. Everyone in white shifts nervously, now that we've seen what happens when we don't have a good enough offering.

After he leaves, the next person steps forward with a pair of tight black briefs. "Professor Kassiel's underwear."

Oh, damn. The thought of Kassiel in those briefs sends a zing of lust through me, along with jealousy too. How did this person get his underwear? Is Kassiel getting involved with another student? I quickly dismiss the thought, since it doesn't seem like something he would do, especially if he can resist me. This person must have snuck into his bedroom to get these.

"Are they clean?" the female in gold asks, sounding almost amused. I hear several snorts and coughs.

"Yes, they are. And it was fucking hard to get into the professor dorms without anyone noticing."

There's a long stretch of silence, and I worry we'll have another person escorted out, but then the leader says, "We accept your offering."

They continue moving through the group, until it's my turn. I swallow hard, step forward, and try to dislodge the book from the bag under my robe. Damn it.

"Hang on," I grunt, but my voice sounds weird. I pause, then realize it's the voice change. Get it together, girl! I manage to get out the book, ready for the strange voice this time. "This is a restricted book from Headmaster Uriel's private library."

The golden-robed figure hesitates before taking the book. "*Daemon Deaths*." The dark eyes behind the mask are familiar to me, but I can't place them. I need to find out more about these people, and a plan hatches. "Do you know this book is cursed?"

I yank my hand back. Good thing I got it earlier today. Who knows what it would have done if I'd kept it in my dorm for weeks. "I did not."

Silence stretches over the clearing, and I hold my breath, worried the object being cursed will be a problem and they'll drag me out of the clearing too. But then the leader nods. "Your offering is accepted."

I breathe a huge sigh of relief as I move back to the line. I've passed the first test. I'm one step closer to finding Jonah.

They continue down the line, sending one more person home, until the last initiate has made their offering.

"Congratulations on passing the first trial. Your next task, if you are up to it, is to guide a human to confession. You must prove that you're willing to help lead humanity down the path we have chosen for them, and take action against humans who commit evil. Many humans have dark secrets and have done things they're not proud of. Find one, convince him or her to reveal his secrets, and then expose them."

"Sorry, but I'm out," the initiate to my left suddenly says. "Stealing an object, fine. Ruining a human's life? Nope. I am not on board with this."

"You must do this if you want to join the Order."

"Yeah, no. This is not my jam. Thanks, but no thanks."

The person walks out of the clearing, while the rest of us stand there, stunned. The golden-robed figures whisper among themselves, shifting around uncomfortably at the disturbance, but the leader holds up a hand to silence them. "It's fine. That person will change their mind and come back to us. If not, they do not deserve to be in the Order anyway."

I'm disgusted by this task too, but I have to do it and it shouldn't be too hard with my succubus powers. Still, I'm seriously impressed by that person for walking away when this didn't feel right to them. That's hard to do, especially in a group like this.

The leader begins to speak again. "A camera will be left for you to record the confession. The camera is a fae relic, just like the masks you wear. You cannot fool it, and there is no way to cheat out of this test. You either do it, or you do not. Once you've completed the mission, leave it here, and if we accept your offering you'll receive an invitation to the next meeting."

With that, we're dismissed, and the others in white robes head back into the forest. I move a little way away from the other seven people, and then bend light around myself to disappear. Then I head back to the clearing. Time to find out who these fuckers are.

With my hand wrapped around my necklace, I double back just in time to see a glimpse of gold through the branches. Hurrying forward, I catch up to the group of masked figures. They walk on silent feet toward the lake, and when I think they're going to walk out of the woods and into the open air, they stop beside a boulder. The first person in the line grabs a branch on a nearby tree and yanks. The boulder rolls to the side as if several large men manipulate it, but nobody is close enough to touch it.

Not creepy at all.

A cave has opened up, and the members file into it one by one. I dart forward, on the heels of the last person to go through, and barely make it inside. The boulder must not be able to sense me with my necklace on, because it tries to roll back as soon as the person in front of me enters. I almost crash into them as I narrowly avoid it, and the boulder slams shut behind me, trapping me inside.

The tunnel behind the boulder leads downward in a sharp slope. I'm not expecting it and nearly trip and fall on my ass. I catch myself on the rough stone wall, and continue into the darkness. The ground levels out as the walls and floor dampen. Based on where we entered and how far we've walked, I guess we're under the lake by now.

The golden-robed figures enter a large cavern with ornate stone benches arranged in a circle. There's a small gap, leading to a large throne made of what looks like gold, carved with intricate designs of angels and demons in battle. It looks ancient.

The members of the Order take their seats on the stone benches, and the person with the crown stands in front. Oddly, he or she doesn't sit on the throne. Is it not for the leader? Who else would sit there?

"We begin another meeting of the Order of the Golden Throne. Has anyone made any progress in our mission?"

Silence. I clasp my necklace harder and stare at the robed figures. Who could they be? Why won't they remove their masks? Does that mean even the other people in the Order don't know who the other members are? Studying height and builds, I can't tell anything. I don't know these people well enough, even after all the time I've been on campus, but I'll figure it out. I've snuck in here once, I can do it again.

"Disappointing," the leader says. "Our master will be most displeased."

Master? Who could that be? I'm dying to know who these people are, but there's nothing I can do but watch and listen. I can't even move, for fear someone might hear my footsteps on the cold stone ground.

One of the masked figures speaks up. "The initiate that refused the second trial and left. She's the one we need, isn't she?"

"Yes, that was her," the leader says.

"How are we supposed to do this without her?" another person asks.

"We'll have to convince her to join after all," the leader says. "Perhaps we'll remind her of the evil of demons, and show her that the Order is the only way to stop them."

"What do you have in mind?" another person asks.

"I have an idea. We'll take action at the football game against the demons."

"Even if we can use her, what makes you think we'll be able to succeed this time? Jonah is still missing. If he failed, what hope do the rest of us have?"

My ears perk up at the mention of my brother. I knew this was the key to finding him. They must know where he is!

"We need to focus on finding Jonah," a different masked figure says. "He's been gone way too long now."

"Has anyone heard from him?" another asks. "Anything at all?"

"No, there has been no contact with Jonah, despite our best efforts," the leader says. "But once we have the girl, we can send a team to find him. Which is why we must convince her to join, no matter what dark deed it requires."

I don't like the way the leader is speaking, and I can't help but wonder who the girl is and why she's so important. How is she going to help them find Jonah? I need to figure out who she is.

"I'll send your orders when I have a plan in motion. Be ready for them. You're dismissed."

The masked figures stand, and some of them begin to file out, while others clump up into groups and whisper to each other. One of them moves to the leader and speaks in a hushed conversation. I really want to listen to what they're saying, but I'm also worried about getting trapped down here. Plus I have an idea.

I follow one of the people up the tunnel and out of the cave, watching when they press a stone to open the boulder. I continue moving silently behind them as they head through the forest for a distance, before pausing to remove their robes and mask. I throw a hand over my mouth so I don't visibly gasp when I see who it is.

Cyrus.

Chapter Twenty-Eight
CALLAN

*I*t's been two months since school started, and there's still no sign of Jonah. Even worse, we haven't kept our promise to him. I graffitied Olivia's door and have been sending her threatening notes, but nothing is working. She isn't scared enough to leave the school, which means I'm going to have to ramp up my efforts somehow.

One morning, I suggest to Professor Hilda that Tanwen should pair up with Araceli that day. Tanwen went hard on Liv last week, which I'm perfectly fine with, but I want a crack at her now.

"You're with me today," I say. Olivia jumps a mile as she whirls to face me, and I can't help but snicker. She didn't realize I was behind her. Good. I'm glad to have the upper hand. Maybe she'll keep being jumpy, and I can use that against her.

"Did you have a good weekend, half-human?" I drip acid into my tone, but she doesn't react.

"I did, thank you for asking. How was your weekend?"

Her polite voice is the opposite of mine and makes me feel like a big jerk. I don't really enjoy bullying her, but I can't let up, though. Jonah would kill us if he knew we still hadn't found a way to get her to leave. He'd been adamant that she had to go for her own safety. And since I can't do a damn thing to bring him back, I have to do this thing for him.

I gesture for her to follow me onto one of the mats. "Today I'm going to attempt to teach you to deflect an attack from behind."

I go through the motions, and she stands there with her hands behind her back, making her breasts push out and look even more noticeable. If I didn't know she hated me, I'd think she's trying to be seductive. Like she needs to try. Even in the shapeless gym clothes, her figure screams at me. I itch to put my hands around her waist. Her curves are what humans sing about. Perfectly proportioned, and a body that would fit mine like a glove.

Frustrated at the direction my mind is going, I attack without warning. Of course, she doesn't have time to dodge me. I've got her pinned to the mat before either of us takes in another breath.

She blinks up at me with big eyes, and I launch off of her. Damn it. Working with her isn't a good idea after all. "Didn't the humans teach you anything?" I growl. "Why don't you go back to them?"

She huffs as she stands up. "I wasn't ready, but I will be this time. Can we try again?"

I grunt, and remind myself I'm supposed to be teaching her. This time I attack slower, giving her the chance to use the move I showed her earlier, and she deflects it easily. We do the move multiple times, until she gets it down. By the time the class is over, I've worked her hard and we're both sweating, but I'm nowhere closer to getting rid of her.

As she walks out of the gym and heads to the lake for Flight class, I rub my palms on my eyes. I keep failing to keep my promise to Jonah, and I can practically hear my dad yelling at me for not living up to my potential. He'd beat the shit out of me if he knew I wasn't keeping my word to someone. As the son of two Archangels, failure is not an option for me.

It's time for some drastic measures. I take no joy in what I need to do, but it's the only way to fulfill my promise to Jonah. I stalk out to the parking lot, where Liv's beat-up old Honda is parked next to my convertible Audi again. I check the area, but no one is around, and even if someone was, what would they do? No one would dare stop me.

I gather light in my palms, and then blast the windshield to pieces with a direct shot. Tiny fragments of glass fly everywhere, covering the car seats and making it impossible for her to drive it until she cleans it out. *Try going on one of your midnight excursions now.*

It's not enough though. She could mistake this for a random act of nature or something. I use my burning light like a laser and write in large letters along the pavement behind her car, "YOU DON'T BELONG HERE." Below it, I add, "LEAVE NOW OR PAY."

I step back and survey the wreckage of her car. There. That should convince her to leave the school. And then my promise to Jonah will be complete.

Chapter Twenty-Nine

OLIVIA

light class is over the lake today. If we fall, we get soaked at best, drown at worst. Enough time has gone by that I don't have to pretend to be a terrible flier anymore. I'm an honest but mediocre flier now and using the class to improve. I'm still not the best, but I don't fall in the lake, so I call it a success.

In Demon Studies, we're learning about Lilim now, which amuses me but also makes me a little nervous that someone in class might figure out there's a succubus sitting only a few feet from them. No one does, of course.

"Imagine needing sex to survive," Marcus says with a grin when we walk out of class together. "Doesn't seem so bad to me."

I roll my eyes. "Of course you'd think that. But it also means the Lilim can never settle down with anyone."

"Not unless they had a harem or something, I guess." Marcus wiggles his eyebrows. "Don't tell me that doesn't appeal to you."

I shake my head, but can't help but smile. "But then the trick is finding people who are okay with sharing you with others."

Marcus grins and starts to reply, but then Grace runs over to me. "Liv! Your car!"

My good mood instantly vanishes. "What? What about it?"

"It's been attacked. You need to go look. I'll go report it to the Headmaster."

"I'll come with you," Marcus says, as we rush down the steps and onto the lawn.

I rush to the parking lot with a hollowness in my chest, and when I get there, I freeze. My windshield's been completely destroyed, and tiny bits of glass cover everything. But that's not the worst of it. No, the worst is the message in the pavement.

My eyes water, and it's hard to hold back the tears. For months now I've stayed strong even when people were mean to me, when they left me threatening notes and tagged my dorm room door, but this is too much. I bought that car myself, scraping together enough money to afford it, and even though it's a piece of shit it's *mine*. Now every time I see it, I'll remember this moment.

YOU DON'T BELONG HERE, the message taunts me. And maybe it's right. I don't belong at Seraphim Academy. I'm not an angel, not like these people are. But I don't belong at Hellspawn Academy either. I belong nowhere.

For a second I'm tempted to say fuck it and leave. Give the haters what they want. It would be so much easier to return to my old life and forget about all of this. But I can't. I won't.

Not until I find Jonah, anyway.

Marcus wraps an arm around my shoulders. "I'm so sorry, Liv."

I nod absently. "Who could do this?"

"That's the work of an Erelim. They're the only ones who can burn with light like that."

My hands clench at my sides. Tanwen. It has to be. That bitch is going to pay.

Marcus takes my face in his hands and stares into my eyes. "Don't listen to them," he says. "You do belong here, as much as any of us do."

His kind words are my undoing, and before I know what I'm doing, I press my lips to his. It was either that, or burst into tears, I guess. He kisses me back like he's been dying for this moment as much as I have, wrapping his arms around me and holding me tight. I slide my hands along his strong back, and for a second I feel safe and loved with him, a feeling so rare and nice I never want it to end. But it has to. It's an illusion, because everything between us is a lie, and nothing like this can last.

I pull away from him and run off, leaving him behind, along with my broken car. As I do, I feel the after-effects from the kiss, sending power through my veins. Marcus is the son of an Archangel, and thus stronger than most other angels, and even a kiss is enough to give me a boost and hold off the hunger for a while. Except now that I've had a taste of him, I only want more.

———

I ditch Angelic History, because I can't face Kassiel with lust running through my veins, but I calm down enough to meet Bastien for our special classes. I'm distracted, totally focused on my car being vandalized and the kiss with Marcus, and he can probably tell.

He meets me outside the library today. "Since nothing has worked so far in finding your Choir, we're going to do something different now. Today we'll go to the Ishim class and watch them practice to see if you feel anything. Then next time we'll go observe a different Choir and on until we find the one you belong to."

I nod, but my stomach twists. Why did we have to start with the Choir I should belong to?

The Choir classes are held in a large building on the other side of campus, set back against the forest. I've never been to this building before, but it's divided into four sections. We head down a hallway that leads to both the Ishim classes, and the Malakim training area and school infirmary. On the rare occasions an angel is sick or injured, they come here and the Malakim fix them up.

Bastien takes me inside a room that appears to be empty except for one man, with pale skin, pale eyes, and pale hair. He looks like an angel that's been bleached by the sun.

"This is Professor Nariel, and he teaches the Ishim classes," Bastien says, introducing us. "Olivia here hasn't found her Choir yet, and we wanted to observe some Ishim at work to see if she feels anything."

"Nice to meet you," Nariel says, shaking my hand. "We were just practicing hiding groups of people and objects."

He makes a gesture, and suddenly half a dozen students appear around us, making me jump. They were invisible the entire time, and I had no idea. Bastien doesn't appear surprised, but I bet he saw through their invisibility with his Ofanim sight. Only my necklace prevents him from seeing me when I sneak around.

Grace is one of the students in the class, and she gives me a little wave, her eyes sympathetic. I don't know the other students, but they stare at me with openly curious expressions.

"As Ishim, we bend light around ourselves to turn invisible," Nariel says, telling me nothing I don't already know. "We can also extend this power to other objects and people, with training. The strongest of us can hide entire buildings from view."

"I bet that makes you good spies," I say, sounding impressed. *And assassins*, I silently add.

"Spies and scouts, yes, but we do a lot more than that. We move through the human world more than other angels do, and often act as messengers. Some of us also work as guardian angels, watching over important humans to influence and protect them as needed."

"Oh wow. I had no idea angels were so involved with the humans. How do you pick who to guard?"

"The Archangel Council assigns us the humans," Nariel says.

"Can we show Olivia some Ishim powers in action?" Bastien asks.

"Of course." He gestures at Grace and the other students. "Continue, Grace."

Grace vanishes into thin air, and then the other students do the same. Seconds later, the desks on one side of the room disappear one by one, along with the bags and jackets hanging on them. Soon the classroom appears completely empty, except for the three of us standing there.

"Impressive," I say, my chest tightening. I can make myself invisible, along with anything I'm holding, but that's it so far. I could learn so much more if I was in this class with the others of my kind. But if I reveal my Choir, that would link me to Father and Jonah, and I can't expose my connection to them. For now, I must remain the powerless half-human girl with no Choir.

Grace suddenly appears at my side, though I didn't even hear her move. "Did you feel anything?"

"Nothing." Looking at Bastien, I shrug. "Sorry."

My necklace keeps him from detecting the lie in my words. "Thank you for your help," he tells Nariel. As we walk out of the building, Bastien arches an eyebrow at me. "You truly felt nothing?"

"Nope. Were you expecting me to?"

His cold eyes narrow at me. "I was testing a theory. Don't worry, I have plenty more. Tomorrow we'll watch the Malakim heal people. Don't be late."

As I walk across campus to my dorm, a memory of Jonah comes back to me. It was his second visit after starting Seraphim Academy, and I remember how he flopped on my bed with a big, dreamy sigh.

"What's that about?" I asked.

He came out of his fog with a silly grin on his face. "Hmm?"

"Your goofy smile." I pushed him over, so I could sit beside him. "Let me guess. You met a girl."

"How'd you know?"

"A succubus can tell these things," I said with a wink. "Tell me about her."

"Her name is Grace. We met in Ishim training, and she's just...the best. So smart and kind, and she has the prettiest big brown eyes. Here, let me show you." He scrolled through photos on his phone, and then showed me one. He wore a baseball uniform, except this one had the Seraphim Academy logo on it, and he stood in front of a lake with his arm around a strawberry blond woman with a pretty face. They were both grinning like idiots, and Jonah beamed just looking at the photo.

"We started dating a few weeks ago and everything's been great. I seriously think I might marry this girl one day."

I rolled my eyes and threw a pillow at him. "Let's not get carried away, lover boy. You haven't known her that long."

"Yeah, but sometimes you just know. You just do."

My brother, the romantic. He really loved Grace, and after spending time with her these last few months, I can see why.

I vow again to find him. Not just for me, but for the sadness I still see occasionally in Grace's eyes.

But first...I need to get back at Tanwen for destroying my car. Tonight I'll sneak into her room while she has dinner with the Valkyries at their normal table. Tomorrow, when she goes to get dressed for Combat Training, she'll find every single one of her gym clothes has been cut to shreds. It's the least she deserves. Sure, she can go get more at the student store, but it'll be a hassle for her, and she'll know I'm not going to sit back and take the abuse anymore. I'm done being bullied.

Chapter Thirty
OLIVIA

*I*t's been two weeks since my car was vandalized, and tonight's the football game against Hellspawn Academy. Tanwen is one of the cheerleaders, because of course she is. She must suspect that I'm the one who pranked her, but she hasn't said anything to me about it. I keep waiting for some kind of retaliation, but all I get is mocking insults and the regular beatdowns in Combat Training, although I've gotten better at fighting back. On rare occasions I even manage to knock her on her back.

We head out to the field behind the gym, and on the way there we run into Darel, who's wearing his football uniform. Lately he's been spending more time in our dorm than his own. When he's in Araceli's bedroom, the lust coming out of there is more than I can refuse. All I do is sit on the couch and absorb it, even though I feel like a fucking creeper. Like having a light salad, it's great nourishment, but it doesn't fill you up for very long. I need another real meal soon.

I smile at their joined hands. I'm so glad Araceli has found someone that accepts her for who she is.

As soon as we walk behind the gym, we see the huge field there has been transformed. Bleachers line either side and at first glance, it's obvious the visitors are not mingling with the home team. There are easily seven or eight hundred angels crammed into the bleachers. Maybe a thousand. On the demon side, probably half that.

I turn in a circle with my jaw slack. I've never seen so many angels and demons in one spot. "Wow."

"Yeah, I guess it's a lot if you've never been here," Darel says. "My dad took me to a bunch when I was a kid. He's thrilled I made it onto the team this year, even though he had to miss this game. He'll be at the next one though, and then you can meet him."

"That would be great," Araceli says.

"I need to get going. The game's starting soon." Darel gives Araceli a long kiss, and I pointedly look away.

"Good luck!" we call out, as he jogs away to join the rest of the team. Professor Hilda barks some orders at him, and he disappears into the gym.

"Let's find a seat," Araceli says.

We get some beers and find some seats just as the football team comes out onto the field to the major cheers from the crowd. They don't have their helmets on yet, and I catch sight of Callan. I can't help but stare at his ass in those tight little pants as he runs down the field. Even though I can't stand the guy, I have to admit he fills those out nicely. Yum.

I gaze across the crowd and spot Bastien and Marcus in the audience, and a little way behind them sits Kassiel with Nariel and Raziel. I make a mental note to avoid looking that way again, or risk my lust flaring up again. Grace and Cyrus wave at us as they walk by, and grab seats a few rows ahead of us. Ever since finding out Cyrus was a member of the Order, I've been super careful with what I say around him, and Grace too in case she's a member also.

The crowd quiets down as the demons come out. Their bleachers erupt in cheers, but it's nowhere near as loud as the angel side. I guess if we were at a game at Hellspawn Academy, we'd be the lesser represented, too.

"Do they have games at Hellspawn Academy too?" I ask. I can't wait to visit there. In theory, I could've gone to that academy if I could've hidden my angelic side from them. It would've been nice to have been able to learn from both sides of my heritage.

"They do, and normally this game would be held there, but their field was flooded this spring. It should be back in shape for their game against the fae though."

"Why not hold it at the fae school? Ethereal Academy, right?"

"They don't allow us to go to Faerie. I've never even been myself."

"Oh, too bad."

The game starts, and we cheer when Darel makes a touchdown. "He's the best one on the team," Araceli says dreamily. "Even better than Callan."

"It's nice to see Callan isn't the best at something. The Princes think they're so damn good at everything."

"They are. Most things. But football takes more than natural-born skill. It takes practice and learning."

The football game is close, but Callan, big and fast, heads up the angel's defense and blocks many of the demon's attempts to score. Darel is the hero of the night, scoring thirteen touchdowns. When the angels win, I cheer as loud as everyone else.

At the end, the teams shake hands, and even from a distance it's easy to see the tension. There is no happy banter, no real sportsmanship. It's barely-veiled hostility between the two teams.

Darel runs over to Araceli and I smile up at them as he lifts her off her feet in a huge hug. Their fondness for each other is uplifting to see, but it also makes me feel like something of a third wheel. I can't help but be jealous of them for having something I'll never be able to have myself.

"Are you two coming to the party after this?" he asks us.

"Wouldn't miss it," Araceli says.

"Cool, I'll meet you there." He gives her another kiss, and then runs back to celebrate with the rest of his team. My gaze follows him and then lands on Callan. Tanwen stands beside him in her cheerleader uniform, clutching his bicep, but his eyes are on me. I blow him a kiss, just because I know it will annoy him, and I'm rewarded with a sharp scowl.

"I think I'm going to head back to my room," I tell Araceli.

"You're not coming to the party?"

"No, I'm not feeling up to it. I think that hot dog didn't agree with my stomach."

"Oh no! Want me to try healing you?"

I laugh. "I'll be fine. Seriously. Go have fun with Darel."

"Ok, but if you feel better you should come over."

"I will."

I start to head back to the dorms, but I'm stopped by Marcus blocking my path. He's wearing a black shirt that hugs his muscles, his gorgeous hair ruffles in the wind, and his mouth looks deliciously kissable. It hurts to look at him, because I know how good he tastes, and it takes all my power not to take more from him.

"Liv," he says. "You haven't shown up to work on our project. What's the deal?"

I stare at the grass under my feet. "I didn't think we needed to meet anymore. We're pretty much finished with it."

"This is about that kiss, isn't it?" he asks. "You've been avoiding me ever since. Don't deny it."

I sigh. "Fine, I've been avoiding you. That kiss shouldn't have happened."

"Why not?" he steps closer, within dangerous touching distance. "I thought it was pretty amazing, and I'd love to do it again sometime."

My heart squeezes painfully. "Look, Marcus, it was a good kiss, but I'm not looking for anything serious right now. I'm not in the right place for a boyfriend or anything."

"That's fine. I don't want anything serious either. We can keep it casual."

Except my idea of casual would be sleeping with him and a couple other people too. Not because I want to, but because I have to do it to survive. Somehow, even with his joke about a harem, I don't think Marcus would agree to anything like that. Besides, I can't tell him about that anyway, not without revealing my succubus side, and risking everything.

"I'm just not interested," I say, with a nonchalance I don't feel. "Sorry."

His jaw drops, and I bet I'm the first girl who's ever rejected him. He can't even form a reply as I walk away. *Score another point for Liv,* I think, although it doesn't give me any comfort this time, knowing I put another of the Princes in his place.

———

I make it back to the dorm room and settle down in my pjs with a cup of decaf coffee and my Angelic History textbook. We have a test tomorrow, and even though Kassiel and I meet regularly, I know he's not going to let me off the hook if I don't pass.

Hours later, our dorm room suddenly bursts open. Araceli stands there, obviously distraught. "Have you seen Darel?"

"No, I thought he was with you at the party."

"He never showed up! I waited and waited and he never arrived!"

"That's odd. Maybe he was tired and passed out after the game?"

"No, I checked his dorm and he's not there. No one has seen him. He just...disappeared after the game." She bites her nails, something she does when she's nervous. "Do you think demons took him?"

"I doubt it. Why would they do that?"

"I don't know!"

It tears me apart seeing her so upset, and even though I'm sure there's a simple explanation, I stand up and grab my coat, then toss Araceli's to her. "Come on, let's go look for him."

We spend the rest of the night combing the campus for

Darel, but there's no trace of him anywhere. It's like he just vanished after the game...like my brother did.

———

*D*arel's body is found the next morning in the forest. Upon hearing the news, Araceli collapses against me, screaming and crying. I hold her as her body shakes, and I cry with her while hating myself a little for being grateful it wasn't Jonah's body they found.

Rumor gets out that Darel's body was torn apart by what looks like animal claws, and there were fang marks in his neck. All signs point to a demon attack after the game, and people are out for blood, even though all Uriel says is that the investigation is ongoing. Darel was liked by everyone, not to mention he was the star of the football team, and his death hits everyone hard. Especially Araceli.

Her normal light has dimmed, and now she hides in her room most of the time. I can hear her crying through the walls. I give her some space, because there's not much else I can do, and bring her her favorite tea and cookies whenever I can.

I find it hard to believe demons would kill Darel, but there doesn't seem to be any other explanation either.

Two weeks after Darel was found dead, Araceli emerges and sits beside me on the couch.

"Oliva, I need to tell you something. Something secret."

I put down my favorite mug and sit up straighter. "Anything."

"You asked me one time if there was a secret society on campus, and I lied to you and said no. But there is one, called the Order of the Golden Throne, and they're this fanatical pro-angel, anti-demon group. They invited me to join them, and at first I was so excited because I've always been such an outcast among the angels, and it felt good to be wanted and accepted. But then they had us do things I didn't agree with. Like stealing from a professor."

"You did that?" I ask. Even though I know this was the first task, I find it hard to picture Araceli stealing anything.

"Yeah, I stole Professor Kassiel's underwear cause I thought it would be funny, although I felt horrible doing it. I passed that test, but then they said we had to get a human to confess to something on camera, and then expose them. I refused and walked away."

Oh shit. She's the one who left that night—and the one they said they needed.

"Since then, I've been getting notes telling me to come back, and I got one again after Darel died. It's obvious it was a demon attack, but the authorities aren't doing anything so far. The Order says they can help me get revenge against the demons who killed him, but only if I complete the second test and join them. And I do want justice for Darel, I really do, but I don't know if I want to get involved with the Order again." She turns her big, kind eyes on me. "What do you think, Liv?"

I take her hands in mine and give them a squeeze. "I think you were right to walk away from the Order when you did."

She bites her lip. "But should I join now? For Darel?"

"No, I don't think you should. He wouldn't want that."

"He wouldn't?"

"No, he wouldn't. Uriel will make sure that the people who killed him are brought to justice, I'm sure of it. Meanwhile, you can honor Darel by living your life the best you can and staying true to yourself. That's what he would want."

She throws her arms around me. "Thanks, Liv. I knew you would understand. And I'm sorry I lied to you and didn't tell you about the Order. I just wanted to protect you from them."

"It's okay." I feel a pang of guilt, knowing how much I've lied to her about, including this. I'm tempted to tell her I was invited too, but decide against it. That would only open me up to even more questions, and I'm not ready to confess everything to Araceli yet. Besides, it's better for her if she's kept in the dark about all of this. Araceli's heart is so big and pure, and I can't let her get corrupted by the darkness inside the Order. That's my job—and I've already got plenty of darkness inside me anyway.

"I'm going to go make your favorite tea," I tell Araceli. "You just relax here and watch some TV."

She sniffs. "Thanks."

As I head into our mini-kitchen and heat up some water, my mind wanders back to that night I snuck into the cavern below the lake.

"We'll have to convince her to join after all," the leader said. *"Perhaps we'll remind her of the evil of demons, and show her that the Order is the only way to stop them."*

"What do you have in mind?" another person asked.

"I have an idea. We'll take action at the football game against the demons."

My hand trembles as I clutch Araceli's mug, and I nearly drop it. Could the Order be responsible for Darel's death? Would they really do something so extreme as to kill one of their own? Thank goodness I steered Araceli away from them. But why do they need her? The only explanation is because she's part fae, and they think that will help them find Jonah somehow. Could he be in Faerie?

I need to pass this next test. The camera arrived a while ago, but I've been putting the task off because I don't want to do it. It's time to suck it up and get it over with, especially because I only have a few more weeks before the deadline. I feel it in my gut, all of this is connected, and I'm getting closer to the truth. The Order is the key to this mystery—and I'll do whatever I have to so I can join them.

Chapter Thirty-One
OLIVIA

*A*s soon as night falls, I double-check the map and take off from my balcony, using my necklace and inborn abilities to leave campus undetected. It's almost summer now, and the air is warmer as it filters through my black feathers. I stretch them wide and savor the feel of flight. I've never traveled this far before, but all that practice in Flight class has been paying off, because it isn't a problem.

The church is empty by the time I get there. I step up to the door and push, finding it unlocked. The large wooden door creaks as I push it open. "Hello?"

Nobody responds, so I walk farther into the sanctuary. Contrary to what you've seen in the movies, demons won't burst into flames in a church. Lucky for me.

"Anybody home?" I look up at the beautiful stained glass as footsteps echo off the stone walls. The church is pretty old, and for a second I feel like I'm in a horror movie or something, walking to my doom. I shake the thought off and steel myself for what I have to do.

A small man in a black suit walks out of the back. "Can I help you?"

"Are you Father Abram?" I ask.

"Yes, I am." His eyes travel up and down my body, and I can feel a hint of his lust. It makes me want to vomit.

"Can I speak with you somewhere privately?" I ask.

"This way."

He leads me into a back office and shuts the door. "What is this about?"

I set the camera down on the desk and turn it on. There's no reason for me to hide it. Abram gives it an odd look, but then he's distracted when I open my trench coat. Inside, I'm wearing a stereotypical schoolgirl uniform, and with my hair in pigtails, it makes me look younger than I am. Closer to the age this monster likes.

Last time I went to feed, I tried to get people in the bar near the academy to confess, but none of them had done anything terrible enough to warrant exposing them for. Then I met a man who was distraught, nearly drinking himself to death, because his daughter claimed a priest had touched her. No one else believed her, and I silently swore to that man that I'd make things right for his little girl.

"I need to ask you a few questions," I say, as I run my hands down my tight white shirt, which clearly shows my pink bra underneath. I let my powers unfurl, and I'm disgusted by the way his lust tastes. It's rotten and vile, and I can't wait to get out of here.

He stares at me, his tongue practically hanging out of his mouth as he ogles my body. I'm sure the camera is getting a great view of my ass under my short plaid skirt.

Abram is evil, every bit of him, from his shaggy brown hair

to his sensible brown shoes, but he has the nerve to say to me, "You're a sinner."

If only he knew.

"I am," I say, tugging on my skirt, which barely covers my thighs. "I need you to help me."

Abram steps forward, clasping his waistband now. The evidence of his desire is bulging against his pants, and I have to say, it's not impressive. "I can help you."

"Do you want to hurt me, Abram?" Trailing my hands up my waist, I throw my hair back and moan. "Do you want to make me pay for my sins?"

"I do."

"Except I'm not young enough for you, am I?" I can't bring myself to touch him where he wants me to, but I reach out and touch his hand, and my power latches onto his lust and draws it out.

"You'll do for tonight," he says, as he pulls out his cock.

"You want me, Abram?" I slide a hand under my skirt, pushing it up, revealing more of my bare thighs. "Then tell me the truth. You touch little girls, don't you?"

"They need it," he says, stroking his cock as he stares at me. Ugh, he's disgusting. "Someone has to punish them for their sins."

"And it has to be you, of course."

"I'll punish you too, you little demon."

I laugh, and the sound is evil. "Oh, I'm so much more than that, Abram." My voice lowers. "I'm an angel."

He falls to his knees and reaches for my legs, his desperation to have me so strong he can't help himself. "Please, demon, angel, whatever you are. Let me punish you."

"Tell me the girls' names first."

"Caroline. Melody. Amanda."

I nearly barf with each confession, but this is what I need for the video. When he's done, I reach over and shut it off.

Then I reach over and wrap my hands around this monster's neck. I want to squeeze the life out of him, but instead I throw more of my power into him. He jerks on his cock, unable to stop himself, until his orgasm shoots out of him. I needed him to come, but I was definitely not fucking this guy. Just touching him for a second is horrifying.

"If you want more, you will get up, put your dick back in your pants, and go straight to the police station. Confess everything you told me tonight to them." His eyes are on mine, and my power has done its job. He's glassy-eyed and totally in my thrall. "Do that, and I'll come to you again."

He nods and as soon as I let go of him, he jumps up, running for the door as he stuffs his dick in his pants. I grab my coat and camera and follow, unfurling my wings and going invisible. He's already in his car and pulling out of the parking lot. Damn. I've never unleashed my magic like that before—I usually try to hold it back, so that humans won't be harmed by it. But once I let the magic work, it really did.

I follow Abram to the police station, and when he disappears inside, I creep to the window and turn the camera back on. As it records, I watch the priest speak to a police officer behind a desk. His face goes from bored to pale to furious.

Mission complete.

I need to go home and have a long, hot shower to get the feel of his desire off of me. The Order had better let me in after that—and now there will be one less predator out in the world too.

Chapter Thirty-Two
MARCUS

*D*uring second period, we head to room 302. Bastien unlocks the door with the key he swiped from the office, and I glance around warily. He shut the cameras in the dorms off, and even if someone was here, they wouldn't stop us or question us. Why would they? We do what we want without any consequences. Olivia's the only one who ever gives us any grief at all.

Maybe that's why I can't stop thinking about her. She's the only woman who's ever rejected me before, and it stings. I know she wants me too, but she's holding back, and it drives me crazy. For once, I don't know what to do about a woman.

I'm pretty sure breaking into her room isn't it, but the guys never listen to me on these things. "This is a really bad idea," I say anyway. "We shouldn't do this."

"Nothing else is working," Callan says. "It's been months and she's still here. We have no other choice."

Bastien pushes open the door, and Callan pushes past him and stomps inside. I pinch the bridge of my nose and follow behind them. It was bad enough when Callan was just sending her notes and being rude to her, but then he went and trashed her car. Now this.

But maybe he's right. Jonah made us promise him we'd keep Olivia away from the school for her own safety, and I trusted my best friend to my core. She was obviously important to him, which makes her important to me. If this is how we keep her safe, I guess we have to do it. I just don't like it. At all.

The living room is neat and unadorned, except for a few cozy pillows they've added, plus some art on the walls with splashes of paint. There are textbooks stacked on the coffee table and a few dirty plates in the sink. Both Olivia and her roommate Araceli have class right now according to Bastien, so we knew they'd be away, but it still makes me feel like a total creeper for being in their room uninvited.

Callan and Bastien don't seem to be bothered by it though. They find Olivia's bedroom and get right to work, first closing her curtains so no one will see. Meanwhile, I keep glancing at the door and wondering if I can sneak out.

Olivia's room is surprisingly boring. There's nothing on the walls, and her bedspread is plain gray and from the student store. Even so, her presence is imbibed into its fabric, and I can practically smell her in the air. Knowing how she affects me, I don't give her unmade bed a second glance, besides thinking how typical it is that she doesn't make her bed.

"She's undisciplined," Callan says, his voice disgusted. "People without proper structure never make their bed in the morning."

I roll my eyes. "I bet you make yours every day."

"Of course I do. It sets the tone for the day. Order and control."

From what Callan's told us, I wouldn't be surprised if Michael drilled that into him. Everyone thinks the former leader of the Archangels was a damn saint, but Callan's hinted at another side to him. A dark side.

Bastien digs around in her desk and looks under her bed, while Callan throws open the closet doors and begins pulling out her clothes and tossing them on the ground. I cringe at this major invasion of privacy, but I don't stop them.

Callan glares at me. "Why'd you come if you're not going to help?"

"This is wrong," I mutter. "Seriously wrong."

Even as I say it, I move to her drawers and begin pulling them open. The top drawer holds her panties and bras. She likes dark lingerie, the color of jewels, and there's not a granny panty in sight. Lace the colors of rubies and sapphires tempts me, but I only look long enough to make sure there's nothing hidden in the drawer.

"Fuck." I slam the drawer shut. "Leave that drawer alone," I warn Callan, but of course, my words make him come straight over and open it.

He sucks in a fast breath. "That's..." Looking at me out of the corner of his eye, he slams it shut, too. "No big deal. Pull the drawer out and sling them around the room."

Nope. Can't do it. If I touch those frilly things, I'm going to run out of this room and find Olivia immediately. Instead, I pull out the next drawer, which holds several pairs of jeans. I can handle that. Taking my time, I pull them out one at a time and shake them to unfold them, then fling them around the room. Meanwhile, Bastien has found Olivia's planner, and is studying it like it might hold the secrets of the universe. From what I've seen of Olivia's room so far, I doubt it contains anything important. She's too careful. Almost like she knew something like this might happen.

By the time I'm done emptying out her jeans and socks, Callan has pulled out the rest of her closet, and Bastien's ripped out all the pages of the planner and scattered them around the room.

"No sign of any white robes," Callan says. "She must not be an initiate."

Well, that's a relief. The last thing we need is for Olivia to be mixed up with the Order too.

Bastien examines her shoes carefully, and then picks up one of her sexy little heels, the ones she wears when she sneaks out at night. He presses something inside of them. "There, now we'll be able to follow her next time."

"What was that?" I ask.

"A tracker."

It keeps getting worse and worse. I feel like the biggest jerk in the world. "Can we leave now?"

"One last thing." Callan picks up a mug, half-full of coffee, from her bedside table. It has a phrase on the side. "I'm a fucking angel," he reads, and then snorts. He pours the coffee out on her bed, then throws the mug against the wall, hard. With a crash, it breaks into a dozen pieces and falls to the floor. He looks at me with hard eyes. "Now we can go."

Chapter Thirty-Three

OLIVIA

*A*fter Flight, Araceli and I head back to our room to change and heat up some leftovers for lunch while we study before our next classes. It's been over a month since Darel was killed, and she's doing a little better, although I worry she'll never return to her once-perky self.

When we walk into the dorm room, my bedroom door is open. That's odd. I always close it. As I stand in the doorway, my heart freezes and jaw drops. It's totally trashed. There are clothes thrown around everywhere, the pages have been ripped out of my planner and scattered around, and there's coffee all over my bedspread.

"Liv?" Araceli calls out, sounding worried. She peers over my shoulder and gasps. "Oh my gosh. What happened?"

I shake my head as I survey the destruction. I don't even want to walk into the room, but I take a step forward. It was bad enough when my car was attacked, but now this. I'm sure it's retaliation for going into Tanwen's room and messing with her gym clothes, but everything she's done to me has been so much worse than what I did to her.

"Oh, Liv, your planner." She picks pieces of paper off the floor and sighs.

Tears threaten to fill my eyes, but I take in a deep breath and blink them back. These are only things, and I'm not that attached to them. There's only one thing I'm attached to, and I glance around for it. My mug from Jonah was on my bedside table. Where is it?

I pick up clothes around the room and then I spot the mug on the floor.

In pieces.

The tears fall then. Everything else in this room meant nothing to me, but that mug? It was the one connection to Jonah I allowed myself. My most valuable possession. And now it's gone.

Araceli puts her arm around me. "I'm sorry someone did this."

My hands clench at my side. "It has to be Tanwen."

"Probably." She sighs, and then throws my empty planner in the garbage can. "Come on, I'll help you clean this up, and we'll go shopping this weekend."

"Thanks, Araceli." I pick up the tiny pieces of my mug, wiping the tears from my eyes as I drop the shards on top of my destroyed planner.

After she leaves the room, I shut the door, and pull the desk out from the wall. Behind it is a little hole I made where I keep my Order robes and mask, plus a huge wad of cash. Luckily it's all undisturbed.

———

J report the break-in of my room to Headmaster Uriel, and he says he'll investigate it, just as he said the same thing about my car. So basically he's no help at all. I'll have to deal with Tanwen on my own.

I'm five minutes late to my meeting with Bastien, and he gives me an icy stare.

"You're late."

"Deal with it," I snap. I'm so tired of getting shit from everyone, I can't even tell you. "Someone trashed my room, and I was busy reporting it to your dad."

"I see." He pauses, and I think he might actually say something nice for once, but then he starts walking. "We're going to watch the Malakim work today."

"Fine, whatever."

We head over to the infirmary, in the same building as the Ishim classes. A blond woman wearing a flower-print flowing dress greets us at the door. "Hello Bastien. What can I do for you?" Her face grows concerned. "Are you injured?"

"Not at all, Professor Lydia. We were hoping to observe the Malakim at work to see if it helps us identify her Choir."

"Of course. You're in luck, actually. We had a mishap during Erelim training today and have a young lady in here needing to be healed."

We step inside and I look around for Araceli, but she must have Malakim training during another period. I spot Marcus immediately, and when our eyes meet, his forehead creases in concern. It must be obvious from my face that I'm both hurt and pissed.

He's sitting beside a bed, and lying on it is a Valkyrie girl a year ahead of me, whose name is Gwen. I've never spoken to her, but she's joined in on Tanwen's taunts, and I glare at her. It's hard to be too mad at her though, because she's holding her arm and wincing, and I can see a painful-looking burn running along it.

"Gwen here was burned during class, and although her body would be able to heal this in a few days, it'll be very painful until then. As such, Marcus here is going to practice his healing and help it along. Go ahead, dear."

Marcus lifts his hands and they begin to glow, almost too bright to look at. He holds them over Gwen's arm and within seconds the burn disappears, soft pink skin knitting over the spot where the blisters were.

"That was amazing," I whisper. I don't have to act. Watching an instant healing is impressive, even if it's not my affinity.

"Did you feel anything?" Marcus asks.

"No, sorry."

Bastien lets out a huff and walks away, no doubt disappointed I've foiled him once again. Gwen thanks Marcus, and then gets up and heads to talk to Professor Lydia, without even giving me a second glance.

"Are you okay?" Marcus asks, lightly touching my arm.

I run a hand through my hair with a sigh. "Yeah, just having a rough day. Thanks."

"I can help you with that."

"If you're offering sex, I'm so not in the mood."

"Not this time, though I'm open to that too." He winks at me. "We Malakim can help soothe the mind and the body in other ways though."

"I don't know..."

"C'mon, let me try. It'll be good practice for me anyway."
He tilts his head toward Professor Lydia. "Make me look good
in front of the boss."

"Okay, fine."

He rests his hands on my upper arms and closes his eyes.
Warm light surrounds me, and the muscles in my back and
neck begin to relax. I didn't even realize I was so tense, but
Marcus basically gives me a full-body massage with his magic,
and I let out a long exhale.

"Wow, that was..."

"Almost as good as sex?" Marcus asks with a grin.

"Almost," I agree. "Thank you, Marcus. I feel a lot
better now."

"You're welcome, Liv."

As I walk out of the infirmary, my steps are a lot lighter,
and my body feels all loose and warm, like I just stepped out of
a hot tub. I'm still upset about my room, but it doesn't bother
me as much anymore.

I find Bastien waiting outside with his arms crossed and a
sour expression on his face. "What's your problem?" I ask.

"You. You're my problem." He pokes a finger into my
chest, in the spot just above my breasts. "My father gave me a
task, but you thwart me at every turn. I know you're hiding
something. Just tell me what it is already, and we can end this
ridiculous game."

"Sorry, but you didn't say please." I take his hand and go to
move it off me, but when we touch, lust flares between us. I
hate to admit it, but he's sexy when he's angry like this, and I
long to melt his cold exterior.

"You're impossible," he says, but then he tightens his hand
around mine and pulls me closer. His mouth is near my ear as

he whispers. "I'm going to figure out your secrets, little angel. I promise."

"I'll enjoy watching you try," I reply.

And before I know what he's doing, his mouth lands on mine, and he's giving me a thorough kiss that makes my knees weak. If this is his way of finding out my secrets, sign me up.

He pulls back and lets go of me. "Interesting," he says to himself as he walks away, rubbing his chin. "Very interesting."

Okay, then. I guess that was another test. I'm just not sure if I passed or failed it.

Chapter Thirty-Four
OLIVIA

Summer in the mountains of Northern California is like something out of a movie. Everything is green, the sky is bright blue and cloudless, and the lake is perfect for swimming after class. My angelic side loves all the sunshine, and drinks it in hungrily.

On Saturday, Araceli and I take a day trip to go to Redding to shop for some new clothes. This time, I don't buy new, and Araceli delights in finding thrift store gems with me. She's never been secondhand shopping before, but I'm pretty sure I've converted her.

On Sunday, I head out to my morning yoga class, and it's already so hot I'm sweating by the time I get there. These weekly yoga classes have been a true blessing, except for the fact that Tanwen is in them too.

I stretch my mat out as far away from her as possible. As class begins, I focus instead on the instructor as she moves us through the complicated positions of advanced yoga. Using the time to meditate and drink in the light, I think about my brother and what I know so far.

He disappeared after the championship game against the fae. The Order knows where he is, and are worried he hasn't returned yet. They need Araceli for some reason, probably because of her fae blood. It doesn't seem like a stretch to come to the conclusion that my brother is in Faerie.

I need to know more...and find out if my theory is correct.

I turned in my camera the other week and received a note that I'd passed the second test, and now I'm waiting for the third trial. If I pass it, I'll be invited into the Order and can find out more about what happened to Jonah. Then I can make a plan for finding him.

After class, I roll up my mat and turn toward the dorm, only to run headfirst into Tanwen.

"Get away from me," I snarl. After she destroyed my dorm room, I have no patience for her whatsoever.

"Whoa." She holds her hands up and takes a step back. "Hostility from the half-human."

"Where's your entourage, Tanwen? They can't stand the heat?" She's not so tough without her Valkyrie cronies backing her up.

"They prefer more strenuous exercise, but I've learned that the key to being a good fighter is flexibility."

"Whatever." I don't know why she's trying to explain herself to me. I don't want to hear it. Pushing past her, I take the high road and squash the urge to use my powers on her to make her want me so bad she can't think of anyone else ever again.

I could do it. But I won't. I'm better than that.

"Hey, hang on." Tanwen catches up to me. "What's your deal today?"

I round on her. "You destroyed my car, trashed my room, and you're asking *me* what my deal is? You call me hostile? You've been nothing *but* hostile to me, Tanwen. I'm sorry about the gym clothes, but you've gone way too far. I can't help the circumstances of my birth, and I can't leave. They made that perfectly clear. So, *back the fuck off.*" By the time I finish, I'm shouting and everyone on the lawn stares at us. After shooting them a glare, I stalk off to go have a shower and change.

"Hey, wait!" she calls, as she follows after me. I can see I won't be able to shake her so easily.

"What?" I ask, stopping on the path and crossing my arms.

"I didn't trash your room." She holds up her hands. "Or your car. I swear."

"Yeah, right. And you didn't send me threatening notes either, right?"

"I didn't. Although maybe I should have done all that stuff, if you're the one who tore up my gym clothes. I mean, what the fuck?" She tilts her head and grabs onto her straw-colored ponytail.

I huff. "I only did that in retaliation for what you did. But I'm done with this shit. Seriously over it, and all the insults, and everything else. That stops now."

"Fine, I'll lay off the trash talk. I don't dislike you as a person, Olivia, but you don't belong at Seraphim Academy. I'm obviously not the only one that thinks that if someone trashed your room." She lets out a haughty sniff. "Trust me, I wouldn't want to touch your stuff."

I roll my eyes as she walks away. What a bitch.

Except...I believe her. But if she didn't do all that stuff to me, who did?

———

I head to the lake and breathe in the warm night air. Even at night the campus is beautiful, and I listen to the sound of crickets chirping. Instead of sitting in my normal spot on the bench, I opt to sit in the cool grass instead.

Before I even have time for my thoughts to collect, Kassiel's voice interrupts my quiet meditation. "Fancy meeting you here."

"How are you?" I ask, as he sits beside me on the grass, stretching out his long legs.

"Good. How are you doing? Getting enough to eat?"

His eyes flash in the moonlight, and I can't help but think he wishes he could help provide me some nourishment. "Sure. The cafeteria here is great."

We both know that's not what he means, and he grins. "You did well on your last Angelic History exam. Good work."

"Thanks. I have a pretty good teacher."

He looks at me out of the corner of his eye. "Perhaps. I try to teach history in a way that doesn't paint angels or demons in a negative light. Do you think I've succeeded?"

My time in his class has been difficult at best. Not because of the subject matter, but because watching Kassiel move and talk has been a lesson in suppressing my succubus powers. I answer his question with a question of my own. "Why do you do that? Why do you care?"

He hesitates. "I... I've known demons over the years. They're not so different from angels. Most of them aren't evil or anything, and just want to live their lives peacefully, the same as we do. I've learned it's possible for anyone to be good or evil, even angels. Plus, I was alive for the last several decades of the war."

My eyebrows fly up. "Of course. I should have realized. What was it like?"

"It was horrible. So much death, and for what? Because angels and demons have been enemies for centuries, and no other reason." He shakes his head. "It was the best thing to happen to both races when Michael and Lucifer made the Earth Accords and stopped the war."

I can hear the depth of pain in his voice, and it breaks my heart. "You lost someone, didn't you?"

"My mother."

"I'm sorry."

He nods. "That's why I became a professor here. If I can teach younger angels about what happened, perhaps I can prevent the war from starting again."

"You're doing a good job of it."

"I hope so."

"I'm glad the war is over too. Although I can't help but wish I could have seen Heaven before it was closed. What was it like?"

"Bright."

I laugh. "Obviously."

"During the day, the sky there was the color of dawn, when everything is a soft orange and a golden yellow. It sounds odd, but it was beautiful."

"I can imagine. And Hell? Did you ever go there? What was the sky like there?"

"Yes, I've been there." He stares out at the lake, his face

distant, his eyes lost in memories. "You know that moment after the sun sets and the sky is a deep indigo? That's what Hell was like during the day. And at night... it was like living in the space between the stars."

"I can tell it had a strong impact on you."

"It did, yes." He clears his throat. "Maybe one day we'll be able to visit the two other realms and rebuild."

"What about Faerie, have you been there too?"

"No, I can't say I have. Maybe someday, though." Kassiel lays down on the grass and puts his hands behind his head, which pulls his shirt up a bit so I can see his toned stomach and dark happy trail. Urges that have nothing to do with hunger rise in me. Urges that are getting harder and harder to resist the more time I spend with my professor.

I need to feed. Tonight.

Chapter Thirty-Five
OLIVIA

I end up back at the bar I've visited many times before. It's not ideal, but it's probably been a month since I last came here. I've been avoiding feeding as much as possible, surviving on sunlight and little lust snacks from people around school, plus the kisses from Bastien and Marcus. But I've gone too long since I've had a real feed, and now I'm desperate.

Naturally, the bar is fucking empty. Nobody but the bartender, and I've been avoiding using her. Employees of places like this are the worst option. If I sleep with her, I can never let her see me again, or she'll want more. I can't give her more.

Damn it.

I sit at the bar and signal her to bring me a beer. I'm so hungry, I may be forced to seduce the bartender after all. I'll give it a few minutes and see if anyone comes in. Maybe I'll get lucky.

Checking my phone, I see it's after two on a Sunday night. I'm not going to get lucky.

As I finish my beer and prepare to lay the lust on the bartender, the door opens and a good-looking guy walks in. He's no movie star, but he looks clean at least, and isn't wearing a wedding ring. I call that a win.

"Hey, Chuck," the bartender says. "How goes it? You still with Louann?"

He sits on the other side of the bar. "No. She took off with that guy from Redding that sold us the Mustang."

"Tough luck."

The phone distracts the bartender, and I take that as my cue. "Hey." I hop up in the seat beside Chuck and trail a finger along his arm. "Want some company?"

Hitting him hard with desire, I make sure he won't say no. His mouth opens into a slow grin. "Definitely."

With one eye on the bartender, I grin at Chuck. "Meet me in the bathroom," I whisper. "Hurry."

The bartender has her back to us as she speaks into the handset, so I hurry past with Chuck right behind me. As soon as we enter the bathroom, I'm on him. I wore a skirt and no underwear just for this. He steps forward, and I grab the waistband of his pants. I'm not interested in kisses or caresses, I just want to get this over with as fast as possible.

I hate that I have to do this with him and not one of the guys I want to be with. After kissing both Marcus and Bastien, I'd much rather be sleeping with one of them tonight. Or Kassiel. But that isn't an option, and I need to feed.

I can't help it. I have to do it to survive.

I didn't choose the Lilim life. The Lilim life chose me.

Before I can get started, the bathroom door bursts open. I shove Chuck back as a tall man walks in. It's the hot guy I spotted the first time I came here, the one who somehow rejected my seduction, and he smiles at me like a cat who just caught a mouse.

"Hello, little succubus. We've been looking for you." He's tall, and seduction rolls off of him. I can feel it, even though it bounces off me. An incubus. A full incubus. Oh shit.

Chuck is caught in a daze of lust, unsure if he should look at me or the new guy. I shove him toward the door and *push* with my magic. "Get out of here!"

He runs out the door, and I enter the fighting pose Callan taught me and prepare to defend myself the best I can. I can't use my Lilim powers against this guy. They won't work. Equally, though, he can't use his against me. Unfortunately, that does me no good when two other men walk in the bathroom, and although I'm pretty sure they're both demons, I'm not sure what they are.

One of them suddenly shifts into a large black bear. A shifter, which Raziel would say represents the Sin of wrath. He definitely looks pretty wrathful as he lets out a terrifying roar, and I can't help but shrink back.

The other one lets out a burst of darkness and multiplies, until I'm staring at three identical versions of him. An imp, like Marcus and I are studying for our project. He's using illusion magic to make copies of himself. I'll have to find the original one to stop him.

Fuck, I am way out of my league here.

"Come with us, and we won't hurt you," the incubus says. He's wielding a big ass knife, which kind of contradicts what he just said.

Father and Mother warned me this would happen one day

if I ever revealed myself, and now it's happening. I need to get out of here, fast.

The incubus rushes me, and I try to deflect him the way Callan taught me. It works and I spin away from the knife, but then the bear raises up and knocks me back with his giant paws. I hit the side of the bathroom stalls and stumble, and the three imps grab my arms. The incubus stalks forward, playing with his knife, and he leans close and breathes me in slowly. I have a sudden fear he might kiss me. I have no idea what I taste like, but I don't want to risk him figuring out I taste like an angel.

They can't know what I really am.

I jerk in the imps' arms, and one of the hands moves onto my bare skin. I blast him with a bolt of power, making his emotions flare and dazing him for an instant, giving me a chance to spin around and knee him in the groin. I choose the right one, and he yells and lets me go, while his clones vanish. I dart away, but the bear blocks my path.

The bathroom door bursts open, and I spot three men standing in the doorway with their wings spread, their eyes burning with light, looking every inch like sexy avenging angels.

The Princes have come for me.

I can't believe a strong, capable woman like myself is so relieved to see three Princes riding in on their proverbial white horses, but here I am.

Callan blasts the bear with a bolt of burning light, and Marcus and Bastien rush forward to fight the incubus and his knife. The whole place suddenly goes black, courtesy of the imp's illusion magic, putting my guys at a disadvantage.

Wait. Not my guys. Just guys.

The imp suddenly grabs me and paws at my skirt. The one I'm not wearing underwear under. Damn it, I blasted him too hard and now he wants me. I use my meager skills to fight him off, but then he pulls out long blade. It glows with eerie darkness, like nothing I've ever seen before.

"Get back!" Marcus yells, but then the bear knocks him aside, and he crashes into one of the tables in the bar.

The imp lunges for me with the blade, and I dodge out of the way, but I'm not fast enough. It slices along my side, and I let out a scream of pure agony. Bastien grabs me and drags me out of the bar, and into the cool night air, but it doesn't help. My side is on fire, and all I can do is hang onto him and moan.

"You were hit with a dark-infused blade," Bastien says, sounding way too calm considering I'm squirming with pain. "Don't worry, Marcus can heal you."

Callan and Marcus bust out of the bar an eternity later, and I've never seen them look so angry before.

"We took care of them," Marcus says.

"Fucking demons," Callan growls. "We need to report this."

"No, you can't!" I can't have any questions about what I was doing out here. But then another dose of pain hits me, and I cry out.

"Olivia is injured," Bastien says.

"What happened?" Marcus asks, moving close to inspect the wound.

Callan huffs. "She didn't listen in combat practice, that's what happened."

"I promise to do better next time," I manage to get out, but I'm so weak. Worst of all, my hunger grows so strong I can't contain it. My body is trying to heal itself, but it can't, because

I was already so low on power. If I don't get out of here and find someone to feed on, I'm going to do something I regret.

Marcus's hands glow and he heals my side, and the pain fades a little, but it's not enough. I waited too long to feed, hoping that my kiss from Bastien was enough to tide me over, but I was wrong. I squeeze my eyes shut and try to hold my succubus side at bay.

"She's healed," Marcus says.

"There's still something wrong with her." That's Callan. "Try again."

"Whatever it is, it's nothing my magic can fix."

"Please," I find myself begging.

"What do you need?" Bastien asks.

Marcus's tender, masculine hands touch my cheek. "Tell me, Liv. How can I help?"

My eyes suddenly fly open, and I grab Marcus's face and kiss him hard. I can't stop myself, the hunger is too intense, and my succubus side has taken over. I suck the lust from him that springs up when we kiss, and it's oh so delicious, but it isn't enough. The thing I want to do most is spread my legs and let him settle there between them.

"Her eyes are black," Bastien says.

In the back of my mind, I know this is bad. Really fucking bad. But I can't stop myself from rubbing up against Marcus like a damn cat. I reach for his jeans and pop them open, trying to reach inside for his cock.

"Whoa now," he says. "I am all for whatever this is, but maybe we should wait 'til we go somewhere more private."

"Can't wait," I manage to get out. "Need. Now."

Bastien suddenly grabs me and kisses me, and it's enough to calm me down a bit. But I need more, more, more. I paw at his chest, and he pushes me toward Callan, who steps back at the sight of my black eyes.

"Kiss her!" Bastien yells.

"What?" Callan asks, taken aback.

"Just do it!"

I grab Callan's face and pull it to mine. I'm a bit stronger than I was before, but if he fights me at all, I won't be able to feed from him.

Callan resists at first, but then he can't help himself, and he presses a hand to my back and kisses me hard. I suck all the sexual energy I can from Callan through the rough kiss, and he's so powerful his energy fills me up just enough to take the edge off.

When we're done, my head clears a little and I no longer feel so weak. I'm still hungry and will have to feed soon, but I might be able to make it a few more nights before things go bad again.

Bastien glances back at the bar. "We have to get out of here. I'm sure they called the human police."

"She's too weak to fly," Marcus says.

Callan grunts, looking pissed off, but he scoops me into his arms. I cling to him as he takes off, his powerful white and gold wings beating the night air. Curling my face into his neck, I breathe in his spicy scent. I never thought I'd be grateful for the Princes spying on me, but if it weren't for them, I'd be with the demons now...and I have no idea what they would do with me.

"I'm sorry," I whisper against Callan's thick neck. I know he never would have kissed me if Bastien hadn't made him.

He doesn't reply, or if he does, I can't hear it over the

sound of the wind whistling past my ears as he flies. He does tighten his grip though.

I doze as we fly, and only wake when Callan lays me down on the couch. They've taken me to their private lounge in the bell tower, and I would feel honored if I wasn't so tired. Callan steps back, and I sit up and press a hand to my side. That blade really messed me up.

As the three men stare at me, I realize what I've done, and my stomach sinks.

Bastien manages to speak first. "You're a succubus."

Chapter Thirty-Six
BASTIEN

Olivia's eyes are no longer black, but I can see the truth in them, and I don't even need my Ofanim powers for that. "Yes," she replies to my statement. "Half succubus, anyway."

Callan backs up from her and swears under his breath. "You're a demon. Fuck."

I always knew there was something suspicious about her, but I thought I would feel more satisfaction upon uncovering the truth. "How is this possible?"

She sighs. "My father is an angel, my mother is a succubus."

"But demon-angel relations are forbidden," Marcus says.

"That's why I've been in hiding my entire life. My parents told me if anyone found out what I am, I'd be in danger."

"Why did you come to Seraphim Academy then?" I ask.

She hesitates. "I got tired of hiding. I wanted to learn to use my powers, and it seemed safer here than at Hellspawn Academy."

I get the feeling there's more to it than that, but I'm not done with my interrogation. She's deceived me for months, and it shouldn't have been possible. I need to know more. "How were you able to hide your succubus side from me?"

She touches the aquamarine stone at her neck. "My mother gave me this necklace. It allows me to lie undetected and to hide the truth from anyone. Even an Archangel."

"That looks like a fae relic." I rub my chin. That would explain a lot. What would I see in her aura if the damn thing was removed? Now I want to find out.

"Are you going to expose me?" From her spot curled up on the couch, with her eyes wide and her dark hair mussed up, she looks more vulnerable than I've ever seen her before—and scared. She's terrified that we know the truth about her.

"No, of course not," Marcus quickly says, as he covers Olivia in a blanket.

Callan shakes his head and paces back and forth in front of the window. "We should. We definitely should."

I'm not so sure. I find it hard to believe my father doesn't know, or at least suspect, what Olivia is. "One last question. How do you know Jonah?"

"Jonah..." she says slowly, tilting her head. "The guy that disappeared last year? How would I know him?"

"You're lying." My lips press into a tight line. Another secret of hers to uncover. I have to admit, I'm glad the game isn't over. I like playing with her. Finally, a worthy opponent.

"Sorry, not sure what you're talking about," she says.

"Take off your necklace and tell me that," I snap.

Marcus holds out his hands to separate us. "Okay, that's enough. Liv has been through a lot and she can barely sit up. She needs to rest, not be interrogated by the three of us."

I huff and cross my arms. "If we're going to protect her, we need to know the truth."

"I don't need your protection," she mutters.

Callan snorts. "Obviously you do. Those demons tonight wanted to take you somewhere."

"They somehow knew I was a succubus." She stares off into space. "How did you find me there?"

"Bastien put a tracker in your shoes," Marcus says, his voice guilty.

She sits up at that. "He *what*?"

I shrug. "We knew you were sneaking off and wanted to know why. Be glad I did. It's the only reason you're here and not with the demons."

She narrows her eyes at me and pulls the blanket up to her neck, but doesn't reply.

"We need to report the attack to Uriel," Callan says.

"You can't," Olivia says quickly. "If you do, there will be too many questions, and someone else will find out what I am."

'The Archangels need to know," Callan insists. "First Darel, now this...the demons are growing bolder. We need to prepare for battle."

"Okay, let's not jump straight to war," Marcus says, rolling his eyes.

"I agree, we should keep tonight's events between us for now," I say.

Callan shakes his head. "You're all making a mistake. Olivia's a *demon*. She's one of *them*. And you're just okay with that?"

"She can't change what she is," Marcus says.

"Fuck this, I'm out of here." Callan throws open the balcony door and launches off before his wings are even fully extended. Marcus runs after him, his bronze wings flapping against the night.

I pinch the brow of my forehead. Someone needs to go deal with those two. "I'll be right back."

I fly to the top of the bell tower, where Marcus and Callan are facing off. Callan paces back and forth on the old roof, looking pissed. "She's a demon."

"Half," Marcus reminds him.

"That's a pretty big chunk." Callan's hands are starting to glow. He's gathering an Erelim's burning light and if we're not careful, he'll release that power on something. Or someone.

I don't try to get in front of him or calm him down. He's got to get control of himself, and there's little I can do to help. Marcus though, he's a bigger idiot than I am, and he steps towards Callan. As a Malakim, he can calm Callan down, but it's risky when he's in a state like this. He might explode instead.

"Callan," Marcus says.

"What?" he roars.

"She's half angel, too." Marcus lets that sink in for a second. "Think about what that means. She's supposed to be impossible. Forbidden."

Callan's chest heaves as Marcus's words break through the rage clouding his mind. "She's an abomination."

"She's a woman." Marcus laces light into his words, just enough to have a slightly calming effect on Callan. And me, but I shake it off easily. "She's a person. She has feelings too."

I stand to the side and wait. I'm as useless as Marcus against Callan in combat. Both of us are well-trained and can hold our own in a fight. Against each other, either of us would have a fair shot. But Callan is an Erelim, and he's the son of

Michael. He's a warrior, born and bred. It's in his very DNA.
Some humans are good at making music. Some are good at
math. Callan is very good at fighting. The only thing we can do
is work together to restrain him if he loses it.

Callan stares across the dark sky as his chest heaves.
Marcus is calming him down, but not enough. Callan has more
reason than anyone to hate demons, since they killed his father
and his half-brother. Finding out Olivia is part-demon shook
him, hard.

"Tell me something you know about Olivia," I say.

"She's a demon."

I roll my eyes. "Something not related to her being
a demon."

He sighs, and his glowing hands dim again. He's calming
down, and I nod at Marcus. He cuts off the flow of magic to see
how Callan does on his own. It's still best for him to come back
from this as much as he can on his own. It will help him learn
to control it in the future.

Sucking in a deep breath, Callan manages to say, "She's a
horrible fighter."

Marcus smiles. "She is. For sure. She's also too stubborn
for her own good."

"And secretive," I add. "But I can understand why now."

"We're not asking you to accept her." Marcus steps
forward again, getting within swinging range of Callan's fists.
"You don't have to be her friend. Just don't expose her either."

Callan glances at me. "What do you think?"

I rub the back of my neck and scowl. "I think it's likely my
father already knows. He probably wanted me to figure it out
as a test. Which I failed."

Callan's glow vanishes, and he rests a large hand on my

shoulder. "Don't be too hard on yourself. She's spent her life deceiving people."

"Why'd you carry her back?" Marcus asks.

"She needed help," he says, as if that explains everything.

"Jonah must have known the truth about her," I say. "That's why he wanted to keep her away from the school. He worried if she came here someone would find out what she truly was."

"Yeah, he said it was for her safety," Marcus adds. "Now we know why. But how do they know each other?"

"That's what we need to find out, but she's playing innocent. I'll get it out of her in time though."

"Jonah obviously wants her to be safe," Marcus says. "That means we should keep her here and protect her."

"I disagree," Callan says. "Jonah made us promise to get her away from the school. That promise still stands, even more so now that we understand the danger she's in."

Marcus points in the direction of the bar. "She's in danger out there too! You saw those demons tonight."

"Then we'll find her somewhere safe to hide her," Callan says. "We have enough money between the three of us to make sure she lives a life of luxury, at least until Jonah is back."

"I don't think she'll go for that," I say. "The best thing we can do for now is to keep her close and try to figure out what else she's hiding. Then we can decide how to proceed."

"Fine," Callan says. "I trust your judgment. But we can't forget our promise to Jonah either."

"We won't."

"I'm going to take her back to her room," Marcus says, his wings flaring. "Maybe I can heal her a little more too."

I raise an eyebrow at him. "You do know what she needs in order to heal?"

He gives me a cocky grin. "If that's what she wants from me, I'm more than happy to provide."

He's totally missing the gravity of this situation. One quick fuck is not going to cut it. "From what I know about Lilim, she was completely starved tonight. She's probably not getting enough sustenance from the few times she's sneaked out of school. She'll need to feed more often or she'll continue to grow weak."

"Feed?" Callan asks. "Like on sex?"

"Exactly."

"I'll take care of it," Marcus says.

I shake my head. "One person won't be enough. I'll have to sleep with her too."

Marcus's jaw drops. "You?"

I wave my hand dismissively. "Don't worry. I'll only be doing it out of necessity to keep her healthy and safe, as part of our promise to Jonah. I don't have feelings for her or anything preposterous like that."

Marcus relaxes a little and laughs. "Of course you don't. You're as cold as ice. Sex with Olivia will be like a business arrangement for you."

His easy dismissal annoys me, especially as I remember my kiss with Olivia. I definitely felt something then, though I'll never admit it.

"It would be best if three of us provided sustenance for her." I glance at Callan pointedly. "Succubi must feed on multiple people or risk injuring them."

"No fucking way," he snarls. "I am not touching a demon."

"Fine, Marcus and I will handle it. We're much stronger

than humans, and we can deal with it later if it becomes a problem."

"Assuming she's on board with this arrangement," Marcus says.

I flash back to the way her lips felt on mine and how her body molded against me. I know she kissed Marcus too—I saw it on camera. Somehow I don't think she'll have a problem with this proposal. "She will be."

Chapter Thirty-Seven
OLIVIA

While the boys are off somewhere discussing my fate, I drag myself off the couch and pull myself together. I'm still weak and hungry, but I'm not going to sit here and wait for my judgement to come.

I draw out my black, shining wings, and then launch off the bell tower. I'm covered in blood from that demon's blade, and all I want in the world is a hot shower. Then I'll start packing a bag. Just in case I need to make a quick getaway.

When Marcus arrives on my balcony, I'm wearing only a robe and brushing my hair. I cautiously let him in.

"What happened?" I ask.

"We've decided not to tell anyone about you," Marcus says.

My shoulders slump in relief. "Thank you."

"We've also decided we need to help you with your succubus problem. Well, Bastien and I will. Callan isn't a fan of the idea."

I raise my eyebrows. "Is that so?"

"As long as you're okay with it." He reaches out and strokes my cheek. "I understand why you pushed me away after our kiss. But you don't have to do that anymore."

I grab his hand and squeeze it. "Then you know I can't have a real relationship either. We can have sex, but that's all it can be."

"I'll take whatever I can get of you." His hands slide around my waist and he pulls me against his hard chest. His mouth finds mine, and his kiss instantly makes me stronger. I grab his shirt and bring him closer, as his lips and tongue do wicked things to mine.

But then I have a thought, and I pull back to look up at him. "Are you okay sharing me with Bastien?"

His thumb runs along my lip as he gazes down at me. "I don't love the idea, but from what I remember from Demon Studies, you need to feed on multiple people, right?"

"I do. If you were human, I could only feed on you once without killing you, but I can feed multiple times on supernaturals without draining them too much." Or so I'm told. I've never tested the theory.

"That's where we come in. Bastien and I are the sons of Archangels. We're stronger than most supernaturals. Between the two of us, we'll keep you satisfied." He gives me a sinful smile that makes me want to rip his clothes off right this second. "Besides, I'd rather you feed from us than from strangers."

I can't believe the two of them are on board with this plan, but I'm so ravenous and relieved I don't want to say no. Maybe the two of them could actually keep me full without any problems. We won't know unless we try, anyway.

His lips trail down to my neck. "We're going to take care of you. I promise."

In his strong, protective arms, I'm actually willing to believe that fantasy, if only for a few minutes. He grabs the tie of my robe and slowly pulls on it, allowing the terry cloth fabric covering my naked body to fall open. His dark eyes look me up and down with obvious pleasure, and the lust coming off him is so strong it makes my succubus side go into overdrive.

"Damn, you're beautiful." He grabs his shirt and lifts it off him, then tosses it to the side. I lick my lips at the sight of his muscled chest, like some kind of ravenous beast. He grins at my reaction. "Bastien said you've been starving yourself."

"I didn't want to get caught."

"Then tonight you're going to have a five-course meal." He pops open his jeans and slides them down without hesitation. His black briefs go next, and then he's as naked as I am. The size and shape of Marcus's cock is absolute perfection. I've touched so many in my life, and his is one of the best I've seen. Long, thick, and delicious.

I step forward and rest my hands on his chest, unable to stop myself. I press my face into his neck and breathe him in. "Marcus, I need you now, please. I can't hold back the hunger."

"Take whatever you need."

I push him down on the bed and climb onto his lap, wasting no time sinking down onto his cock. I cry out as he fills me up, and he feels like heaven inside me. His sexual energy hits me like a jolt of lightning.

He grunts and grabs my ass to pull me closer, but he lets me lead the show. Swiveling my hips, I ride him hard and fast, positioning us so that his head hits my spot every time I press down on him. It's been so long since I slept with someone I actually liked—since Kassiel actually—and it's amazing how different it feels. You'd think after sleeping with so many people it would get old, but this is like having sex for the first time all over again...except with someone who knows exactly what they're doing.

My orgasm builds fast, and I cry out as it hits me, cascading over me along with Marcus's power. I slump down onto his bare chest as he heaves. He moves to kiss me, but stops just before our lips meet. "Whoa. Your eyes."

I pull back and clap my hands over them. "I'm sorry."

"No, no." He takes my hands away from my face. "Don't be sorry." He kisses my eyelids with the softest touch, brushing his lips against them, feather-light.

I breathe in and open my eyes. "They don't bother you?"

Marcus grips my hips. "On the contrary. They're kind of sexy."

I can't help but laugh. "Oh, so you've got a demon fetish."

"Seems that way." He grins. "Or maybe I just have an Olivia fetish."

"Thank you. I feel a lot better now. Feeding from you is... intense." Marcus's energy is strong enough I'll be able to go for weeks before feeding again, just like when I slept with Kassiel. Their energy tastes different somehow, though. Maybe because Marcus is a Malakim and Kassiel is... Actually, I'm not sure which Choir Kassiel is a member of, come to think of it, but perhaps that's the reason. Marcus and Kassiel are the only two angels I've fed from, but it sounds like I'll be sampling Bastien soon, and then I can see if that's the difference. I doubt I'll get another shot at Kassiel, unfortunately.

"We're not done yet." Marcus grins and lifts me off him, then spins and plants my back on the bed. He hasn't come yet, and I'm ready for him to enter me again and finish us both off, but he has something else in mind. "Like I said, this is going to be a five-course meal. Time for round two."

"What—" I start, but then he's spreading my legs wide and dipping his head between them. His tongue begins to do sinful things to me, things I've rarely had done before. I usually go straight for sex to get it over with as quickly as possible, and don't have time for foreplay. Plus most of the guys I pick up give zero fucks about making sure I'm satisfied. Marcus, though? He's a real man, and he definitely knows what he's doing and likes to make sure his woman is very pleased. As his mouth and tongue bring me to new heights, I see why he's so popular with the ladies around campus.

I cry out and dig my hands in his glorious hair as he works magic on my clit, and then he slips two fingers inside me and brings me to climax all over again. Two orgasms in one night? I'm a lucky girl.

But he's not done yet.

I'm in a daze of pleasure, when he lifts his head and grins at me. "You taste delicious. I could go down on you all night long."

"I certainly won't stop you," I say with a laugh. "But I think it's time you came too."

"Is it?" he asks, as he slowly stalks up my body.

I nod. "To feed fully, I need you to have an orgasm too."

His eyes gleam with desire as his cock nudges my entrance. "Well, I can't let you go hungry, now can I?"

He's still slick with my juices, and his entry is fast and hard. It takes my breath away when his cock fills me up, and then he sets a relentless pace as he plunges into me. It's exactly what I need from him, and I arch up to meet his every thrust. He captures my mouth as he fucks me hard, and it's somehow both intimate and dirty. I love every second of it.

Another orgasm builds, and we finish together, crying out at the same time as he thrusts his cock into me harder than before. He pushes up on his arms and looks down at me as we both breathe heavily. "Fuck, that was good. But we have another two rounds to go so I make sure you're nice and full."

I laugh. "Should we take a break?"

"No way." He pulls out of me, flips me over, and enters me from behind, already hard again. "Angel stamina, baby. I can go all night."

And he does. We end up having more than five rounds, until I'm so full I feel like I just had Thanksgiving dinner and I need to unbutton my jeans. I finally kick him out just before dawn so we can both get a little sleep, but it's hard. I want him to stay. That's new.

Other than that time with Kassiel, I've never wanted so badly to roll over and cuddle with someone before. But I have to push the urge away, and it unnerves me. This is not a relationship. I can't have one of those. This is just fucking. Really, really good fucking.

Hopefully on a regular basis.

Chapter Thirty-Eight
OLIVIA

A knock wakes me up.

"You coming down for breakfast, Liv?" Araceli cracks my door open as I sit up. "Hey. You hungry?"

"Yes," I croak. "Starving." And thirsty. Although physically I feel like I could fly from here to New York. Marcus's sexual energy crackles inside me, and I've never felt so... powerful before. I'm even more excited about feeding from Bastien, whenever that happens.

I use the bathroom and run a comb through my hair before throwing on my gym clothes and walking out to meet Araceli. No time for a shower.

The cafeteria is packed. We're having one of those crazy California heat waves, and even at 8am it's crazy hot out already, even for an angel. Everyone wants to sit in the cool air-conditioned cafeteria instead of eating outside. Only one table is open in the entire room, so we grab our food and then hurry over to it, plunking our butts down before someone else can claim it. Seconds later, three trays plop down across from us.

My gut tells me what my eyes haven't seen yet. I look up. Sure enough, I drink in the sight of three gorgeous angels hovering over me. Marcus gives me a knowing grin, his dark hair still messy from last night, while Bastien stares at me with eyes that are slightly less cold, although still inquisitive. And Callan? He glares at me like he wants to wrap his big hands around my neck and squeeze.

"Shit," Araceli breathes. "Sorry, we can eat somewhere else."

She starts to stand, but I shake my head and stare back at the Princes. "I don't remember inviting you to sit with us. Besides, I thought you guys never eat in here."

"These are the last three seats in the entire room, as you can see." Bastien sits down first, on my right. Marcus sits on the other side of me. Callan sits across, next to Araceli, who subtly inches away from him.

"We wanted to see how you're doing this morning," Marcus says, with a naughty gleam in his eye. "Are you feeling well-rested?"

"I'm fine, thank you."

"You do look better," Bastien says.

Araceli is staring at us like she's very confused.

"I ran into the guys yesterday after having a run-in with Tanwen," I explain. "It was nothing."

"Right," she says slowly, but I don't think she buys it.

The rest of breakfast is super uncomfortable. Marcus keeps grinning at me and sneaks in a few light touches on my arm or hand, Bastien stares at me like I'm the most fascinating thing he's ever seen, and Callan throws food in his mouth while glaring at me the entire time.

"Well, as fun as this is, it's time for class." I stand up and grab my tray. Araceli breathes a sigh of relief and follows me. "I guess we'll see you there, Callan."

He grunts as we walk away. I have a feeling he won't be giving me a break in Combat Training today. And Tanwen? I'm not sure where we stand either after our talk.

As soon as we're outside and sweating instantly in the heat, Araceli whirls around on me. "What was that about?

I shrug. "I don't know. It's weird they sat with us."

"No shit. And Marcus was all over you. Plus last night I definitely heard some sounds coming from your room along with his voice. Are you guys a thing now?"

"No, definitely not."

"But you totally fucked."

I hesitate. She is my roommate, and the walls are not thick. I heard everything she and Darel did together, that's for sure. "Yes, we did."

"So why aren't you dating? Marcus is hot and nice, for a Prince anyway, and he's obviously into you."

"It's...complicated. I'm not looking for something serious right now. He's just a fuck buddy."

Araceli snorts. "Fuck buddy. Right."

"Seriously."

"Okay, Liv. Whatever you want to believe." She slings her bag onto her shoulder and starts down the path. "Let's go."

We head into Combat Training, which has been Araceli's least favorite class since Darel died. For a long time she skipped it entirely, but then Hilda came to our room and talked to her, and she started going again. I think it's actually helped her to be able to take out her grief and anger... Usually on me. I became her regular partner, which at least saved me from more Tanwen beatdowns.

Tanwen and one of the other Valkyries are sparring, and she gives me a little nod as I move to the mat. I guess we're in a truce now.

"Olivia, you're with Callan today." Professor Hilda calls. "We've got to get you up to par."

Callan argues with Hilda in a low voice, but she shakes her head. He scowls, before stomping over to me. "Until you're able to show at least a modicum of an ability to defend yourself, we're going to be working together."

"I didn't do too badly the other night," I say in a low voice.

"You got stabbed. By a dark-infused weapon. How is that 'not too badly'?"

I huff. "What is a dark-infused weapon anyway?"

"It's a weapon made by the fae to hurt angels. There are light-infused ones also, which do extra damage to demons."

"Great," I mutter. I'm probably susceptible to both of them.

Callan looks me up and down slowly, like he's trying to decide what to do with me. No way I'm going to make this easy on him, so I cock one hip and breathe deep so my breasts will push ever-so-slightly against my shirt.

"See something you like?" I place a pinch of husk in my voice, a great touch when seducing someone overtly. The trick is to be seductive without the target realizing you're *trying* to turn them on. It must seem effortless and natural. I could just send some of my succubus magic at him, but where's the fun in that?

"You're not my type," he growls. Liar, liar, pants on fire.

The desire coming off Callan is enough to wake up my succubus side. Even knowing I'm part demon, he still wants me—he just doesn't want to admit it.

"Put your hands here," Callan says, lifting my arms at the elbow. His fingers on my skin cause bolts of fire to shoot down my body, making it really damn hard to hold my arms exactly where he wants them. He's affected too because he lets go of my arms as fast as he can.

"Now, when I move toward you, put your arms here." Showing me how to best deflect his attack, I try to pay attention. Not an easy task.

We walk through the motions several times in slow motion, until Callan says, "This time, I'm coming at you at full speed. You ready?"

"I don't think the bad guys will warn me."

He takes my point and rushes me. Throwing my hands up at the right moment, I'm amazed to see him flip over my shoulder as I twist and curl.

"Nice work," Callan says. Then he realizes he's congratulating me, and his face darkens. "It's about time."

Jumping to his feet faster than I can follow with my eyes, he straightens his clothes and runs at me with no warning this time. I sidestep him, grab his arm and twist around, flipping him again. I wish I'd learned this move before fighting the demons the other night.

A flash of pride crosses his face, just for a second, and then it turns hard again. I hear a smattering of applause from around the gym and look away from Callan to see Professor Hilda and Araceli clapping. Even Tanwen gives me a little nod.

"Great job," Hilda calls across the gym. "Practice the rest of the period."

I turn triumphantly to see Callan giving me a deadpan stare, but the emotions coming off of him betray his thoughts.

He's thinking about doing things to me that don't include me flipping him over my shoulders. He runs at me again without warning, and this time I don't move fast enough.

I hit the ground and look up at him without any breath in my lungs. He looms over me, deadly and handsome, and I grin. "You just wanted to get me on my back, didn't you?"

He grunts and gets off of me quickly. "No, I expected you to fight me off. Guess I should have known better."

Whatever. I still managed to flip him twice, even if he got me the third time.

Through the rest of the class, he pins me two more times, but I flip him another three. And even though toward the end I'm growing exhausted, I'm triumphant. If those demons come for me again, I have another way to defend myself, thanks to Callan. Turns out, he's actually a pretty good teacher, when he's not being a dick. Maybe he'll keep it up.

"Thanks for the help."

"It's my job." He gives me a hard stare. "You obviously need a lot of help defending yourself."

I roll my eyes and walk out. Nope, he's still a dick.

Chapter Thirty-Nine
OLIVIA

*O*nce the Princes take interest in me, the rest of the school notices. The whispers and weird looks stop, and instead everyone starts acting really nice to me and Araceli. Suddenly the outcasts become the cool kids on campus, and all it takes is a couple of overprotective guys following me around all the time. They even invite the two of us up to the bell tower, and I find myself studying up there whenever I can.

As summer turns into fall, the football game against the fae rolls around, but Araceli isn't up for it after what happened to Darel. I skip it to keep her company and watch movies while eating pizza, even though I'm dying to see a full-blooded fae in person. Faerie might be the key to finding my brother, but it's not like I can just walk up to one of the fae and ask them if they've seen him. I highly doubt I'd learn anything at the game, and Araceli is more important.

It's a shame I can't watch Callan run around in those tight pants though.

I keep waiting to hear from the Order of the Golden Throne about the next trial, but so far they've been silent. I'm anxious to confirm my theory about Jonah, or uncover another member or two of the Order, but for now all I can do is wait.

We're watching the newest X-men movie on the couch when Mystique takes the form of a politician, and I grin and nearly turn to Araceli and tell her about my brother. Then I remember she doesn't know he's my brother, and mentioning him now doesn't seem like the best time somehow. Not when she keeps turning the volume on the TV louder and louder to drown out the cheers from the game outside.

But my mind wanders, and I can't help but remember the last time I saw him.

Tap tap tap.

Jonah was flying outside my window, like he did the first time we met, except he was a lot bigger now. I opened the window up and laughed. "What are you doing out here?"

"Coming to see you, obviously."

"You're too big to fit through the window. Come to the front door like a normal person."

"Oh, fine." He went invisible as he floated to the ground. I waited a few minutes, and then he knocked on my apartment door.

I threw my arms around him before I could stop myself. I hadn't seen him in months, not since he told me about Grace. He spent all his time at Seraphim Academy now.

"Hey now," he said, surprised by my rare show of affection. "I missed you too."

"Sorry, it's been a rough day."

"Rough? How come?"

"Oh, the usual stuff. Weirdos at the bar. And all I got was a

card from Mother and a note from Father saying he'd be coming by to teach me to use my angelic powers soon."

"Sorry, but I'm here now, so let's get the party started." He was carrying a brown shopping bag, and he pulled out a bottle of champagne. "Happy birthday, Liv!"

I laughed. "Thanks."

"Have you gotten your wings yet?"

"No, not yet."

"I'm sure you will soon. I heard most don't pop out for two weeks. Hey, I got you something." He reached into the bag again and handed me a pink mug that said, "I'm a fucking angel" on it. "It's not much, but I thought it was appropriate."

I clutched the mug with a grin. "Wow, Father is going to hate this."

"That's exactly why I got it. Along with a large tin of your favorite fancy coffee."

"I love it. Thanks." I gave him another hug.

He popped open the champagne, and we crashed on my bed and toasted to my 21st birthday. Then I asked him about school and he caught me up on things, like how he was still seeing Grace, and how he'd been studying up on the fae.

"There's something I need to show you too," he said, sitting up. "Check out this thing I learned how to do."

As I watched, his skin seemed to shimmer and crawl with light, and then his appearance changed, until he looked exactly like Father. I jerked back in surprise. "What...how? Is that an Ishim power? Father's never mentioned that."

"Nope," when he spoke, he sounded like our dad too. Creepy. "You know how Father has special powers because he's an Archangel? Turns out I have one too—I can change my *appearance however I want. It's easiest to copy someone I've seen and heard before, but I'm still experimenting."*

"Wow, that's incredible. Do others know?"

"Only Grace and my friends."

"Be careful. With a power like that, everyone will want you to be their spy."

"Don't worry about me." He paused for a second, and then frowned. *"Although there is something going on at school."*

"What do you mean?"

His face darkened, which was unusual for him. *"I'm not sure, but I think it's a good thing you're not going to school there too."*

"Why?"

"They're not a fan of demons there, for one thing." He stared off into the distance, and I could tell something was troubling him, but then he turned to me and smiled. *"But I'm probably worried over nothing. Let's pour some more champagne."*

He must have been talking about the Order then. He knew they were up to no good, and was glad I wasn't there to be involved in it.

It's almost my 22nd birthday now, and all I want is to find him. I'm close though, I can feel it.

———

"*Y*ou're feeling hungry again, aren't you?" Bastien asks me.

It's been weeks since I had sex with Marcus, and even though he's hinted many times that he wants to do it again, I keep turning him down. Not because I don't want him, but because I'm worried about what might happen to him if we have sex a second time. I've never tested it before, and though I think he'll be okay, I don't want to hurt him.

"How can you tell?" I ask.

We're having one of our afternoon library sessions, although since he found out I'm half demon he's given up on uncovering my Choir and instead questions me about being a succubus. The guy is relentless, and I have to be extra careful with what I say around him, especially since he keeps bringing up Jonah.

"You're more distracted than normal and your eyes are a little wild. Not to mention, you keep looking at my neck like you want to take a bite out of it."

"I'm not that kind of demon." He's right though, and I hate that I'm so obvious. Then again, no other person has ever studied me as closely as Bastien has. It's kind of an honor, having someone so focused on me. He's borderline obsessed.

"No, but vampires and Lilim share many similarities. The hunger, for example." He stands up and begins closing the blinds, even though the library is pretty empty. "You need to feed."

"But Marcus—"

"Not on Marcus." He finishes with the blinds, and moves to sit on the edge of the table in front of me, forcing me to look up at him. "On me."

I swallow. I can't say I'm not tempted, especially after our kiss, and Marcus did say he was okay with it, but I still hesitate. "Are you sure?"

He begins unbuttoning his shirt slowly, and I revel in every inch of skin he reveals. "Yes. But don't take this as anything more than what it is—a business arrangement. I don't have feelings for you. I don't want to date you. This is just sex, and I'm only doing this because it needs to be done. Understand?"

My eyes narrow at him. "Fine with me. I don't have feelings for you either."

"Excellent. Let's begin."

I can't stop myself. Reaching out, I slide my hands up his chest, enjoying the strong muscles underneath. He's not huge like Callan or full of natural sex appeal like Marcus, but his sharp jaw begs to be licked. So, I do. In our private library room, I nibble Bastien's jawline and barely contain my desire as he reaches around and lifts me by my ass. Wrapping my legs around him, I press my mouth to his. He kisses me thoroughly, just like he did the other time, and he's such an expert with his tongue that it makes me wonder what else he could do with it.

He sits me on top of the desk, his fingers digging into my butt cheeks as he stands in front of it. Pressing his groin into mine, he grinds, causing delicious friction. It's not enough and it's too slow. I'm suddenly starving for him, and I'm not sure it's all succubus hunger.

"More. Now." Pushing him away in a show of strength that surprises him, judging by the look on his face, I grab his belt buckle and pop it open. I've had some practice at disrobing a man, and I've got his cock out within seconds. My mouth waters. I want to taste it, but I think that might break the "just sex" part of our arrangement.

But Bastien's not content with letting me take charge, and he pushes me down. My back hits the desk with a thump, and then he's yanking off my flats and tugging my jeans down my legs. My panties slide off next, and then he drags me down the desk until my ass is at the edge of it, and he's spreading me wide. His fingers slide between my legs, and he finds me dripping wet. A wicked smile crosses his lips as he feels how hot I am for him, and I'm so over the arrogant look in his eyes. Or maybe it turns me on more, I'm not sure. Either way, I reach between us and grab his cock, positioning him so my wet slick slides down his length with ease. He fills me completely, large enough to give me a bit of stretch, which is delicious.

I'm lying back on the desk and he's standing over me, looking down at me with his inscrutable gaze. The first time he moves inside me, I gasp. Bastien is excellent at everything he does, and I can already tell he's not going to disappoint in this area either. He pulls out of me almost completely to the hilt, then slides back home so smoothly it makes me moan. He hits me deep inside with expert precision, and I'm tempted to touch him, but I grab onto the desk instead. I've still got my shirt on, his black slacks are still hanging off his ass, and everything about this encounter says this is just a quick fuck, except for how amazing it's making me feel.

He starts moving faster and harder, slamming into me over and over, and I can't help the sounds that erupt from my mouth. I wonder if any librarians or other students will hear us, and decide I don't give a flying fuck at this moment.

I think he's going to make me come without touching me at all, but then his fingers dip between us to find my clit. With a master's touch, he takes me to new heights, even as he fills me with his cock. With his other hand, he slips under my shirt and begins teasing my nipples, almost like he can't stop himself.

I can't help myself either, and I wrap my legs around Bastien as I feed off him. With his fingers and cock stroking me, I scream out my orgasm, and he follows me a second later. His eyes close and his face changes, losing that cold exterior for just a second, as he pulses inside me. Drawing in his orgasm with mine, I suck the last little bit of sexual energy from him as he finishes us both off.

As soon as it's over, he pulls out of me and turns away, tucking his cock back in his slacks. "I trust that will be sufficient to keep you sated for a while."

He's all business again. That was fast. Meanwhile, I'm still panting on the desk, my naked legs hanging off the edge of it, with my shirt pushed up to my breasts. I manage to sit up and smooth my hair at least. "Yes. Thanks."

He buttons his shirt back up, still not looking at me. I wonder why. Is he afraid I'll see a hint of emotion in his cold eyes? Or is he worried he might actually feel something if he looks at me? "You're welcome."

He walks out of the room without another word, and I'm left to pick up my clothes alone. Try as he might to act unaffected, I can tell I'm starting to melt that hard, cold exterior of his.

Chapter Forty

KASSIEL

I've been waiting on the bench for an hour before Olivia shows up. It's been a while since she visited me by the lake, and I was starting to think she wasn't going to come anymore. When she sits beside me, I'm relieved. I see her every weekday in class, but that's different because we don't really interact. I've come to appreciate these quiet chats we have by the lake, and I felt almost hollow when she missed a few of them. If there wasn't this power imbalance between us, I might even call us friends now.

"I haven't seen you here in a while," I say, studying her closely.

"Sorry, I've been kind of busy."

"So I see." For once, she looks like a well-fed succubus. Her hair is extra lustrous, her lips look fuller, her eyes are brighter. Even her breasts seem perkier. Olivia is always beautiful, but now she's downright stunning...and I'm suddenly awash with envy knowing she's this way because she's been feeding regularly with some of the other students. "You've been spending a lot of time with the Princes."

Her eyebrows dart up. "You know?"

I smirk. "Yes, we Professors do notice these things, and Hilda and Raziel love to gossip." My voice turns serious again. "It's good to see you looking healthier. I was worried you weren't feeding enough before."

I wait for her to deny it, but she lets out a long breath, and I sense she's done with that game. "Thanks. It's been a challenge to feed while I've been here, but it's going better now."

I sigh, knowing she spent months struggling while I did nothing. I feel like a total jerk, but I couldn't risk getting caught. "I wish I could have helped you with that."

Her eyes widen at me. "You do?"

I can't help but reach out and touch her cheek, stroking her soft skin. "I've never stopped wanting you since that night. If it wasn't forbidden, I would take you to bed again. Many times."

She presses her hand against mine, holding it to her face. "I'd like that."

I swallow and yank my hand away before I throw her down on the grass and have my way with her. "Maybe once you're finished with school. It's only another two years. That's nothing for people with our lifespan."

She nods, her face disappointed. "Maybe."

We sit in awkward silence again as we fight off the sexual tension between us, until she asks, "Does that mean I can sleep with an angel multiple times without hurting them?"

"Yes, you definitely can. You're not the first succubus I've been with."

"Really?" Now she looks intrigued.

"I've lived a long time," I say quickly, hoping she doesn't

dig further. "Plus the Princes will be extra strong since they have Archangel blood. They won't be as weakened when you take their energy."

"That's good to know."

"Do they know what you are?" I ask.

"Yes, they found out."

"Are you sure you can trust them?"

"No, not really. I'm not sure I can trust you either, though."

"That's probably smart. Just...be careful. If word gets out about what you are, both the angels and demons will want to control you. Or they'll want you dead."

She swallows and nods. "I'll try."

I reach over and squeeze her hand. "I'll do whatever I can to protect you also. I swear it."

She gives me a heart-stopping smile. "Thanks, Kassiel. Being able to talk to you about this has really helped me a lot. I'm glad you walked into my bar a year ago."

"Me too." I stroke her hair softly, just once, and then I stand up. I'm so close to kissing her, I need to get away. Resisting a succubus at her full power is difficult, especially one I like as much as Olivia. "I should go. Good luck on your test tomorrow."

She groans. "Don't remind me."

With a flash of my black-and-silver wings, I'm in the air, and flying back to my room. Like the student dorms, it has a balcony so I can land on it and walk inside, without having to go through the rest of the building. I purposefully left it unlocked, since I knew I'd be coming back here.

But when I step inside, I see I've had a visitor while I was gone, and now an ivory envelope waits on my bed. Inside is an invitation to the third trial to get into the Order of the Golden

Throne. It's during the half-time of the championship football game against the demons, which I was planning to skip anyway.

Finally. Father's been waiting for news on my mission to infiltrate the Order of the Golden Throne, and it's been ages since I had anything to report. Now all I have to do is pass this third trial, and I'll be in. Then I can figure out what they're really up to...and see if they're a threat.

Chapter Forty-One

OLIVIA

*I*t's hard to believe, but the school year is almost over. It's also November 13, and my birthday. I wasn't planning on making a big deal of it, since it mainly reminds me that it's been a year since I last saw Jonah, but Araceli was relentless. It's the first time she's been excited about anything since Darel died, so I caved in. And once Marcus found out it's my birthday, it turned into a *thing*.

Practically half the school has been invited up to the bell tower tonight. I think people are more excited to check out the Princes' lair than celebrating my birthday, but I don't mind. My birthdays usually consisted of just me and Jonah, so it's a nice change to be surrounded by friends.

"There you are!" Cyrus says, as he and Grace make their way through the crowd to me.

"I haven't seen you in ages. Are you avoiding us, or have the Princes been hogging all your time?" Grace asks.

"Neither," I lie. I totally have been avoiding them ever since I found out Cyrus was in the Order, and I'd bet money that Grace is too. "I've just been busy studying for finals. I started out so clueless compared to everyone else, and I want to make sure I do well."

"You're going to do great," Grace says. "Here, we got you a little something for your next year at Seraphim Academy."

She hands me a small gift bag, and I reach around inside until I find a pretty new daily planner for next year in pink and black, with silver edges. "Thank you, I'll totally use this." Especially since my last one got destroyed with my bedroom. Wait...could they know about that? Was the Order behind that? Maybe another test, or trying to find out if I'm loyal... I don't know. But now I'm even more suspicious of Grace and Cyrus.

"Are we opening presents already?" Araceli asks, bouncing over to us with some of her usual inner light. "Open mine next!"

She hands me a little box wrapped in gold, and I give her a big smile before opening it up. Inside is a silver charm bracelet with angel wings. My throat closes up at the beautiful gift, and once again I feel horrible for deceiving her. I'm going to tell her at the end of the school year. I am.

"I love it." I give her a big hug. "Thanks."

"It's nothing for the best roommate in the world."

"That honor definitely goes to you," I say, as the guilt piles up even higher. "You threw me this party and everything."

"No, I had the idea for the party. The Princes did all this." She nudges me. "You should go dance with Marcus."

I glance over at him, where he's leaning on the wall and drinking a beer, while others come and talk to him, like he's holding court for all his admirers. I hate to admit it, but I've become one of them. Marcus is pretty great, once you get past the arrogant side of him.

The other Princes are another story. Bastien and Callan stand in another corner, glaring at anyone who dares to come close. Callan still hates me, more than ever now, but he's oddly protective of me too and has worked hard to make sure I can defend myself in Combat Training. My situation with Bastien is even more confusing. He doesn't hate me, but he doesn't seem to like me much either, even though he also wants to help me in his own way. The sex is good though, so at least there's that.

I head over to Marcus when he's alone, and he grins at the sight of me and then wraps an arm around my waist.

"Having fun?" he asks, as he draws me close.

"Sure," I say. Big parties aren't really my thing, but it was nice of Marcus to do this for me.

"Uh huh. You want to get out of here, don't you?"

"Maybe," I say with a laugh. Am I so obvious?

"C'mon, let's go to my room. I've got a present for you there."

"Is it in your pants?" I ask, raising my eyebrow.

He gives me a wicked grin. "That's not what I'm talking about, but you can definitely have that too."

We fly off the balcony together, and some of the people at the party cheer. Guess it's no secret I'm sleeping with Marcus now. I bet people would be surprised if they knew I was banging Bastien too though.

Marcus lands on his balcony with a thump, and I set down beside him. We slip inside his dorm room, and I remember when I broke into this place to investigate at the beginning of the school year. I glance at Jonah's door quickly, and then look away.

Marcus hands me a box wrapped in balloon-covered paper, and I rip it open. Inside is a coffee mug with a little cartoon devil on it and the words, *"Coffee fiend."* I stare at it, wondering if he knew about my angel mug somehow, but he never visited my room until after it was destroyed. Can it be a coincidence he got me such a similar present to Jonah's? Or was he involved in trashing my room?

"I've never met anyone who loves coffee like you do, so I thought it was funny," he says, rubbing the back of his neck. "If it's too on-point I can get you something else."

He sounds so sincere that I set the mug down and then hug him. "It's perfect. Thank you."

The hug turns into a kiss, and Marcus is ravenous as he presses his lips to mine. We haven't kissed like this since that time we had sex, and even though I don't need to feed yet, I can't help but revel in what he's giving me. Marcus puts off a sex appeal that even a nun couldn't refuse, and to a succubus like me, it's like candy.

"I don't need to feed tonight," I tell him, giving him an out.

"Good," Marcus says, as he pulls off his shirt. "Then this will be just for fun."

Sex for fun? A novel concept for me. I did it to live, and sometimes I enjoyed it, but doing it just because...that's new. I'm definitely not complaining though. Plus, I'm more confident that Marcus will be okay after my chat with Kassiel.

I reach out, splaying my hands across Marcus's chiseled chest. He's not as huge as Callan, but he's still more muscular than most guys I've been with, and I want to lick him all over. Damn.

I'm wearing a little flowy dress with spaghetti straps and a cardigan. While Marcus and I kiss, the cardigan hits the floor, and then he pushes my spaghetti straps off my shoulder. His mouth goes there next, planting kisses on the bare skin, as he tugs my dress down and reveals my breasts. The dress falls away, and I open up his jeans at the same time, then push them down.

His hands wrap around me, pulling me close and pressing my bare breasts against his chest as he swoops in for another kiss. He yanks our hips together, and the desire rages through me, potent and compelling. And for once, it's not my succubus side that's hungry for sex.

Marcus walks forward, moving us toward his bed, and I move with him willingly. He drops me back, and shimmies my panties down my legs so I can kick them off.

I slide up the bed, spreading my legs and gliding my hands down my stomach and around my sex. I arch my back and moan. I'm so turned on my touch is enough to make me soaking wet.

The sharp intake of Marcus's breath makes me look at him. He's got his briefs halfway down his legs, but he's frozen, eyes glued to my hands as they circle my mound.

"Spread yourself," he orders.

I grin and do as he says, happy to tease him this way. It's not much of a tease, because he sheds his briefs and falls on me, cramming his face between my legs.

Spreading my lips to give him the best access, I cry out as he sucks my clit into his mouth. My first orgasm crashes into me quickly, turning me into a moaning mess. As I ride it back to reality, Marcus slides two fingers inside me, hitting the perfect spot like he's done it a hundred times just to me.

Instead of washing away, the orgasm keeps going, like I'm riding on a surfboard, taking advantage of every inch of the wave.

He uses his teeth to put sharper pressure on my nub as he relentlessly strokes the spot inside me that is driving me wild. Moaning and possibly yelling, the same orgasm builds again, going higher and higher. I'm pretty sure by this point I'm screaming and grunting, but I can't be sure. I've lost all sense of propriety. Not that I had that much to begin with, but still.

Marcus's mouth and fingers leave me in the middle of my senseless pleasure, but then his cock slams into me with a force that moves me up the bed. He throws my legs back, putting his hands on the backs of my knees to bend my body in half. It means his cock keeps hitting that spot, that amazing, sent-from-heaven spot, every time he enters me.

His relentless pace makes my orgasm continue, and every time he slams home, the noises I make are truncated as my breath leaves me in a rush. I move my hands above my head, grabbing the wooden headboard of the bed. If I don't brace myself, I'm going to slide up the bed until my head is bouncing off of it.

He's not done. His ferocious pace continues to draw out what has got to be the longest orgasm of my life. It's not the most intense, but I'm not sure it'll ever end. He's getting close to finishing because his thrusts grow wilder and more erratic as the headboard bangs against the wall.

He finishes with a grunt and a whisper of my name, before he collapses on me. Careful not to smother me, he props himself up on his elbows and grins. "Happy birthday, Liv."

"That was...wow." I've never complimented a man on his

performance in my life. It's a night of firsts all around. I'm not sure how I feel about it. "Now get off of me."

He chuckles and pops a kiss on my cheek before sitting up. "Want to stay the night?"

"You know I can't."

He strokes my thigh in a teasing way. "I don't see why not."

Shit, he's getting way too attached to me. He's going to think we're actually dating, and then things will get...complicated.

"I have to go," I say, as I get up and pick my panties off the floor.

He sighs, but then nods. "Let me know when you need to do it again."

"We'll see. I don't want to overtax you."

He grins at me. "Angel stamina, remember?"

I pick up my dress and toss it over my head. It's not his stamina I'm worried about, but his heart. How am I supposed to know if he really cares for me, or if it's a side effect of my succubus powers? Can angels resist the allure? There's so much I still don't know. Where's Mother when I need her?

As I walk out onto the balcony, Marcus grabs my hand and tries to stop me. "Stay."

"I can't."

He presses a desperate kiss against my lips, which only confirms that I need to go. "It's weird that you're leaving."

"No. It would be weird if I stayed." I pull away and launch off the balcony, leaving him behind.

Chapter Forty-Two

OLIVIA

The day of the championship football game against the demons rolls around, and I brace myself for what's to come. After my last chat with Kassiel, I returned home to find an invite to the third trial, and I'm nervous about what we'll have to do now. It can't be good. But at the same time, I'm excited too. Jonah disappeared after this game last year, and I'm so close to uncovering the truth. I just have to pass this one final test.

When I get to the field, I see it's twice as packed as it was at the other game I went to. Araceli opted to stay behind again, and I'm glad. Something is going to happen tonight, and the cold air feels taut with tension. I shiver and pull my hoodie up over my head.

Grace lands beside me. "Exciting, isn't it?"

I nod. "I've never seen this many angels."

She smiles as she gazes across the field. "Imagine the power in this one stadium."

I turn my attention to the other side of the bleachers.

Demons of all shapes and sizes, looking no different than the angels, fill the stands. "There's three times as many demons as there were before."

"That's normal for the championship game. Cyrus has saved us some seats down in front."

We make our way through the stands, zigging and zagging around bodies. I spot a familiar face in the crowd and my jaw drops. I have to quickly compose myself as my father bumps into me accidentally-on-purpose.

"Excuse me," he says as he puts a steadying hand on my arm.

"No problem." I look at him out of the corner of my eye as he walks the same direction I do, seemingly a coincidence.

"You're well?" he asks under his breath.

"As well as I can be," I mutter.

"Did you say something?" Grace turns to me as she walks ahead of me.

"Just that I could go for a drink."

She chuckles. "I'll get us some. You find Cyrus. He's over there."

I nod, and she takes off, leaving me standing next to my father.

"Looking forward to the game?" He doesn't look at me as he asks, and I don't answer. "My son was on the team last year."

"Oh? But not this year?" I pretend to be interested in the stranger's story.

"Unfortunately, no." His voice is heavy with grief. He looks at me for the first time. "You look good," he says in a low voice. "Healthy."

He gestures for me to follow, and we step behind the port-a-potties that have been set up. A ripple of magic releases from him, and he bends light around us both so we're invisible, along with everything we say.

"Are you eating enough?"

"You're worried about that *now*?" I ask. "Where were you the rest of the year?"

"Looking for Jonah. Don't worry, I had people keeping an eye on you here so I knew you were safe."

They're not doing a very good job, since he doesn't seem to know about the demons attacking me. "Has there been any progress with Jonah?"

He scowls. "No. The Archangel Council has officially closed the case."

The news that nobody official is searching for my brother anymore infuriates me. How can he let them stop looking? Jonah is his only son and his only legitimate child. "It's a good thing I'm still searching for him then."

"Have you found anything?"

"I don't know yet. I think he might be in Faerie."

Father shakes his head. "I already spoke with the High Court of the fae, and no one there has seen him."

"That doesn't mean he's not there. If there's anyone who can hide from them, it's Jonah."

"Perhaps." He doesn't sound convinced. "You should give up this hunt already, Olivia. It's only going to get you in trouble."

"I'm not giving up until I find Jonah."

He pinches the bridge of his nose. "Why do you continue with this madness? Are you trying to punish me?"

"I'm *trying* to find my brother."

"We both know that's not going to happen, and you're just

going to get yourself in trouble in the process. At the end of the school year, it's best if you leave this place and never return."

Wow. I can't even reply to him. He doesn't believe in me at all. What must it be like to have a proud parent?

I'll never know.

"I have to go. Don't follow me."

Turning away, I walk back around the port-a-potties and come into view as I leave his magic behind. He better not fucking follow me. I'll blow the whole operation. I'm that mad.

I sit between Grace and Cyrus. "Sorry, stomach problems," I explain.

"Do you need a Malakim?"

"Nah, I'm okay." I grab the beer Grace got me as the teams run out onto the field. My eyes immediately hone in on Callan and his impressive ass. "Besides, the game's starting now."

———

*A*t half-time, I use the same excuse about my stomach, and tell Grace and Cyrus I'm going back to my room to get Araceli to heal me. It's easy to convince them, and I'm sure it's because they need to sneak off too.

I pretend to head back to my dorm, but then go invisible and slip into the woods. I pull my robes and mask out of my bag and throw them on, before going visible again and heading to the meeting spot.

There are only five of us in white robes tonight. I guess two people either failed the last trial or decided not to go through with, like Araceli. I wonder how many will remain after tonight's trial, whatever it is. I swallow hard as we wait.

What did Jonah have to do to become a member himself? I'm almost glad I don't know.

The golden-robed initiates appear, although they seem fewer than last time. I bet some of them are still at the football game.

"Follow us," the crowned leader says, in their garbled voice.

They walk the same way I followed them last time. When they stop near the boulder, one of them turns toward us and hands us each a blindfold. "Put this on over your mask. We will know if you leave a spot to peek out."

One of them must be an Ofanim. Maybe Cyrus. I'm glad I'm wearing the necklace, though I don't need to peek. I know where we're going.

Just to be safe, I put the blindfold on properly, while the other initiates do the same. Then we're told to wait, and I hear the sound of the boulder moving. If I didn't know what it was already, I'd be clueless though.

Someone takes my arm and leads me down the long hallway, and from their nails digging into my skin, I guess the hand is feminine. The initiates are all led down to the main cavern, and then we stop. I wait for them to remove the blindfold, but they don't.

"Congratulations on making it to the third trial," the leader says. "You will each be taken into another room one by one, where you will be given your task. If you fail, you will be escorted out of here. If you succeed, you will be initiated into the Order at the end of the year. Don't let us down."

"You first," someone says to my left. I hear the sound of movement, as the person next to me is taken away. The rest of us have to wait, still blindfolded.

After about five minutes, we hear the muffled screaming.

My stomach twists. I don't know if it's the other initiate screaming, or someone else. What is this third trial? For the first time, I'm questioning whether I'll really be able to do it or not.

One by one the other initiates are led into this other chamber, and then we hear more terrible noises. At one point I think I hear a drilling sound. That's when one of the other initiates turns and tries to flee, then yells, "Let me out!" The person is escorted out of the cave, and then there were four.

I'm the last one to be sent in. When the door slams shut behind me with a heavy *thud*, my blindfold is taken off by a golden-robed initiate. Behind them is a man tied to a chair in the middle of the room. He's covered in blood and his head slumps forward. A few fingers are missing, and I instantly recoil.

"What's going on?" I ask, as I scream a little inside.

"This demon is an abomination," the golden-robed person says.

"Who is he? What has he done?"

"He is no one. A random person watching the games. Does it matter? He is a demon. You will torture him until he gives you any information that can be valuable to the Order. If you come back without this, you will not be initiated into the Order."

The demon is gagged and manages to look at us with furious eyes. Shit. What do I do? I can't torture someone! I am a lover, and getting better at being a fighter, but definitely not a torturer. Besides, the poor guy looks like he's been through enough already.

"We will come get you when your time is up," the golden-robed person says, and then leaves the room, slamming the door shut.

Across the small room is a table with a candelabra and a myriad of instruments of torture. I walk over and examine them, mostly just to give myself time to think, and see all sorts of terrible twisty, pointy objects, many already covered in blood. Including the drill. I cover my hand to stop myself from gagging.

I look around the room, searching for a camera or recording device, but I don't see anything, and I don't think the damp stone walls could camouflage anything. I take out my cell phone and use the flashlight to make sure. It's about the only use it has down here—no reception at all.

I consider using my succubus powers to get this guy to tell me something, but I'm not sure that would work on this demon. I can't tell what he is from looking at him. Like angels, demons all look like humans, until they use their powers.

Making my decision, I kneel in front of the guy and whisper, just in case someone is listening in somehow. "I'm going to get you out of here. I promise. But you have to give me something first."

He tries to talk over his gag, and I remove it carefully. "Bullshit," he says. "You're just trying to trick me."

"I'm not, I promise."

"Why would you help me?"

"Because I'm like you." I was hoping it wouldn't come to this, but this is the only way he will trust me. I remove my mask, then lean in close and touch his arm. As I do, I let my power emerge and draw out his lust for me. It was there, just a tiny bit, and it's enough to activate and feed. As I do, my eyes turn black. He gasps when he sees them.

"A succubus! How is it possible?" he whispers.

"I'm infiltrating the school to find out about what they're doing to demons here. I'll help you however I can, but I'm on a direct assignment from Lucifer, and I can't blow my cover."

"Nope, I've heard that line before tonight. I don't buy it."

"You...what?"

"The whole spying for Lucifer thing." He rolls his eyes. "The guy before you said the same thing."

Whoa. That's...unexpected. Is there another demon infiltrating the school?

I huff. "Fine, don't believe me. I'll just have to torture you, I guess."

He studies me for a long moment, and then nods. "I believe you. Let me free, and I'll tell you what you want to know. Juicy things, things that I didn't even tell your friends who came before you."

I hesitate. It could be a trap, but I also can't let this demon stay down here. I'm 99 percent sure they'll kill him when I'm done with him.

"Okay, but we need to make it look like you overpowered me and escaped."

"I'm a vampire. It won't be a problem."

This is a bad idea, I think, but what other choice do I have? I check out the bindings holding them, and notice they're imbued with light. No wonder he couldn't escape. I find a knife on the torture table that glows when I pick it up, and hope this will work. And if he messes with me, well I can always stab him with it. I know first-hand what these imbued weapons can do.

I saw through the ropes, and then the vampire bursts up

and grabs me. I use the move Callan taught me and flip him over my shoulder, knocking him to the ground.

I level the knife at him. "Information. Now."

He grins up at me, and his fangs are out. The fucker was going to bite me. "I'll tell you a good secret. You're the succubus everyone is looking for."

"Why?" And how? I was so careful.

"There have been rumors of an unknown succubus in the area for months. Many of us were told to be on the lookout for you tonight. The Archdemons want us to bring you back alive." He grins wider. "There's a nice bounty on your head, and I'm planning to collect."

Like I have time for this shit. Seriously.

I lower the glowing dagger to his neck. "Sorry, but I really am on a mission here, and I can't have you messing it up. Now give me something useful, and maybe I'll let you go after all."

"That's all I know, sorry. Everything I told the others was a lie." He laughs, and it's a mad laugh, and I feel bad for the guy again. They really did a number on him.

I stand back. "Go. Get out of here. I'm not going with you though."

He rises to his feet and pounces on me. So much for being nice and trying to help him. I dodge him and roll, then get back to my feet and lunge, using more moves from Combat Training. The vampire lets out a blood-curling scream as the dagger cuts him, and he stumbles back, clutching his stomach. He bares his fangs and backhands me across the face, so hard it sends me flying. Damn supernatural strength.

I hit the side of the cave hard, and fall to the ground. I've still got the dagger clutched in my hand though. Everything fucking hurts, but I will cut that fucker again if he comes close to me. But instead, he throws the door open and dashes out, so fast it's hard for my eyes to follow. I have no idea how he'll get out of the cave, but that's not my problem anymore. He's on his own.

Everything hurts, but I manage to crawl forward and grab my mask and shove it back on my face. There's chaos outside the room and lots of yelling as the vampire makes his escape. For a long time I sit there in a daze, and when it quiets down, someone in a gold robes runs in to me. "Are you all right?"

"I've been better," I say, with the weird muffled voice of my mask. "Did he escape?"

The other person nods. "It seems that way. What happened?"

"I was torturing him but then he overpowered me." I touch my head, which is pounding. "He threw me across the room."

"Did you learn anything before that happened?"

Shit. I need something. I decide the truth is the best option.

"I did." I use the wall to help me get to my feet, but everything hurts, and the hunger is rising in response as my body tries to heal itself. "There's a demon on campus, infiltrating the school."

"What?" the other person asks, shocked.

"It's true. I tricked him into thinking I was going to help him escape, and in exchange, he told me that. But then he actually did escape. I managed to cut him with this dagger though."

"Good work. That will slow him down, and we should be able to find him. Do you need a healer to attend to you?"

"No, I'm fine, thanks."

"Then put your blindfold back on, and I'll lead you out of here."

I do as I'm told, and as the arm grabs me again, I feel the same feminine nails. I'm led out of the cave and into the forest, and I wonder if the vampire got away.

He was a dick, but I kind of hope he did. Otherwise, I'm pretty sure he'll be found dead tomorrow.

"You did good tonight," the golden-robed person whispers to me. "You'll receive an invitation to the initiation soon."

The arm releases me, and when I take off the blindfold, she's vanished and I'm alone in the forest.

I did it. I passed their final test. And I did it without losing my soul too.

Chapter Forty-Three
OLIVIA

The demons win the football game, and I keep waiting to hear about a dead or tortured vampire, but it seems both the Order and the demons want to keep that quiet. I'm paranoid that the demons know I'm here now, and look over my shoulder constantly during the last few weeks of school. Then final exams draw near, and I'm so busy studying, I don't have time to worry. At some point during the school year I stopped being here only for Jonah, and started being here for me, and I desperately want to do well on my exams.

The night before our last day of school, I receive my final invitation to the Order of the Golden Throne. At midnight, I'm to head back to the usual meeting spot, where I'll be initiated into the Order. Finally.

When I reach the designated spot, all of the golden-robed members are there. I think it's all of them, anyway. I wonder which one is Cyrus, and if Grace and the Princes are among them too.

"Initiates, step forward," says the leader wearing the crown.

I move two steps forward along with three other people. Who are they? Maybe Tanwen? Other than that, I don't have a clue. All I know is, I'm glad Araceli isn't one of them. I made sure she was asleep in her room before I left.

"Only four of you were strong and loyal enough to pass all three trials, and become full members of the Order. For your initiation, we require one last test of bravery, loyalty, and faith."

Of course. I should have known it wouldn't be just a simple "here's your gold robe, now we'll tell you all our secrets." Nope, they had to make us do one final thing.

We're taken to the lake, near where I met with Kassiel all those nights, and then we stop. One figure steps forward and places a gold-plated medallion around the necks of the other initiates and me. Once we all wear one, they step back. I look down at mine. It's a golden throne with a sun behind it.

"You will wear these around your neck and allow yourselves to sink into the lake," the leader says. "When you emerge, you will be reborn as a member of the Order."

Nope, this does not sound fun at all.

Suddenly someone is picking me up by the arms, and I'm flown over the lake...and then dropped right into the middle of it. The other initiates hit the water a short distance away, and as I fall, I try to spread my wings, but can't. The medallion around our necks must prevent it. I suck in as much air as I can before I plummet into the water. I kick my legs, but my robes make it hard to swim, and the medallion seems to get heavier, dragging me down, down, down, into the pitch-black depths.

Thanks to my demon side I can see better than the angels can, but that doesn't help me at all down here.

My feet hit the ground, and I glance around for something to help me, but all I see is darkness. Every time I try to swim up, the medallion drags me back down, and the robes only get in my way. I fight, and I struggle, and I try to do everything I can to get back to the surface, but it's no use. None of my demon or angel abilities can help me with this. I can't see any of the other initiates, and I wonder if they're going through the same thing as I am, or if this is some kind of special trick just for me.

I can't hold my breath much longer. Real panic sets in. I am totally going to die down here, and then Jonah will be lost forever.

This is a test of bravery and faith, I suddenly remember.

Am I brave enough to die? For Jonah, yes. And I have faith that I'll find him, even now.

I let my limbs go limp and blow out my last bit of air. This isn't going to be the end, I'm sure of it.

Just when I think I've made a mistake, my medallion begins to glow with a soft light. I suddenly glide up to the surface, as though propelled by a strong motor, and my head breaks through the surface. I cough and suck in a huge gulp of air, and then arms grab me and fly me back to the shore. I'm dropped on the grass, where I turn on my side and spit out a ton of water, then try to remember how to breathe.

The other initiates lie beside me, coughing as much as I am. We all have our masks on still, somehow. More of the medallions' magic? Other members of the Order come around and take the medallions off our necks, and then the leader stands before us. "You have been reborn, and are now members of the Order of the Golden Throne. Welcome, brothers and sisters."

Golden-robed members help us to our feet and pat us on the back. My head is still foggy from almost drowning, but underneath my mask, a big grin splits across my face.

We're taken around the lake to the boulder and shown how to open it, and then led inside the cave to the great big cavern at the bottom. The four of us who have made it stand in our dripping-wet white robes in the center of the room, while the other members form a semi-circle behind us. I'm given a bundle of gold robes and a matching mask.

"Now that you are members, we shall go over a few things," the leader continues. "First of all, you must always wear your robes and masks to the meetings. You shall not know the identities of other members until you graduate, and they shall not know you either. The only exceptions are a few of us who have been chosen to know your identities."

Except I already know Cyrus is a member, and I have my suspicions about a few others. I plan to keep working to uncover other members next year too—especially if they had something to do with Jonah's disappearance.

"Now that you have proved your loyalty and devotion to our causes, we shall reveal to you the true purpose of the Order, and give you your first mission to accomplish over the winter break. We seek the Staff of Eternity."

The Staff of Eternity? The thing Michael and Lucifer used to close off Heaven and Hell? Why does the Order want that?

The leader answers my question without me even asking. "Once we find the Staff, we plan to use it to return to Heaven so that we may rebuild it, and to lock the demons up in Hell for good."

Oh shit. That doesn't bode well for me. Or Mother. Could they really do it though? Hopefully Michael and Lucifer hid that thing where no one can find it.

The leader continues. "For the last few years we have been searching for the Staff, to no avail. We have reason to believe it is in Faerie, but the people we sent to find it have never returned."

That must be what happened to Jonah! I'm practically bouncing on my heels now. I knew I would find the truth once I was a member...except this doesn't make sense. Jonah must have gone to Faerie looking for the Staff, and he would have been able to sneak into that realm better than anyone with his shapeshifting skills. But why would he want the Staff? The Order is opposed to everything my brother believed in. Like Kassiel, Jonah believed we should have peace with demons, no doubt partly because of me. He would never want to find the Staff of Eternity and use it to kick all the demons off Earth.

And what happened to him once he got to Faerie? Did he find the Staff? Or did something go horribly wrong?

"Your mission is to learn everything you can about the Staff over your winter break, including where it might be hidden. Do this without alerting anyone to your true purposes. Return next term with useful information, and the Order will reward your service. Remember, when you graduate from Seraphim Academy, we will help you find prominent, powerful positions in the community. Whatever your dream is, we can make sure you achieve it." He spreads his arms. "You are dismissed."

We file out of the cave with golden robes tucked in our

arms, and as the cold night air hits my damp hair, I do feel reborn...and more determined than ever to find my brother.

I have no clue how to get to Faerie, but I'm going to find a way.

Guess I'll be taking fae studies next year.

$\mathcal{F}$inal exams begin the next morning. My first one is Combat Training, where we have to fight Callan one by one, using all the moves we've learned over the year. It's obvious he's going easy on us, because none of us could actually defeat him in a real fight, not even Tanwen, but he still gives us a challenge.

Araceli does really well, even though she missed a good chunk of Combat Training, and Tanwen of course wipes the floor with all of us. The girl is formidable, I'll give her that.

I'm last.

Callan's eyes narrow as I move onto the mat in front of him. Somehow I don't think he'll go easy on me, but he's also taught me well over the last few months. He rushes me, and I manage to dart out of the way. But then he's back, and there's no use wrestling with him because he's way too strong. I sweep my leg under him, knocking him down, and then land on him with my elbow. He lets out a loud *oof*, before rolling out of the way. Then he's back on his feet almost instantly, and he throws me across the mat. He's on me a second later, pinning me down, and when I look in his eyes I see he's as aroused by this as I am. Luckily he taught me how to get out of this, and I manage to bring my knee up and get him off me. I spin on my back and kick him in his way-too-handsome face, knowing he'll heal fast anyway, and then when he's stunned, I land another one in the chest. He falls back, and I win.

Hilda lets out a little clap. "Nice job, Olivia."

Callan bounces to his feet, and then reaches down to help me up. He doesn't seem to be in pain, even after the entire class beat the crap out of him. Archangel blood is some good stuff, seriously. I wonder what it would be like to feed on him. With two Archangel parents, I bet he's even more powerful than Marcus and Bastien. Yum.

"Good work this year," Hilda says. "You've all improved a lot. See you next year."

We all file out of the gym, and Araceli and I towel off our sweat and then prepare to go take our Flight exam, which is by the lake. It should be easy after all the flying I'm done this year, although we'll be expected to do some fancy maneuvers like spinning and flipping. That stuff scared me before, but not anymore.

"Olivia," Callan says. He gestures for me to follow him.

"I'll catch up," I tell Araceli.

He leads me to the other side of the gym, where we have some privacy from the others. Then he turns on me, and corners me against the wall. "You can't come back next year."

"Why not?"

"It's not safe for you here."

"I'm fine," I try to walk away, but he nudges me back against the wall.

"You're a demon," he growls.

"Half," I remind him.

"You don't belong here."

Not this shit again. "Yes, I do. I'm half angel too, dammit."

"I'll hide you somewhere safe, where no angel or demon can find you. It's the only way to protect you."

"No thanks."

He places his hand on either side of my head, pinning me against the wall. "Why are you so damn stubborn?"

I stare into his eyes, challenging him. "Why do you resist, when you know you want me bad?"

Rage crosses his face. "You don't know what the fuck you're talking about."

"No?" I laugh. "Don't forget, I can sense your lust. I feel it every time we fight. Every time you look at me. And especially now." I wrap my arms around his neck and press myself against him. "Just give in, and this will be easier for both of us."

"Only because you're using your succubus powers on me to make me want you." He yanks my arms off him and pushes me back against the wall. His face is so angry, I think he might explode. "I could never want a demon."

But then he crushes his mouth against mine, funneling all that rage into a kiss so intense, all I can do is let it happen. He presses me back against the wall, kissing me roughly, and it turns me on so much I'm instantly wet and oh so very hungry. Turns out I like it a little rough, from Callan anyway. I can only imagine how domineering he'll be in bed, and if this kiss is any indication, his energy will fill me up for ages.

I didn't feed after the football game, but my body healed anyway, it just left me pretty hungry. Now I take some of his energy through the kiss, my eyes turning black as he devours my mouth like he's just as hungry for sex as I am.

He pulls away and sees my eyes, and that only seems to make him angrier. He stumbles back. "Stay away from me, demon."

He stomps away while I stand there in a daze of his power. His kiss was strong enough to sate my hunger, for now anyway, but I also feel like I only got a few bites of a meal I wanted to really savor.

Stay away from him? He was the one who cornered me and then kissed me! The man has some nerve.

I roll my eyes and pull myself together, then head to Flight for my next exam.

*W*ith Olivia's taste in my mouth, I head to the bell tower and begin to pace in my usual spot. No matter how much I've tried not to think about her over the last few weeks, Olivia's seductive face keeps popping into my head. Every time we fight, I want to pin her down and spread her legs for my cock. And when I kissed her just now, it took all my power not to fuck her right up against the wall.

Why the fuck do I want that? The son of Michael and Jophiel can't want a half-demon. My father will rise from his grave and hunt me down if I get together with Olivia. And my mother? She would probably disown me if she found out. Especially since her first son, my half-brother Ekariel, was killed by demons when he was a child. It was before I was born, but still. Between his death and my father's, I have plenty of reasons to hate demons.

So why can't I stop wanting her?

Plus, there's the promise I made to Jonah. I know now that he wanted her away from this school for her protection, because it would be too dangerous if anyone finds out what she is. I've failed so far at getting rid of her, but I can make sure she doesn't come back next year.

This is my last chance...and I'm going to have to do something drastic.

I text Bastien to meet me at Uriel's house, and he arrives there fifteen minutes later.

"What's this about?" he asks, as he folds his wings away.

"I need to get a video from one of the security cameras."

He arches an eyebrow. "Why?"

"Because I fucking need it, that's why."

Bastien scowls at me, but I'm the boss, and he doesn't question me. Luckily Uriel is gone, and Bastien lets me into the office and goes right to the security camera footage. "What time?"

"About twenty minutes ago, outside the gym."

He finds the footage of me and Olivia there, and we watch as I kiss her and her eyes turn black. Even on the grainy black-and-white footage, it's obvious what she is.

"You kissed her?"

"Shut up," I tell him. "Can I get this on a thumb drive or something?"

"Sure." He looks at me from the corner of his eye as he transfers the video over. "What do you plan to do with this?"

"What I should have done weeks ago." I grab the thumb drive from him. "It's time the truth came out about Olivia. As an Ofanim, I thought you'd be on board with this."

"This is a bad idea," Bastien says with a deep frown.

I ignore him and leave Uriel's house, the thumb drive tucked in my pocket, along with the picture of Olivia that Jonah gave me a year ago.

I don't want to do this, but I gave Jonah my word—and the word of Michael's son is unbreakable.

That's the reason I'm doing this. Not because I'll lose my fucking mind if I have to spend another year with Olivia on campus. Besides, it's for her protection. I'll make sure she has somewhere safe to go, where no demon or angel can get to her.

But by the end of the day, I'll make sure Olivia can never come back to Seraphim Academy again.

Chapter Forty-Five

OLIVIA

I manage to get through all the rest of my exams, and I think I did pretty well on them, even Angelic History, my hardest class. Kassiel gave me a small smile as I walked out, so hopefully I'm not doing too badly in the class, but I won't know for sure until I get my grades when they're emailed to us in a few weeks.

Once exams are finished, we have one final assembly with Headmaster Uriel, and then the school year will officially be over. It's the end of November, and I haven't even thought about what I'll do during my break, which Seraphim Academy takes during the winter, since most angel families like to go somewhere warm during the colder months. Araceli and her family plan to spend the holidays in the Bahamas. And me... I'm not sure what I'll do yet. Stay here maybe, and keep trying to find Jonah. I'm pretty sure he's in Faerie looking for the Staff, but I can't understand why he would do such a thing, or why he hasn't returned yet.

I head to the auditorium, where everyone is abuzz with

end-of-the-year excitement and saying goodbye to all their friends. I see Grace and Cyrus and give them a little wave, then start heading over to them. I'm still suspicious of them, but they're my friends too.

As I'm walking down the aisle toward them, Callan walks out onto stage, and I pause. He has a determined look on his face, his eyes harder than I've seen before, and I'm suddenly nervous, though I can't say why. What's he doing up there?

He speaks into the microphone. "Students of Seraphim Academy, before you head home, you should know the truth about one of our students here. The half-human named Olivia Monroe is not what she seems."

Oh fuck.

"Olivia, what's going on?" Araceli asks me, appearing at my side, while the entire school whispers and turns to stare at me.

I clutch my necklace and shake my head. "I don't know."

Callan's voice booms through the microphone. "The truth is, she's not half human, but half demon. A succubus, to be precise. She's been lying to us the entire time."

It's happening. Callan's exposing me. My worst fear, now come to life, right when I felt like I was finally fitting in. Why would he do this now?

A gasp goes up through the audience, and I begin to back out slowly, trying to make an escape. Araceli, bless her heart, yells at the stage, "You're the liar!"

"I have proof," Callan says. He turns around, and a video begins playing in black and white. There's no sound, and the angle is weird, cutting off everything but my shoulders and up, but it clearly shows my kiss with Callan outside the gym. Along with my black eyes when he pulls away from me.

This is why he kissed me. He was planning all along to tell everyone about me, even though he promised he wouldn't. I feel sick, and dirty, and used. My stomach twists, and I both want to punch something and burst into tears, but most of all I want to run far away and never see him again.

Were Marcus and Bastien part of this plan? I don't see them anywhere, but they must know about this. The Princes never do anything alone, after all, and that only makes this worse. I trusted those guys, even Callan, and thought they truly cared about me. In the last few weeks, they became my friends. Maybe even something more.

Now they've betrayed me.

Araceli's jaw drops, and she turns to me with shock in her eyes. "What...?"

She doesn't want to believe it, but I can't lie to her anymore. "I'm so sorry," I tell her, and then I dart out of the auditorium as fast as I can, while the rest of the place erupts into chaos.

I fly back to my room and start grabbing my things and throwing them into a bag, including the money in my secret stash. The demons know what I am. The angels know what I am. Everyone fucking knows what I am. I need to get out of here, and go into hiding, fast, except where can I go? There is nowhere safe for me, thanks to Callan. I might need to call my parents for help. Shit. I don't think I can handle telling my father I not only failed to find Jonah, but that he was right all along about me coming here. I'm exactly what he thinks I am—a mistake. And Mother? I'm not even sure how to reach her, or where she is. I'm alone, completely and utterly alone, just like I was before I came to Seraphim Academy.

A knock on the door makes me freeze. Shit. They've come

for me already. What will they do to someone whose very existence is forbidden? Kick me out? Lock me up? Execute me?

"Olivia?" Kassiel's voice comes through the door. "Open up."

I let out a relieved sigh and open the door. Kassiel is the one person who might be able to help me. As soon as I throw open the door, he wraps his arms around me and holds me close. I take comfort in his strength and warmth, and nearly start crying, but I manage to hold myself together...barely.

"I'm in trouble," I say against his chest. "I messed up, big time, by trusting the Princes."

"I know, and I'm going to help you however I can...but I'm supposed to take you to see Headmaster Uriel now."

I stiffen and pull away. "How is that helping me?"

"I believe Headmaster Uriel will listen to reason, and I'll help convince him you deserve to be here just like anyone else. Although if you want to run, I can help you do that too, but we need to go now."

I glance back into my bedroom with my half-packed bag and consider leaving. But then I think about how hard I've worked this year, not just to find Jonah, but to learn everything I could about being an angel, and how I'm so very tired of hiding. I'm tired of being ashamed of what I am and feeling like a big mistake. I didn't ask for this life, or to carry both angel and demon blood, but maybe it's time I owned it already.

I draw in a deep breath and nod. I can do this. "Let's talk to Uriel."

"Good choice."

We jump off my balcony, and I hold my head up and let my wings pull me into the air. Kassiel follows, then flies out in front of me, leading me to my fate.

Chapter Forty-Six
OLIVIA

 nce we arrive at Uriel's house, Kassiel walks straight in the front door, through the hallway, and into the office. Inside, Uriel sits behind his desk pinching his nose between his thumb and forefinger.

"Here she is," Kassiel says. I appreciate that he doesn't leave my side.

"Have a seat, Olivia," Uriel says. "You may go, Kassiel."

"With all due respect sir, I'd like to stay."

Uriel glances at me. "If Olivia is all right with that, then fine."

I nod and take a seat. Uriel opens his mouth, but the door opens before he can say anything, and Archangel Jophiel storms in, the angel that recruited me from the hospital to come to the school—and Callan's mother.

"Is it true? Is there a half-demon at your school?" Jophiel asks.

"Yes, it is," Uriel replies.

She stops and looks at me. "You. I questioned you myself. How is this possible?"

"She has a fae relic that allows her to lie," Uriel says.

Jophiel narrows her eyes at him. "You knew all along, didn't you?"

"Of course I did. I know everything that happens at my school."

My eyes widen. Uriel knew all along what I am? I glance at Kassiel and he nods. He isn't surprised by this. He must have suspected all along that Uriel knew. Maybe that's why he didn't feel the need to tell the headmaster about me.

"How could you let a half-demon attend Seraphim Academy?" Jophiel asks, her face enraged.

"She's half-angel as well." Uriel gives a small shrug. "If she wishes to focus on that side of herself in her training, who are we to deny her?"

Jophiel whirls on me, and she's terrifying in her beautiful rage. "What do you have to say for yourself?"

My shoulders slump, but I suck in a breath and prepare to defend myself. "All I want is the chance to learn, like every other young angel out there. I want to attend classes and go to football games and learn how to fly and use my powers. I want to be part of the angel community. I didn't have any of that growing up. Is it so wrong to want that now?"

"You shouldn't have deceived us to get here. You knew you were a succubus from the moment I stepped into your hospital room, and everything you told us has been a lie."

I take a gamble. Callan hates demons, and I'm guessing it partly came from his mother. "I'm sorry, truly I am. But I can't help what I am. What I can do is try to suppress my demon side and overcome it, and that's why I came here instead of going to Hellspawn Academy. I hoped by being here I could bring out my angel half and focus on that."

Kassiel arches an eyebrow at me, and I know he doesn't buy it, but Jophiel softens a little.

"I've taken testimony from her teachers," Uriel says to Jophiel. "They speak highly of her. Even Hilda, and you know how she feels about demons."

"Olivia is an excellent student," Kassiel says. "She has worked hard in all her classes, and done everything that's been asked of her. She deserves to be here."

Jophiel crosses her arms, her nose high in the air. "That may be, but it can't be ignored that she joined our school under false pretenses. Or that you kept her secret this entire time, Uriel. The other Archangels will not be pleased once they find out."

They're not going to let me stay. Where will I go? Soon the whole world will know what I am, and there won't be anywhere I can hide.

Uriel gives her a withering look. "I'm in charge of Seraphim Academy, and how I run it is my decision, not yours, or any of the other Archangels. As far as I'm concerned, Olivia can stay."

I let out a relieved breath, until Jophiel shakes her head.

"Azrael will never allow it," she says. "The girl must leave."

Shit. Azrael leads the Archangels now. If he says I'm out, not even Uriel can stop him.

Footsteps in the hall make Uriel pause. The door flies open, and of all people, my father charges in, looking like he's going into battle. I've never seen his face so determined or his eyes so angry. Holy shit.

"Gabriel!" Jophiel says, dropping her arms. "What are you doing here?"

Gabriel's presence and power fills the room. He was second in command to Michael for thousands of years, and he would be leading the Archangel Council now if he hadn't turned down the job. I can't believe he's here.

"What is the meaning of this?" he demands. He puts a hand on my shoulder and squeezes, letting me know he's with me. "Why is my daughter being questioned like a common criminal?"

"You're her father?" Jophiel asks, so shocked she takes a step back and puts a hand to her chest.

I look up at Father, still in disbelief myself, but he just stares down the other two Archangels.

"Yes, I am."

"I'm sorry, Gabriel," Jophiel says. "We had no idea." Uriel coughs, and Jophiel glances at him. "You knew that also?"

"I had my suspicions," Uriel says.

Damn, is there *anything* Uriel doesn't know?

"Who is her mother?" Jophiel asks.

"That is not pertinent to this discussion, except that she is a succubus," Gabriel says, and his tone leaves no room for argument. He's protecting Mother too now. I've never loved my father more than at this very moment.

"Relations with a demon are forbidden, even for Archangels," Jophiel says, with a hint of a threat in her voice.

"I'll face the consequences for that crime myself, but my daughter is innocent. If she wishes to continue her schooling at Seraphim Academy, she will stay."

"But—" Jophiel starts.

"There is nothing in the guidelines that say demons are not

allowed to attend," Uriel adds. "Only that all angels must attend. That includes half-angels."

Gabriel still has his hand on my shoulder as he speaks. "We have been hard at work trying to create more harmony between the angels, demons, and fae. Having a half-demon, half-angel student here could go a long way to ease tensions with the demons."

Jophiel snorts. "I think we all know the truce with the demons isn't going to last. Especially after the recent demon attacks."

"I know no such thing," Gabriel says. "And whether or not the demon truce will last is not the question here. My daughter has a right to continue attending Seraphim Academy, and that's the end of it."

"Azrael will have many words for you about this," Jophiel says, but the fight in her voice is gone. She knows she's lost.

"I'll deal with Azrael later." Gabriel squeezes my shoulder. "Let's go, Olivia."

I jump to my feet, my head spinning, and say a quick thanks to Uriel and Kassiel, ignoring Jophiel completely, before I follow my father out the door.

Gabriel doesn't stop until we're outside the house, and then I throw my arms around him. He hesitates for a second, and then he gives me a firm hug in return. When was the last time we hugged? Or that he showed any affection for me? I can't even remember.

"Thank you," I tell him.

"It's what I should have done years ago," Gabriel says. "You're my daughter, and I should never have tried to hide you away. I love you, and I'm proud of you, and I'm sorry."

My eyes water. I've wanted to hear those words for so long,

and now I think my heart might explode. Somehow this horrible day has also turned into one of the best days. How is that even possible?

He notices other students watching us and clears his throat. In fact, there's quite a huge crowd gathered outside Uriel's house, waiting for more gossip. I spot Marcus among them, and turn my back on him quickly.

"Let's get out of here." Gabriel takes my hand. Outside the house, his massive silver wings extend and he lifts into the air, letting go of my hand in the process. I spread my much smaller black wings and follow as he flies off-campus and toward Angel Peak.

I have no idea where he's taking me, but I'm pleasantly surprised when we land on top of a hill, on the front porch of a white cottage with black trim. It's super quaint, with a picket fence, square windows, and a cute red door. "Whose house is this?"

"Mine. Most of the Archangels have a house in Angel Peak." He opens the front door. "Let me give you the grand tour."

Inside, I notice how clean and bright everything is. The living room is huge, with a big fireplace and floor-to-ceiling windows showing off an amazing view of the forest stretching out below us. There's a very modern-looking kitchen with granite countertops and shiny new appliances that we walk past, and then Father leads me down a hallway into the rest of the house. He stops in front of a closed door. "This is where Jonah stays when he's not in school."

His voice is sad, and he doesn't open the door, but continues on to the other two doors. "This is my room. And this room is yours. If you want it, that is."

He opens the third door, and I glance inside a bright room with a soft yellow bedspread and white furniture. It's cute, but looks like a guest room that no one's ever used before.

"I can stay here?" I ask.

"Yes. This is your house now too. I actually got the room ready for you a long time ago in the hopes you'd come live with us, but I was too scared of what would happen if anyone found out about you." He shakes his head. "I was a coward. I should have known that keeping you close would be safer for you. You're the daughter of an Archangel, and should be treated like one."

I don't know what to say. On one hand, I'm finally getting everything I've ever wanted. On the other hand, I'm kind of pissed it took him this long to accept me as his daughter, to be honest. I spent my entire life feeling like a dirty secret, and it's hard to suddenly let that go. But at least he's trying.

He presses a key into my hand. "This is yours. I need to go find Azrael before Jophiel puts her own spin on this. I might not be around too much in the future, as my duties for the Archangel Council require me to travel a lot. But I do hope you'll stay here over the break, and perhaps we can spend some more time together too."

"Thanks, Father." I stare at the room that's now mine. I have a home. With my father and my brother. Once I find my brother, anyway.

I turn back to Gabriel to tell him what I've learned about my brother, but he's already teleported away. Damn Archangels. And seriously, why couldn't I get that power?

I'm tempted to throw myself on that sunny little bed and never get up again, but all my things are back at school. Which means I need to go back and face everyone, even though they all know what I am now.

I head outside and spread my black wings under the sunlight. I'm not hiding what I am anymore—and everyone will just have to deal with it.

As soon as I fly into my room, Araceli runs in, her face streaked with tears. "How could you do this to me?"

"I'm so sorry," I say, emotion making my throat tight. I'm the worst friend in the world, and I deserve whatever she gives me.

More tears spill onto her cheeks. "Why didn't you tell me?"

My heart cracks at the pain in her face. "I wanted to tell you, I really did. But I was scared, I guess."

"Of all people, I would have understood!" She angrily wipes tears off her face. "But you told the Princes and not me. Why, Liv? Why?"

"I'm sorry." I don't know what else to say. Everything else feels like an excuse, but I need to try to explain. "The Princes found out, otherwise I wouldn't have told them either. But you're right, I should have told you. I made a huge mistake, and I understand if you don't want to be friends anymore."

"You lied to me all year long!" She plants her hands on her

hips, and she's so upset she's shaking. "And then after demons killed Darel, why didn't you tell me *then*?"

"I should have, but I worried you'd hate me." I swallow hard. I deserve this, but man, it hurts.

Araceli lets out a long sigh. "I could never hate you, Liv. I just wish you trusted me."

"I do!" I sink onto my bed, exhausted after everything that's happened today. "I wanted to tell you so much, but I was scared to trust anyone at first. I've spent my entire life in hiding, worried about what would happen if anyone found out what I am, and I only came here to find my brother, Jonah. Then I wanted to tell you, I really did, but too much time had passed, and I knew if I told you it would feel like a betrayal."

Recognition dawns across her face. "Wait. You're Jonah's sister?"

I nod. "We have the same father, but different mothers. Mine's a succubus, obviously."

Her jaw drops. "That means you're the only true daughter of an Archangel. Wow. Why didn't you tell people who your dad is?"

"He wouldn't let me. My parents were too scared about what would happen if anyone found out about me, so they basically disowned me. I really did grow up in foster care. Almost everything I told you about me is true, other than the succubus bit."

"That's bullshit. You can't help being born to them."

I look down at the key clutched in my hand. "I know. Although that's all changed now. Gabriel came to defend my right to be here, and claimed me as his daughter."

"Good." She sits beside me on the bed. "I'm still upset, but I understand a little better. And I'm sorry about Jonah."

"Thanks. I'm convinced the Order of the Golden Throne has something to do with it." I hesitate, but there's more I've been hiding from her, and it's time she knows the truth about everything. "Jonah was a member, so I joined them too so I could try to find him. I'm sorry I lied about that too, but I wanted you to stay away from them. In fact, I'm pretty sure they killed Darel."

"What?" she practically yells.

"They wanted you in the Order bad, I think because of your fae blood. They thought if they killed Darel and made it look like a demon attack, they could convince you to join them. Luckily you saw through their bullshit and stayed away."

She wraps her arms around herself and trembles, staring off into space as she absorbs my words. "I might have joined, if you hadn't convinced me not to. How do you know they killed him?"

"I don't know for sure, but I followed them after one of the trials and heard them discussing their plans. I stayed hidden using my Ishim powers, and this necklace." I touch the aquamarines. "My succubus mother gave it to me. It's a fae relic that allows me to lie and hide what I am."

"So you do know how to use angel magic after all." She turns to me with wide eyes. "What else have you lied about?"

I hold up my hands in surrender. "That's it. You know everything now. And I've always tried to be as truthful as possible with you about who I am, otherwise. I'm no different than I was before you knew I was part demon, I swear."

"What's going to happen to you now?"

"Uriel says it's okay for me to stay here, so I guess I'm coming back next year. I'd like to be your roommate again, if you'll let me."

"Of course you can be my roommate," she says. "We're still best friends, and next year I'm going to help you find Jonah and take down the Order after what they did to Darel. I just... need some space to come to terms with all this, okay?"

I've held myself together all day, but Araceli saying we're still best friends is what finally makes me fall apart. Tears fall from my eyes, and I'm so grateful to know someone with such a good soul. I truly don't deserve her, and I'll do everything I can to be the friend she needs from now on. I nod quickly through my tears. "I understand."

She wraps her arms around me, and together we cry and rock and hold each other. Then she wipes her face, says good-bye, and leaves the room. As I pull myself together, she gathers her bags and flies off to meet her family. The dorm room feels much darker and emptier after she's gone, but at least I know we're still friends.

There's another knock on my door, and I wonder if it's Kassiel again, but when I open it I see Grace instead.

"Oh, Olivia. How are you?" she asks in a sympathetic voice.

"I'm doing okay," I say, as I let her in.

She gives me a quick hug, and then steps back. "I can't believe Callan did that to you, but at least your father's accepted you now."

"You...don't seem surprised."

"About Gabriel?" She shakes her head. "No, I knew all along. Jonah told me about you. I didn't know about the succubus part though. That was a surprise, but I don't care. You're still Jonah's sister, and that's all that matters to me."

"Thank you, Grace." It's a relief to have another person on my side. I lead her to the sofa, and we sit next to each other, so close our knees bump. "I came here to find him, but I haven't been too successful. I know he was in the Order though—and I'm guessing you are too."

"Yes, I'm the one who nominated you." She gives me a serene smile. "And you're the one who got attacked by the demon at the last trial."

"How did you know?"

"It was me who led you out of the cave, and I had a feeling it was you. Besides, I knew you'd make me proud. You're Gabriel's daughter, after all." She grabs my hands and squeezes them tight. "I'm so glad this is all out in the open now. Next year we can attend Order meetings together, and we can work on rescuing Jonah, plus we'll have Ishim classes. It'll be great."

"You know where Jonah is?"

"Yes, but I only found out recently. He was sent to Faerie to find the Staff of Eternity, but he never returned, and we haven't received any messages from him. I've been so worried about him, and the Order had this plan to send someone back to Faerie, but it didn't work." She sighs and looks down at her hands with sadness in her eyes. "But maybe with your help, we'll be able to bring him back."

"We will. I'll make sure of it."

She nods and stands up. "I need to get going. Did I tell you Nariel is my uncle on my mother's side? Well, we're all going to Orlando for the holidays, and we're heading out tonight. My little brother is going to lose his mind. He's never been to Disney World before."

I laugh at how mundane it all is. Angels like amusement parks too, I guess. "That sounds like fun."

"Do you want to come with us?" she asks.

"No, I'll be okay, but thank you."

She gives me a quick hug and then stands. "Oh, before I go, there's one last thing you should know. The Princes are also in the Order. They know what happened to Jonah too. In fact, they've known from the very beginning. But I guess you already know you can't trust them."

"Yes, I've learned that lesson well today." My anger returns, and my hands clench at my sides.

Grace takes off, and once again I'm alone in my dorm. Soon the entire campus will be empty. It's time to pack my things and leave Seraphim Academy behind for the next few months.

But first, I need to confront the Princes.

Chapter Forty-Eight

MARCUS

I fly toward the bell tower, so mad at Callan I can barely see straight, and totally shocked by what I just saw outside Uriel's house. I need to speak to the other Princes, immediately. They had better fucking be there.

When I arrive, Bastien is arguing with Callan, although they both go quiet once they see me. I land and walk straight to Callan, then pull my arm back and punch him in his face as hard as I can. It's like hitting steel, but I don't give a shit. "How could you?"

"I had to!" Callan says, as his head whips back around after my punch. "You wouldn't listen to me, none of you."

"We told Liv we wouldn't expose her, and then you did it anyway. Without even telling us." I turn my angry gaze onto Bastien. "Or did you know?"

Bastien looks away, and I see a rare flash of emotion cross his face. Guilt? Regret? I can't tell. He's so hard to read, even though I've known him my whole life. "I helped him get the recording of their kiss, but I didn't know what he would do with it."

"You knew it wouldn't be anything good!" I yell. I'm actually shaking with rage now. I care about Liv so much, and I can't believe they would do this to her. Don't they care about her at all? "What is going to happen to her now? She's going to be kicked out for sure, but what if the Archangel Council decides she should be killed or locked up or something?"

"They won't do that," Callan says. "All they'll do is make sure she doesn't come back next year."

"How the fuck do you know?" I'm still yelling and I don't plan to stop anytime soon. "And what about the demons? When she gets kicked out, who will protect her then? They're already searching for her!"

"I was planning to hide her somewhere safe." Callan's jaw clenches. "I know this is extreme, but we had to keep our promise to Jonah. He knew she wasn't safe here, and now we can protect her in other ways."

"You idiot," I say. "Olivia is Jonah's sister."

The announcement hits him in the face even harder than I did. "No fucking way."

"How do you know?" Bastien asks. He's probably annoyed I found out before he did, but he can suck it. He should have stopped Callan before any of this happened. "They look nothing alike."

"I saw her and Gabriel outside Uriel's house. He called her daughter, and then they flew off together. Probably to take her somewhere safe." For all I know, that's the last time I'll see her, and my heart clenches tight at the thought. I think I might be in love with her, and I might never be able to tell her that.

"Gabriel's daughter..." Bastien says to himself, as he stares out the window. "This changes everything."

"No, it doesn't," Callan says. "Jonah still told us to keep her away. Now we know why."

"He wanted us to protect her," I argue. "He would never in a million years want you to fuck up her car, trash her room, or expose what she is to the entire school. That's the opposite of keeping her safe."

Callan says nothing, but he looks away, the muscle in his neck twitching. Awkward silence stretches between the three of us as we remember our crimes against Olivia. I feel like a total shithead for being involved with any of that, and then I have another horrible thought. I've been sleeping with Jonah's sister. After I also slept with Grace after he disappeared. Worst. Friend. Ever. I'm no better than Callan or Bastien, it turns out.

The silence is interrupted when Olivia herself bursts through the open window of the bell tower, her black wings spread wide and her entire body glowing slightly. She looks beautiful and fierce, a perfect combination of light and dark, angel and demon.

"You betrayed me," she says, in a cold voice I've never heard her use before. "Why?"

"I made a promise to Jonah," Callan says. He plucks her photo from his wallet and holds it up. "Before he disappeared, he made us swear to keep you away from this school—for your safety. Nothing else I did worked, so I had to expose you. It was the only way."

"Nothing else—" she starts, and then her eyes widen as she puts it all together. "The notes. My car. My room. You did all that?"

"We did," Callan says.

Her eyes sweep across the room, leveling accusations at me and Bastien. "I can't believe I trusted you."

I step forward and hold out my hands in peace. "I had nothing to do with exposing you, I swear. Or the notes, or the car."

"But you helped trash my room! You broke my mug!"

I hang my head. "Callan broke the mug, but yes...I was there. I'm so sorry."

Liv turns to Bastien. "And you?"

He stands a little taller, like he's resigned to his fate, but he still has that guilty look in his eyes. "I am complicit in all of the same things as Marcus, and I also helped Callan retrieve the video of your kiss. I do apologize. I would not have done such things if I'd known you were Jonah's sister."

"So you all know that too." She shakes her head, her hands in fists. "Jonah gave me that mug. It's the only thing I had from him, and you destroyed it."

"I had no idea know he gave it to you," Callan says. It's probably the closest he'll get to saying sorry. Callan does not apologize. "I figured it was just a silly mug."

"I came here to find Jonah. I believe he went to Faerie, and if he told you to keep me away from this school, then he must have suspected he wouldn't return. Do you know what happened to him?"

Wow, she knows a lot. I open my mouth to tell her everything, but Bastien shoots me a look, before saying, "No, we don't."

He must be trying to protect her, even now. We have to keep her safe from the Order. They'll want to use her or hurt her, now that word's out about what she is. Seriously, what the fuck was Callan thinking?

"Sorry, but I don't believe you," she says. "In fact, I'm pretty sure you're lying and you know exactly what happened to him. After everything you've done to me, I can't trust you at all."

"Everything we've done has been to get you to leave and fulfill our promise to Jonah," Bastien says. "And if we're keeping secrets from you now, that's why."

"We're not bullies, not really," I say, but it sounds pathetic, even to my ears.

Olivia snorts. "Even without the way you treated me, you walk around this school like you own the place. If you don't want to be bullies, try treating people like equals instead of the dirt on your shoes."

Okay, she has a point there.

"I stand by what I did," Callan says. "You don't belong here, and Jonah knew it. Plus you showed up here and turned Marcus on his head, and now Bastien is just as bad. I can't stand the sight of you, but I can't help but want you anyway. We can't have a succubus using her powers at this school."

She puts a hand on her hip and cocks it. "Hey, asshole, I've not sent a single ounce of my powers toward you. So, if you can't stop thinking about me, guess what? It's because you want me for who I am, not because of what I am. But I'm happy to tell you that your plan failed. I'm coming back next year. And the three of you? Can stay the hell away from me."

"Liv, wait." I reach for her, but she pulls away, and her glare shuts me up fast.

"No. I thought we were friends, or maybe even more. But we are done."

She flies out of the bell tower, and I'm half tempted to follow her, but sense it would be useless to try to talk to her right now. I spin around and face the other two Princes.

"We're done too. I want nothing to do with either of you. I'm over your bullshit." I shake my head at them in disgust. "Olivia deserves better."

I don't wait for a response before I take off. I need to figure out how to get Olivia back, and I have a feeling it's going to involve a lot of groveling.

Chapter Forty-Nine

OLIVIA

I head back to my dorm room and finally let myself fall apart. I cry, and I hit a pillow, and I eat up the last of the ice cream in the fridge, then drown myself in coffee —after throwing the mug from Marcus against the wall. It doesn't break, because even my fucking mug is against me. It's obvious he got it for me as a guilt gift, and I want nothing to do with it.

Or with any of the Princes. I'm certain they're lying to me about Jonah, especially after what Grace said, and I can't forgive them for what they did to me throughout the year. I blamed so many things on Tanwen, and even pranked her in return, when it was the Princes all along. Specifically Callan. He vandalized my door. He sent me horrible notes. He ruined my car. And they *all* trashed my room.

Then they committed the ultimate betrayal by exposing me, after getting me to trust them and promising they wouldn't tell anyone what I am. Marcus might be innocent in that crime, but Bastien is as guilty as Callan is, and I can't forgive any of them. I'm not sure I ever will.

Next year, I'm going to make them pay.

By the time I pull myself together, it's gotten late, and the campus is pitch black and empty. Everyone else has left. But there's one last person I want to talk to before I go, and I have a feeling he's waiting for me too.

I set down by the lake, and Kassiel is already waiting there, still wearing his suit from earlier. He jumps up from the bench and steps toward me with a worried expression.

"Olivia, are you all right?"

"It's been a rough day, but I'm...okay," I say. "Thank you so much for your help today. I appreciate you standing up for me and for just being there."

"Of course. Everything I said was true. You do deserve to be here, and I'll always do whatever I can to help protect you."

All year long I worried he might expose me, but in the end, he proved to be one of the few people I can trust. It's a strange realization that I have only two real friends at Seraphim Academy, and he's one of them.

"Why help me?" I ask softly, stepping close to him. He's so ridiculously handsome, and it's been a while since I really allowed myself to fully take him in. The moonlight enhances the highlights in his dark hair, and his lips look so soft and kissable. I can't stop staring at them.

He reaches up to stroke my hair. "I care about you, Olivia. You know I do."

"I care about you too," I whisper. Originally it was just lust and attraction, but over the last few months it's turned into more. Our little midnight meetings by the lake became one of the highlights of my week, and I wished so many times that he wasn't my professor, even though he was also a damn good one.

He's looking at my lips too, and then our eyes meet again. He looks as conflicted as I feel, and he's still touching me, trailing his hand down my cheek now. We're standing close together, very close, and I'm not sure how that happened.

"Fuck it, I can't wait two more years," he suddenly growls, and then our mouths meet at the same time. His arms pull me against his chest, and I circle his neck with my own, never wanting this moment to end. Our kiss is desperate and hungry, filled with months of longing and the memory of that one night we spent together, and then his energy hits me, hard. He's so incredibly strong, maybe equal to Callan, but he tastes totally different from the Princes, just like I thought. They taste like light, and the finest wine, and hardy potatoes.

He tastes like whiskey and filet mignon.

And darkness.

I pull away from him and stare up at his green eyes. Eyes a lot like mine.

Demon eyes.

"You're a Fallen," I whisper.

He looks down at me in the darkness, seeing me perfectly, and his lips press into a tight line. "How did you know?"

"You taste different from angels. Before I thought maybe I was remembering it wrong, since it had been a while since I fed on you, but now I know for sure—you're a demon. But you have wings too, so you must be a Fallen." My eyes widen as I connect all the dots. "The other demon, the vampire the Order tortured—I told him I was undercover on a mission for Lucifer, and he mentioned another demon at the school said the same thing. That's you, isn't it?"

"It is." He tilts his head and studies me. "You're a member of the Order?"

"I am now, yeah. And so are you."

He nods. "I started teaching here to find out if the Order is a threat. But you're not on a mission from Lucifer."

"No, I just thought it would be something the demon might believe, especially once I showed him I was a succubus."

"You told him that?" he asks, his face concerned. "That means the demons know you're here."

"Yeah, it seems the cat's out of the bag now. Everyone knows about me."

"Things could get very dangerous for you now. Be careful. Why *are* you here anyway?"

"I'm trying to find my brother Jonah, who disappeared last year. The Order sent him to Faerie, and I'm going to bring him back."

He takes my hand. "Then we'll work together. I can't let the Order get the Staff of Eternity. They'll start another war, and I won't let that happen."

I squeeze his hand. "Me neither. And I promise I won't tell anyone what you are. You can trust me."

He leans down and brushes his lips against mine. "I know."

"Uriel knows you're a Fallen though, doesn't he?" I ask.

"Of course he does. He knows everything, and he thought it would be good to have a demon professor on campus." He hesitates. "I'm not sure we'll be able to hide a relationship from him, and I can't afford to get fired. Now you know why I've had to resist you this year."

"I understand." I take his face in my hands and give him

one more quick kiss. "We can't be together. Not yet. But maybe someday."

"Someday," he says, then kisses me again. Harder this time, like he can't stop himself.

I'm the one to pull away. I want him so badly, but I can't get him in trouble either. I need his help. "Until then, we're allies. We'll stop the Order together."

A dark smile crosses his lips. "With the two of us infiltrating them, they have no chance."

"I'll see you next year," I tell him, and then launch myself into the air before I throw him onto the grass and take what I need from him. I have no idea how I'm going to resist him for the next two years, especially when I know he cares about me as much as I care about him, but we'll have to find a way. He's the only one I can count on to help me fight the Order from the inside.

I fly back to my father's cottage and begin to make a plan for my second year at Seraphim Academy. First, I'm going to bring the Princes down, and then I'm going to rescue Jonah. I'll learn everything I can about Faerie and the Staff, and I'll do whatever it takes to find him. He's alive, I know it, and if anyone can bring him back, it's me.

Because I'm not just a succubus. I'm the daughter of an Archangel too.

ABOUT THE AUTHOR

New York Times Bestselling Author Elizabeth Briggs writes unputdownable romance across genres with bold heroines and fearless heroes. She graduated from UCLA with a degree in Sociology and has worked for an international law firm, mentored teens in writing, and volunteered with dog rescue groups. Now she's a full-time geek who lives in Los Angeles with her husband, their daughter, and a pack of fluffy dogs.

Visit Elizabeth's website: www.elizabethbriggs.net

Printed in Great Britain
by Amazon